Dedicated to all who suffer and all who wish release from suffering.

Diana's Life

2005

near Toronto

Diana kept her voice low, but the intensity and underlying rage were not lost on the middle aged man who lay on the dock beside her.

"You come here to visit me and maybe you're thinking this will be easy picking. You men believe that's all we want, a man to hang around and make our lives complete. Well, listen up. My life is complete already. I don't need you if what you have to offer is half measures, I'm waiting for a man who's got the guts to give a complete commitment, dedication to me.

"This is my dock, and my little cottage up there and no man is going to come along and mess up what has taken me most of this sodden life to put together." In the brief pause she gave to gather her breath, she watched Jake roll over onto his side on the wooden planks, to face her.

For a moment she dreaded he might be getting up to leave. 'Well, then let him,' the thought came fierce and fast. "Better to get it over with now than linger in some fantasy." As she thought this, his green eyes returned her gaze and she felt those snakes of sensation that meant she was falling for him.

Forging forward, her harangue carried on, "Make no mistake. If you decide after this to stay with me, it will be because you want to support MY life, not the other way around. The days when I gave and gave and used my best energy to transform some man's nasty moods are over. I'm done with all that."

Energized by her tirade, Diana turned her body to lie front down on the warm wood. Her eyes focused just over the edge of the dock on the water, clean and clear.

"I'm waiting for someone. He's been gone from me a long, long time, and I thought David was him. This man loves me. He knows who I am and he loves me. He's been looking for me. For ME. Not for me as a stand in until some young thing comes along, not me as good enough because I make life easy for him, but for me. He will be true to me and committed and will stay devoted. He will not be interested in any other women, now or ever. If you believe you'll get close to me, then give me some meditation rap about "non-clinging" as the reason you get to stray, fuck off. I've heard it all before in every guise going.

"When he gets here, he will take care of me. I'm waiting for him. I've spent a lifetime looking after others. Not interested any more. I've got too much going on in my life to be ready to babysit another man. I want someone man enough to help me, support me and if that isn't you, get the fuck away now because you better understand there'll be another just like that, another man with a hard luck story, a hand full of gimme and a mouthful of much obliged, coming along again in five minutes. If that's who you are, get out of here now.

"I'm waiting for the one I was supposed to meet in this life. He's the one I've been waiting for and he will be here for me." Diana's voice dipped almost into a soft sob on those last words. She paused and lay with her eyes still focussed on the water where they had been since she rolled over.

Jake was also on his stomach, his eyes on the waves below him. "The water is clear here," said his voice, softened by the water lapping on the wooden supports of her dock.

She wondered, not for the first time, if he knew what he was saying. They lay in silence, their faces toward the waves, then, fighting a desire to run from this moment, from him, Diana turned on her side, lifted her hand to hold up her head.

"Well?"

"I said I wanted to know about your life." Jake smiled gently, sitting up.

Diana looked out over this small lake she loved, watching the waves cap unevenly in bright sunlight. Those waves might rise to four feet, huge for a lake this size but then the forces of nature are not reckoned by human numbers. She took a deep breath, flickered her eyes in Jake's direction, let her breath go, sat up.

She started slowly, "Madness... isn't what you, what most people, imagine...it's like the torn edge of a mental fabric, like a piece of cloth you know should fit stitch by stitch, the way you see all the other material around you fitting evenly, smoothly. Part of the agony of madness is knowing that others so easily make their material all fit together. At least, enough of it to blend in." She looked into Jake's eyes.

"Yes, go on." His voice was even, nonjudgmental, his eyes remained full of light.

Turning her gaze to the lake in front of them, Diana considered how much more to risk telling him.

"I have studied states of consciousness deeply, from meditation, to prayer, from writing, dreaming at night..." Diana's eyes rested on Jake's face as she continued. "Dreams have always been so important. I have a recurring dream..." Diana knew most people were fascinated by night dreams, always wanted to tell her about the 'one dream they'd had that one time.' She weighed up the chances of Jake following the pattern and bet it was likely.

Jake's smile did not change. He just looked at her, then shifted his focus to the waves lapping gently under the dock.

When he faced her again, he turned on his side, his body moving with a liquid sensuality that Diana found irresistible. She felt again that strong clenching in her diaphragm, not uncomfortable, just very strong, as she had when she first saw him, two months before at a meditation gathering. Now she wondered how much would he take in of her life story, her wild and almost unbelievable life story before she saw that glaze in his eye, the one that signaled the man was no longer interested in listening, but wanted to impress her with something about himself. Five minutes, she thought. He'll listen for five minutes and then be out of his depth and to cover his discomfort, he'll start talking about himself.

Since Jake didn't respond directly to her mention of dreams she plunged on. "My recurring dream takes place in a meadow, a spring meadow with flowers everywhere. It's beautiful and I always feel so happy to be there, so excited and joyful even though...even though I feel some darkness at the edge of the place, like shadows, things I can't see that mean sorrow, pain.

"I've had this dream since I was a child. It has changed some, the time of day changes, or the season, sometimes there are many people there, sometimes I am alone, the dream itself, the meadow, always comes back..."

Diana paused again, took a deep breath and looked again into Jake's eyes. She saw a quiet acceptance there that increased her confidence.

"Some of what I'm going to tell you has to do with time travel."

Jake didn't blink.

"Time travel, dreams..." Diana continued blushing slightly, "You see if you say to people, oh yes, time travel that's what we really mean by space travel and oh, by the way, under steady conditions with the right people, it's quite easy to achieve. If you say that, people don't sit back and say,

'By Einstein, I'm in!' as they adjust their watches."

Jake's broad smile and light chuckle brought warm relief to Diana's mind.

"No. It's easier to just believe anyone who says this is crazy. So...you said you wanted my life story? Well, get ready. Lots of adventures including time travel...strange stuff."

"Sounds better than T.V."

"I don't know if that's a compliment or not."

The silken rope of bright, soft energy between them that had been so clear to her right from the start now pulled around her evoking vague memories, and emotion. Strong emotion. All that and the heat of sexual desire.

Although Jake seemed to be aware, conscious of what he said and did, Diana still wasn't sure. She knew so many people, very bright, successful people still hadn't the quality of being self-aware.

"I'm still here." Jake spread his square, fleshy hands out. Diana saw the pouches under his eyes, noticed the cut muscles across his shoulders. She wondered what he saw? At fifty-three she was still slim, somewhat in shape, but her flesh was beginning to loosen from her bones and her face crinkled even when she wasn't smiling.

Two months. They had been at a meditation group together once a week for only two months, and she knew he, like her, was there only because that's where they met.

At their age two months was a long time. On the other hand, a little caution in opening up demonstrated some wisdom gleaned, lessons learned from all that life already lived. So Diana told herself.

"I'm going to sound like I'm reciting something as I tell you the worst of it, what happened when I was 16, what caused my...the madness." She expected a response of some kind, some slight movement of his eyes, or a shift in his body or his breathing at her confession. Expected but did not see anything stir even on the surface of his finely balanced features.

"That's because I have written it many, many times, so often I have the words memorized."

Jake's face opened with empathy, "Don't talk about it if you don't want to."

Diana smiled, "I do. I want to talk about IT because talking and writing and writing and talking have been major ways for me to heal. They are also..." her lips pursed primly, "methods I use with my own clients. So yes, I want to."

Diana paused for a moment, took in a full breath, down deep as she had practiced for so many years. Her earlier harangue, or rather her outburst, was a symptom of how much she wanted Jake to feel for her. At the same time she desperately wanted him to only be a friend, to leave her life in the simple, uncomplicated rhythm it had become. She dove in.

"I'd been walking the boardwalk in Toronto's Beaches, which was then a working class neighborhood. I'd probably had a fight with my mother. Early afternoon, September sun. This skinny, agitated, man, pale blue eyes full of void, knew of kittens, trapped, sounded wounded or ill, maybe starving, would I help him? His words targeted my sixteen year old heart.

"He created his own world in that deserted basement, where dust motes lay in silent pews of sunlight, in which he tied my body to a chair, alternately gagged my mouth, then released it so I might speak the words of love and devotion he demanded from me, my skin his ashtray, my breasts his teething ring.

"Understand, rape is an admission of defeat, an act of helplessness, a declaration of the rapist's frustrating impotence. The act signals the rapist's lack of skill, lack of masculine ability to wield power to seduce. Rape trumpets the puerile insignificance of the rapist, tells of his undeveloped manhood, his childish flailing, a blunt attempt at what requires a mature, seasoned and tempered approach. Rape is flaccid emotion, unable to penetrate.

"He was flaccid, as I said, until he finally felt fear in me. That is what excites. He engorged almost enough to enter my body. Almost but not quite enough. Just as I had some fear, but not quite. He grabbed my long hair, wound it around his hand hard enough my head and neck were at an angle, then used this pressure as a stabilizer while he pounded, attempting to enter me, attempting to stuff with his hand his crumpling genitalia into the door of my body, my bare back struck by the cold cement floor." Diana paused briefly here, before resuming.

"You might assume the torture was more difficult, his teeth landing over and over upon the surface of my breasts, sucking purple, blue-black petals ringed in red tooth marks from the dark earth of my body or the small, hot ember of his cigarette floating forward, a blood planet in the twisted, toxic night of his need. His voice intoned like a mother crooning her baby to sleep, 'If you press the heat against skin until it starts to smell, then pull away, the mark does not stay. No one can prove anything. This,' he carried on in a confessional tone, 'is a prison trick. Everyone who has been in prison knows this,' as the red distorted eye of his intention gazed mercilessly on my flesh.

"He had tied, as I said, my arms behind my back, had made sure the rope tightened each ankle, one against the other, bone arguing with bone. He had gagged my mouth, my jaw open at an angle to maximize the ratio of pain over time. My arms soon refused, refused signals about their twisted state. I smelled briefly the dank dust of the basement, then nothing at all.

"His angled ears, his large, excessively soft lips appear before me still. His scrawny, tautly excited body guided the small missile toward its target. It landed, repeatedly, burning through the first layer of my skin, evoking orange-red circles, like eyes that have seen too much. He went on for hours, believing his cigarettes, his teeth landed on me.

"With the first burn my senses reduced themselves, sight to a smaller, tighter focus of only his eyes, his pale, pale blue eyes behind the round red ember. All sound resolved to the literal content of the words he spoke, not their emotion. Likewise my nostrils received air only between where the scent of my own flesh burning might register.

"My skin knew to reconnoiter with its inside seam, to remove sensation from the outer layers, reduce itself to what was true internally: organs, blood, lymph, marrow, nothing I might consciously register.

"For hours. I lost circulation, lost time. In retrospect it felt endless, but not in the way you might imagine. Not endless and hopeless, just endless. It had to be endured.

"Of that I was certain. I had..." Diana stopped abruptly, aware the next bit of information may brand her in Jake's eyes as a kook. "I had heard a rustling about the air, a kind of tinkling as though soft bells were being played. I knew by this and the sudden calming warmth I felt all around me the Angels were present. I...I have always seen or heard Angels, or Higher Energy or whatever name you want to give the Intelligence..."

"Diana, it's all right. I studied Catholicism as part of my search. Angels? I'm good with that."

Diana went on, "It was the Angels" she said evenly, "who saved me that day. How I wrote about it goes on...Thus when he stopped surface branding my skin, my brow unfurled from its pained expression, I gazed at him, a look of calm tolerance without recrimination, without blame. I waited for him to speak."

"You know I...I had to do that," he said.

"Yes. I sighed lightly, as though sharing with him a secret. I don't know what made me know this was the way to respond, to agree, to make him believe I was on his side.

Whatever provoked that response in me probably saved my life. I knew I had to get him to believe I was his friend or at least not freaked out by what he had done."

"You had to make him your friend?" Jake's voice was incredulous.

"I told you. This is the impossible stuff, the not to be believed stuff. Yet it happened, just this way."

Diana saw Jake's doubt weighing against his desire. Whether that was his desire for her or his desire to believe her she didn't know.

"Go on."

Diana looked at him, her lips slightly tightened as she anticipated his rejection. "He walked aimlessly around the room, pretending to look for something. Part of me registered fear, but that part slipped below the blank horizon of my inner, senseless planet and I felt again the nothingness required of this moment.

"'You,' he said coming to stand in front of me, 'might run. You...you might even go to the police.' He spoke slowly.

'Why?' I waited two beats. 'Why would I do that?' I had already cleared my mind of what he had just done, dumped it into some void where no memory remains. I truly did not recall.

I wasn't on the ceiling or sitting in a far corner of the room, the kind of thing we usually call an out of body experience, so it wasn't dissociation. I just found every moment slipping away into a place without form, without sight or touch or smell, just slipping away and being totally gone from me. I had no memory.

"'I don't know if I can let you go.' That's what he told me. 'You might go to the police. I...I don't want to go back to jail. Or, if I am going back, it must be...for something...worth it.' His watery eyes stared into mine."

Jake exhaled slowly, purposefully, bringing Diana's attention to this moment, their conversation.

Diana watched his chest rise and fall, then brought her eyes to his, his warm acceptance still visible.

"All right?" he asked softly.

"Yes, yes, I'm good." Diana was feeling many things from this story, her story. She wanted to believe Jake accepted it all. It would mean the emotional strength she felt from him was real.

"From there...I glanced at his face while he stepped heavily about; I noticed his breath coming faster. I registered the slightly twisted look of anxiety under the smile he pasted over his concern.

"'Yes, I see...I have to make a decision,' he announced. Then I started humming but he cried viciously, 'Shut up, just shut up!'

"I did.

"Too much responsibility, too much human interaction, too much near clarity, a threatening weather pattern, like neon hail or black snow fell about my prison-keeper, my torturer. What to do? He circled that room seventeen times, before coming again to stand in front of me, his mind made up.

"'Here.' He laid a knife on my lap. 'By the time you get to it, I'll be long gone anyway.' A flash of sunlight through the door then darkness. I pushed the chair over on its side, bearing the bruising crush against my flesh. The knife clattered a short distance away. I wiggled myself around so the back of the chair faced the knife, my flesh refusing knowledge of pain. Then I slowly began working the knife back and forth."

"You are a good writer," Jake's small smile, soft voice and the hand he reached out to cover hers brought a warm flush to the center of her chest.

"Thank you." Diana felt Jake's fingers explore her hand. She raised her eyes again to meet his, and he withdrew his fingers.

"Are you all right?"

"Yes." Diana smiled at him, "Let's go up. I'll show you my house."

They walked up the wood steps to the dirt road, crossed it slowly, and entered the house, a cottage really, where she lived.

"Tea?" she offered from the kitchen.

"Just water." Diana made herself a cup of tea and sat on the far end of the couch from Jake. "What about you? What life medals have you won in fifty plus years?" Diana registered Jake's appreciation of her humour.

"Oh, not much...LRP in 'Nam, soldier here at home..," To her puzzled look, Jake said, "Cop. I was a cop for a few years, then switched to Immigration where I chose every morning what guns to wear that day."

The air between them held the weight of their opposing lives. Hers, having been threatened, his having been a force of stability and when needed threat.

"Surely you dressed in something else," she joked, easing the strain.

"A uniform. I dressed in a uniform, you know, badge, jacket. Later I went undercover and dressed in blue jeans, t-shirts."

Diana just kept looking at him. Her turn to wonder if he was telling the truth.

"Hair down to there and a large beard. Wore those clothes for years."

"And guns."

"Yup. Every morning I'd look and say, "today, the snub nose 38 in my boot, derringer in the waist of my pants at the back, a 45 in my blue jean jacket inside pocket...or some days, just a shot gun."

"I like the way you say that, just a shot gun."

"That was my life." He exuded that same calm sense of being in control, of being confident about everything that so attracted her.

About an hour later she watched him drive away in his old mustang, sleek sunglasses pushed dramatically down over his eyes after he waved to her one last time. Did he really linger?

Diana said out loud, "You can't be feeling this way. You know what happens. Besides, you're not free."

Tahni's Life

1640's

Tonawanda

Humming softly to herself, Tahni dipped doeskin bags into the gurgling clear stream. Far away this stream joined with a large rushing river, creating the area known to her people, the Iroquois, as Tonawanda "Swift Water."

Carefully pushing out air bubbles so each bag took its fill, so engrossed was Tahni with the water, its splashing sound, the color of the rich blue, early spring sky lighting with the stark rays of the rising sun, the white birch forest to her right now distinct in its shades of darkness and light, sand, soft and wet under her bare feet, she did not notice at first.

The pungent smell of horse caught on the edge of her nostrils and she turned. He sat as before, astride the magnificent white beast, this warrior chief she had seen so often this past moon cycle she almost expected him. He sat silently, his lithe body topped by wide strong shoulders, his eyes intent upon her. As always she looked back, feeling that trill run up and down her stomach. Then, for lack of knowing what else to do, she returned to her tasks.

This day however he did not melt into the forest as before but walked his horse down to the river's edge. She heard him slide gracefully to his feet, and felt his eyes still watching her. She kept her eyes down, on the soft rushing water, on the skin bags she was filling.

He saw her beautiful young body, both strong and feminine, her full bosom beneath her tunic, the thin waist and graceful legs.

"The water is clear here." He said this softly, close to her ear.

She knew the ways of life: if he decided to carry her off, she would have no one to hold out for her. Yet although he was a stranger she felt good in her stomach, a sign no danger was near.

He picked up her water bags easily and keeping the reins of his horse loosely in his hand, followed her back to the wigwam of her parents.

Once there he hung the bags on tree branches. Then he turned towards her father who watched from his place by the fire where his wife was cooking breakfast.

The Warrior Chief, so noted by the feathers on the staff he carried, stood respectfully, waiting for his hosts to speak first.

"Welcome to our home," her father began with the hospitality always offered one who was not a threat. "What comfort may we bring you?"

"A drink of water for my horse and a cup of water for me." In spite of his obvious rank, this Chief took time with each courtesy, demonstrating his intent would be revealed slowly, with humility.

Her father spoke again. "You have come some distance. Would you like to rest near our fire?"

The Chief threw the reins lightly over a tree limb, walked a few steps and sat a respectful distance from the fire.

Tahni's mother signaled her to move away and together they walked toward the children and dogs playing among the other eleven tepees that made up this tiny village.

"Do not look back at him," her mother warned softly.

Beside her mother, Tahni held her breath, feeling her skin prickle and her stomach flutter, both signs she recognized. Something was going to happen.

The two men conducted business, then the warrior rose and left without looking at her again. Tahni felt disappointment snag inside, but heard her father state, "We will see you again three suns from now." Her heart fluttered and she tried to steady her mind.

That night the dream returned. In this dream she stands next to a beautiful meadow, stands watching. Some shadows flicker off to the edges of her sight, but the center of this dream is the meadow and the happiness she always feels. She woke with the same happiness and marveled not for the first time that the dream never failed to come back.

Three days later Tahni watched as the eyes of the old couple standing side by side never left her. They watched silently as the child they had adopted fifteen years ago rode off on the back of a pony led by the Chief. The old woman sighed and put her hand on the arm of the old man.

The young bride had done well, more than satisfied the hopes and desires her adopted parents had had for her. The most they'd imagined was marriage to one of the richer warriors of their own small village. Instead, she had been claimed by a neighboring chief, a fierce warrior, loyal to his tribe and by all accounts, noble.

He had brought gifts, meat and other bounty, as though he had to prove himself, like any ordinary man, capable of providing for their daughter. He had sat at fire with them, stated his wish and waited patiently by his horse as her parents considered and then asked her what she herself felt.

It was a formality. His eyes had made captive of her heart, soul, mind and spirit, as though he had known who she was before they met.

Now a group of children, women, dogs and two or three ponies from this, the village Tahni had known as home, scattered around the Chief and the teen bride who was now also his. She swayed on the back of his pony, accustomed to riding and the warmth of the animal's body that spread up and into her own.

Tahni's thoughts turned somber, "If in some way he is cruel, or violent, I will still not return to my parents' wigwam. That would invite the wrath of this husband, and his warriors, upon them."

She turned her mind to the positive loving feeling of Great Spirit, the loving Nature from which they all came and back to which they would all return someday. Surely Great Spirit had sent this man to her. If so, the outcome would be good.

They headed off toward the morning sun and as they left her small village she had one fleeting moment of sadness before her young heart sang out again to the handsome chief who rode before her.

She had been to the edge of her village many times, but never crossed into the deeper part of the forest, even though a path existed. As she crossed those limits for the first time she felt a freedom in her heart, the intoxicating sense of possibility, of her own new life.

The warm spring sun splayed down through maple trees, showering beams of golden light through the opening leaves. Early growth sent up a scrunching noise as first his horse's hooves, then her pony's, stepped along. The action released deep, musky fragrance from the forest floor into her nostrils.

They approached the deepest part of the forest and continued, his back to her, his feet in moccasins swinging loosely along the belly of his horse. He rode bareback with only the suede of his pants between his skin and the back of his large mount. Tahni watched the rhythm of his body. She saw the muscles, the clear cut flesh of his back and arms and found herself imagining those arms around her. It made her smile softly in anticipation of what would be, that night, her first night with her husband.

After a ride that took them from the sun in the East to the sun well behind them, he turned the nose of his horse to the right, up and away from the stream he had been following. A large meadow rose before them. He stopped at its side and slipped off his horse's back.

Tahni dismounted. With reins in his hand, her companion led both horse and pony slowly, with great care, around the perimeter of this beautiful place. Full of early spring wild flowers, the land rose slightly toward the center where she saw a large fire pit. Her body flushed with a familiar joy. It was the meadow from her dream! Goose bumps dimpled her flesh.

"We have our ceremonies here." He turned to watch her expression. Tahni stood silent, intent on the sight.

"As a small child," she said, "I dreamed of fighting, terrible sounds, horses frightened, neighing and bucking. I watched it all, then woke with sweat and fear. The next day a warring party suddenly attacked my parents' village.

My adoptive parents pulled me from the forest where I had run to hide. I was crying. They took me in, cared for me. The two people you met." She turned to look again at this beautiful man who would be her husband. "I have dreamed always of this meadow, but always as a place of joy and warmth..." Tahni's voice faded a little as she recalled the dark shapes around the outline of the meadow in her dream. Those too, those shapes and their darkness were contained in her dream, but most of it, she continued aloud, "...a place I felt I belonged." She blushed slightly and lowered her head.

"I hope," Takoda's tone was serious, a little concerned, "it was a pleasant dream."

Tahni smiled. "Always, always my favorite dream. It felt so good. And now, here, too..." she shyly looked up at him, then swept her eyes across the lovely scene, budding shrubs, grasses and early season wild flowers starting to show blue, purple and pink.

As Takoda noticed Tahni's long eye lashes, the sweet curve of her mouth, the rise and fall of her ample breasts, he felt his knees start to weaken.

"You have had many dreams. The ones that have come to be." He recognized with a small start this was a statement.

"Yes," she replied, solemnly. In that one word he heard, with a slight shudder, a portion of what had so magnetized him toward her.

She would be a Medicine Woman.

He led them carefully around the perimeter, Tahni absorbing every detail. Then he took them back into the forest on the other side, the stream to their left. She was aware of a distance surrounding him, as though he was listening to something far away.

Takoda was focused deeply on the majesty of this natural world. He honoured and revered those trees, the river and especially the meadow. He felt a deep kinship and gratitude to the natural forces, to Great Spirit who had given him health and vitality, even into his thirtieth year, despite so many battles with animals, humans and yes, the forces of nature.

He was aware, also, of her scent, slight, barely there, but to him deeply stirring. It was enough for now. He had to prepare himself for the battle ahead. He trained his mind away from thoughts of her and prayed for success.

He took a path down along the bank of the river flowing smoothly over many small boulders. The water splashed, gurgled as it played against the unyielding rocks before spilling into small eddies and whirlpools.

The glint off the water captured Tahni's eyes and heart in an instant. She had lived near water all her life, but only the small stream of her village. If she had had one wish for her new home, it would have been to be close to water.

Then Tahni heard dogs barking, people shouting, children's laughter, sounds as familiar as her own voice but here thick as thunder. The river still to their left, they crossed farther to the right through a small copse of white birch trees, walking in that easy, sedate and graceful pace he had set at the beginning. Suddenly they cleared the forest.

There before and a little below her, spread like several skins ready for working, lay the village, her new home. She was dazzled. The sheer number of wigwams, people thronging here, there, children spilling in every direction, ponies, horses, smells familiar and strange at the same time made her a little dizzy.

"How are you?" he asked, without turning his gaze away from the villagers who were beginning to gather as they noticed their Chief returning.

She startled slightly at hearing his voice, deep in his chest, gravely yet clear, and registered a warmth between her legs that was not from the animal's back. She felt he knew her confusion, and this made her blush.

"I am grateful."

She kept to formal language as an indication of her respect for him. She saw the corners of his mouth turn up slightly and although she could not see his whole face, she had the strongest feeling they were looking only at each other.

He made his way ceremoniously through his villagers. Everyone's eyes were on him as he led her pony through to the center of the first cluster of people. So many! She had never imagined so many people might live in the same place!

Once among them he dismounted and coming to her side, took her hand. She slid off the pony and stood next to him. With a small shock she realized the most known feature to her in this, her new world, was him. He took the reins from her hand and walked with her by his side to a small grove of trees opposite the stream just outside the village perimeter.

No one followed him, although all clustered where he had first stopped their horses. With the eyes of the whole village upon them, he slipped the reins of their mounts across some low branches, and with a slight smile at the corners of his mouth said, "Welcome to my village. As you see, there are many of us."

She smiled up at him, already too in love to speak easily.

"I hope," he continued, seriously this time, "you will be happy here."

Her heart opened her mouth. She said, "I already am."

His face softened and the light in his eyes leapt.

He led her to one wigwam, beautifully painted with the outlines of suns and stars, full and sickle moons. Takoda pushed back the flap and walked straight through without having to bend. Tahni hid her amazement at the size of the doorway and walked, her head high, as though she was accustomed to this.

In the cool semidarkness of their new home he said, "It will soon be dark. I will bring food." Then he slipped outside into the deepening dusk.

Tahni looked around. Bear skins had been arranged on the floor with extra care. A few dishes hung on some branches at the back of the space. A small fire warmed against the growing chill of the early spring evening outside. She walked forward and put her hands toward the flames.

He returned with a pot of steaming food and two spoons, sat on a mat near the fire and indicated with a nod she was to sit on the other mat, close by but not touching. Then he offered her the first meat, an honour to be given once in her life, this night. After this she would serve him first, a sign of respect for the warrior who faces death to provide life for others.

With a slight tremble in her hands she took the meat and ate. It was delicious. She would have chewed and swallowed, would have demonstrated appreciation even if it had been tough skunk meat with fur in it, but the deer meat was tender and well cooked, spiced with dried sage and oregano.

After her first mouthful, she said softly, "Thank you." He heard her meaning more than the food. She finished and waited, her eyes on him. He gazed into the fire as though alone. Then he stood and to her surprise said, "I will take care of the horses." His voice was warm and kind but she felt her heart sink.

After he left she gathered their dishes. She stacked the dishes neatly to one side, put another small log into the fire pit and lay down enjoying the feel of bear skin beneath her bare legs and arms.

Soon he returned. It was late dusk with the blue-grey glow of almost night. Calm and sure in his movements, he made his way toward her. Her heart raced.

He sat easily beside her. She turned to look at him and he saw again the most beautiful young woman he had ever seen, strong, capable but at the same time, delicate, vulnerable.

"Are you happy here?" he asked.

She nodded, smiled and the light leapt again into his gentle eyes.

"Do you want for anything?" he asked in a husky tone.

Tahni, confused, shook her head slowly.

"I will be at my brother's wigwam, then." With that, Takoda stood lightly to his feet and slipped out of her sight.

Her thoughts circling, her heart flooded in sadness. Did I do something to displease him, to make him not like me? Why did he leave? She wanted more than anything to please him. Did he not find her attractive? What had she said or done? Tahni's mind raced; her heart constricted in an anguish new to her.

Tahni stepped out of her wigwam on the first morning of her new life to find the sight of people, dogs, horses, children filled her eyes. Her ears picked up the sounds of many lives being lived as one and this brought her comfort. For that remained the same: in the village which had been her home, in this new village which was now hers, the people belonged to a single soul, cared for ultimately by Great Spirit, but overseen and cared for in this realm by the Medicine Man, the Medicine Woman and led by the Chief of each Village.

The Chief! Her husband-to-be! Tahni stood awed by these thoughts when a toothless old woman shuffled up to her.

"Come," the Grandmother said softly.

Saying, "Good morning, Grandmother," Tahni followed. All old women, whether they had ever given birth or lay as virgins on their death bed were called "Grandmother." All were given respect and treated with extra dignity, because each had outlived Trickster, Coyote in his mystical form of Death. Although everyone knew Trickster would win in the end, the ability to outfox him was venerated as wisdom.

Grandmother led her into a large home. In the sunlight slanting through the opening in the center of the wigwam's ceiling, sat many women of various ages. For a silent moment, one longer than any she remembered, they all looked at her.

Then the Grandmother reached an old gnarled hand out and placed it on Tahni's forearm. At that, all the women surrounded her, everyone talking at once and every comment about her! Every comment except the ones full of ribald humour about her upcoming marriage.

"The Chief has a very large horse," said one, smiling like an imp.

"The largest in the village, it is said," offered another.

"Oh, and so easy to ride, the Chief stays so still!" This one clasped her hand to her mouth, giggling.

Hands touched her hair, shoulders, arms, one touched her face. Another brushed her leg. All the time these women chattered as if she wasn't really there: wasn't her hair the most silky anyone had ever seen? Didn't her eyes match the morning sun? Wasn't her figure, so young, firm and full of curves the best shape for love and for making the babies which would surely come? In doing this, the women were accepting her into their community, and without knowing they did so, encouraging her body to smell like theirs, encouraging her moon blood to flow with theirs.

Tahni stood quietly. Her small village of only twelve wigwams had not offered much in the way of different customs, but she had been taught to pay attention and pay respect to others. These two qualities held her well in this new situation.

Suddenly, one voice from the throng asked, "Does she speak? Can we hear her voice?"

Just as suddenly all the women stood again silent, looking at her. Her eyes fell into the eyes of the woman in front of her, warm, laughing, brown eyes, full of strength, humour, energy and intelligence, everything Tahni wanted to be as a woman. Tahni also felt emanating from this woman a sharpness, a vital force that made her a natural leader.

"Hello," Tahni said. Immediately all the women sang praises to her voice, to her soft voice flowing like a stream in the spring woods, like a bird's early morning song, one woman even said her voice fell like mare's milk! That comment made everyone laugh and Tahni felt herself relaxing a little as the self-deprecating humour of these people removed her from the center of their attention.

"Yes, I remember my mother's voice," one began.

"Oh, sure, your mother's voice is one even Raven would recall!"

Eventually the women filed out, duties calling them. Only one young woman remained. She stood and looked at Tahni without speaking, but Tahni thought she heard words, inside her head, words of friendship. The two were about the same age and height. A sliver of kinship beyond village boundaries, wider than one life, ran between them, not entirely smoothly but with a deep sense of familiarity. The young woman held out her hand and asked, "Do you want to see the river and the forest?"

Little Bird led Tahni back down the same path the Chief had used to veer away from the stream. Today as yesterday the water spoke with gurgles and chuckles as it lapped around many rocks and boulders. They crossed the path and scrambled down the shrub strewn hill. Little Bird stripped her moccasins off, was knee deep in water calling to Tahni, "Come on, it's not too cold."

Tahni put her feet in, then yelled, "What do you mean, not too cold? It's freezing!"

"Ah, you're just not used to it. We come here often."

Tahni suddenly realized there was so much she needed to know, "Is this where you come to bathe?"

Little Bird's laughter spilled above the sound of the water. "The boys would like that fine. Then they could sit on top of the hill and watch all the women get naked!"

Tahni flushed but Little Bird did not notice and continued. "We have another place behind the village where most of us go to bathe. I'll take you there."

They passed many wigwams, rounding in front of the one with stars and moons and Tahni realized she felt a bit of comfort seeing Takoda's home. From there Little Bird passed by the horses and ponies that stood patiently, tied and waiting. Tahni saw with a pang the Chief's horse was not there. He had gone somewhere, and not told her.

Disappointment welled up along with tiny snakes of anger. Instantly she squashed those snakes, whose entry into thoughts led to destruction. She tried to ignore the stabbing feeling in her heart, her disappointment, by concentrating on what Little Bird was saying, "We go through the ponies and trees, and then walk behind the village and away from it." Little Bird almost sang the directions as the two young women walked through a very large field.

Crossing the field they came down a small hill through a grove of white birch trees. True to her name Little Bird seemed to flit from slender trunk to trunk weaving through the maze of trees. The high sun fell in short shadows dappling the forest floor beneath Tahni's feet.

Suddenly Tahni stood at the shore of a large body of water. A dark fringe of birch trees lined the lake except for the far side where the waters' edge blended into hills of granite rock. Tahni felt a shiver, not related to the elements, pass through her body as her eyes scanned the horizon.

"You'll find this suits you better," Little Bird chattered on as she again stripped her feet bare and waded in up to her knees. Tahni peeled her moccasins slowly from her feet, put her toes just into the water's edge. It was warm! She sank her feet onto the water's floor and stepped, thick warm mud rising as she stepped into deeper water.

"The water stays warm from the mud and from the sun," Little Bird explained. "At least that is what I'm told. I don't much think about these things."

"Who tells you this?" Tahni realized she had been keeping her shoulders taut. She took a deep breath and let go.

"Well, I'm told this by the Medicine Man, or at least, he tells us when he comes into the village."

"You have a Medicine Man? In my village we have Medicine Women, who live among us."

"Yes, we have those too. Macawi, the woman you saw in front of you this morning, she's our main Medicine Woman but here, in the forest, lives a Medicine Man. Sometimes he comes to sit at a village fire and tell us things." Little Bird spread her hand to indicate where this magic man lived.

Tahni's inner vision filled with the warm laughing eyes of the woman she had seen this morning. So she was Medicine Woman, her name Macawi. Next a barrage of questions poured out from Tahni, "Where does this Medicine Man come from? Why doesn't he live among you? How does he help you? What are his methods?"

"All right, all right," Little Bird laughed. "I'll tell you the story. He came from our village. It is rumored he is related, maybe a cousin, maybe even a brother, to the Chief. He was in battle one day, a brave warrior, some say even more brave than the Chief." Here Little Bird lowered her eyes a bit, and looked out the corner of them at her new friend.

"These two men had been in competition since childhood. Sometimes one, sometimes the other was more brave." Little Bird grew more serious, although the corners of her mouth still curled up just a little. "During this one battle the Chief found his brother lying on the ground, a large wound through his groin, blood everywhere. The Chief tried to pick him up, to bring him back to the village, but his brother talked to him, saying if he moved, he would die.

"The Chief believed if he stayed on the ground like that, he would die anyway. But his brother convinced him, saying he didn't want to go back to the village like a cripple. He preferred to die in the open air, on the ground where battle took him with honour. So the Chief left him there.

"It is said the Chief sat in his wigwam for two days after that, no food, no water, even though they had won the battle and the neighboring tribe leaves us alone until now. Instead of making forays into our village to steal food, children, ponies, whatever they can get their hands on, they leave us alone. Our warriors beat them so badly they stay away. To this day. That's what happened."

"But he didn't die. What happened there? How did he stay alive?"

Little Bird looked across the water, her eyes focusing on the dark within the grove of birch trees. "No one of us knows for sure. The rumors are a Wolf came by and licked the wound clean. The Medicine Man had Wolf as his totem so some believe this is what happened. Others say Medicine Man himself pulled himself away and healed himself. How he did that no one is clear."

"Can't you ask him how he did it?"

"Oh, no, you don't just ask Medicine Man any old thing. He comes when he is ready and he leaves when he wants and he doesn't speak unless he wants to and no one has ever tried to ask him these questions."

To the silence of her new friend, Little Bird continued, "See, a Medicine Man is not like you and me. He is not even like the Medicine Women. He is one who has healed himself, by ways we don't know and who comes back to help us whenever he can. Or if he wants to. Some of the village women say they have seen two eyes looking at them from the forest when they bathe here." Little Bird stopped and looked at her new friend to see if this news had any effect.

"So he might," she continued looking into the trees, "be watching us right now."

Tahni's eyes searched the tree-lined shore. Nothing. But it wasn't her eyes that told her no one was there, it was her skin and belly. No sensation, just normal feelings. She knew they were alone.

By late afternoon inside Takoda's wigwam, and hers now, she reminded herself, Tahni stared into the fire. Someone had come while she was gone with Little Bird and lit a fire. The warm room felt oddly welcoming, already like home.

She looked into the fire and was so intent on her thoughts about Medicine Man, she did not hear him until the flap opened. She turned and saw Takoda's body, lean, tanned and tall, outlined by the fire's glow and her heart jumped a beat. Her legs again tingled and a warmth spread through her lower belly.

"Oh," she jumped up.

"No, no, I startled you." He was chuckling a little. "You

were far away. Were you thinking of home?"

"No. Besides, this is my home."

She saw his face light up a little. "I saw," she started to speak, then stopped, then started again, "I saw your horse gone. I thought maybe you had left…"

He moved swiftly to her side and put his hand on her arm just below the shoulder. "No, I will not do that. When I go, I will tell you first. I will not just leave."

His intentions were so clear tears clouded across her eyes.

"Have I made you sad?" his voice, low and gentle, was also full of emotion.

"No, no, not sad at all. You make me…you make me very happy." Tahni's face lit up softly as she spoke these words in a near whisper.

He leaned over to hear her better. His skin smelled of leathers, horses, reminded her of spring rain. She felt a bit dizzy, his face was so close to hers. He turned his head and brushed her lips with his. She startled. He stopped and stood to his height.

"I'll go get us some food."

"But, but that's my job…" she protested. Her head cleared a little and she kicked herself mentally for not being on top of this.

"And where will you go to get this food?" he gently mocked her.

"Oh, yes, of course," she murmured.

He brought back another meal full of flavor. This time they sat side by side on the same mat in front of the fire pit; this time she waited until he was full before beginning her food. When she had finished she placed her bowl down. His hand on the small of her back startled her, and she tightened up a bit.

He kept his hand where it was. "Are you finished eating?" he asked softly.

She felt ashamed of her fright, and confused about what else she was feeling. That growing warmth in her belly didn't come from the food, a tingling rose in her legs and now she felt her nipples pucker as the warmth of his hand on her back spread upward. She nodded, keeping her face down, afraid he would know what she was experiencing.

He sat very still, waiting. Finally, she looked at him. His face was turned to the fire. She studied his profile. A strong forehead, deep-set eyes, a large nose with a bump in the middle. 'Like a hawk's beak,' she thought. The most sensuous well-shaped mouth she had ever seen sat above a strong chin.

Her eyes roved his profile, detailing the small scar at the edge of his jaw, the hairline. She noticed how every now and then his nostrils flared slightly as though a thought of particular importance passed by.

Without turning his head he asked, "Do you approve?"

His words shocked her. What did it matter if she approved or not? He was the Chief, a great warrior and he had chosen her. It was up to him to approve of her. She didn't want to say anything wrong. She considered his tone and realized he was serious. From the circling thoughts whirling around she picked one. "Yes."

She thought she saw the corners of his mouth turn up, but what she was sure about was the racing in her heart, the increased heat in her legs and belly and how quickly her breath was coming, as though she had been running. He turned to look into her eyes, keeping his hand on the small of her back. He seemed to be considering something. She was going to ask in turn if he approved, but he leaned in and once more brushed his lips against hers.

This time she felt steadier. She had an impulse to put her arms around him but did nothing, since she had been taught it was up to the man. That was all she had been taught, but she held to it like a canoe in turbulent waters.

He stood suddenly then and she saw the bulge in his pants. He was at the door when he said, “I will be in my brother’s tepee if you need me for anything.”

Again Tahni sat alone, waves of disappointment rising within her, rising and falling.

Mary's Life

1885

London, England

Mrs. Sheldrake, keeper of this home for the indigent and insane, eyed the small, brown skinned man in front of her. He was talking, but what she noted was his personal warmth, which felt to her very like hope. Hope rose in her heart as a ghost, dangerous, wailing, pulling bitter disappointment right behind. She curled against this, unconsciously lifting herself to her full height and leaning her body away from him. The man's voice pierced through to Mrs. Sheldrake's brain.

"Mary Eagleton is her name. I believe she was registered with you several months ago," he was saying. His different skin and gentlemanly demeanor provoked in Sheldrake a sense of high society which her own cockney accent denied.

"Yes, yes, I know the one you speak of. She's up on the rafters, that one." She raised her eyebrows, her wrinkled face following the gesture until every line moved toward her greasy, gray hair.

"Yes, I'm sure it's been difficult," he acknowledged. "Here, if you would be so kind as to accept this..." and the small, soft palm of the gentleman opened, depositing a few shillings into her own hand, although she did not recall offering it to him.

"Of course you must want to see her yourself, you've come such a long way."

Mrs. Sheldrake's assumption, that the gentleman had travelled great distances from an exotic point of origin, provoked from her the use of formal names. "She'll be in the Recreation Room."

He turned silently and followed her through to a heavy door which she unlocked using a key from many dangling off the large metal ring at the side of her apron. They stepped a short way down a dark, narrow hallway where she beckoned with her hand that he look through a small, barred window on a door to his right.

People, maybe twenty, some shuffling slowly around the perimeter, any number of them moaning, or shouting suddenly, populated this dark den. Three small high windows on the opposite side opened directly to the elements. Years of snow and rain had flooded portions of the room and now moss grew beneath those far windows as though to remind those on this side of the green growing life outside. Yet no eye might take comfort by looking at trees or grass because the opening was too high. Only a scrap of sky for any who looked up, a scrap of sky and the moss, green and damp, lining the wall in a dingy, downward pattern.

No one looked in any case. They walked slowly, or rocked themselves or leaned against the walls, staring off to some other place, another time, or to nothing at all.

Mipham, whose native land India with its many meditation masters had afforded him training in observation, focus and attention, instantly absorbed the entire scene. His eyes however never stopped searching for Mary.

The former beauty huddled against the back wall, swaying slightly, her eyes distant, unfocused. He took in the matted, unwashed hair, swollen, infected skin, and the curve of her arms around an invisible baby to which, as he walked closer, he heard her humming.

What Mary experienced was a sunlit meadow just beyond the trees she saw in her inner world. She was trying to get to the meadow, to that safe, warm place.

"Mary," he called softly. Then again, "Mary."

The thin veil of possible comfort receded as she heard her name. The last syllable of her name yanked the next, Theodore, from her. Theodore who had loved her, Theodore whose child she had, Theodore gone from her, this name dredged with it an intolerable anguish.

"Theodo....ahrhg," the wail erupting from her thin body sounded part animal, part human, part from another dimension.

Mipham stepped back, reconfiguring. Clearly Theodore's callousness had cleaved her psyche more deeply than Mipham had understood. Now it was going to take time to bring her back, coax her back to the land of the living, "...if that is even possible," he thought. His training in meditation as a path to cure the mentally ill told him it was possible, but the depth of Mary's anguish and the loss of the child argued against it.

Mrs. Sheldrake, eager to ease this exotic and wealthy looking stranger's way, tried to soothe. "Now, now you didn't know she were as bad off as this…she comes and goes, she does and best left to being gone for all as ever 'appens is that wailing and moaning."

Her solid frame led Mipham back through the large door and out to the reception area.

"I'll come again, if that is quite all right," he said.

Anticipating the warm feel of shillings across her palm for whatever small favors she might apply to this man, Mrs. Sheldrake eagerly responded as her eyes followed her hand in replacing the key on its large ring, "Come as often as ye like, then. We'll take good care of her, our Mary, yes, we will, you can be sure of that, as best as…"

Mipham was already out the door.

For the next few visits he again crossed the sodden, grimy floor, stood a few feet away from Mary's side, watching. Mipham absorbed every detail including her breath, which came in and left from the top of her chest, stopping altogether for long periods of time. These two signs, her breath coming in and leaving through the top of her lungs, and the large gap between breaths demonstrated deep mental and emotional disturbance within the young woman.

He deliberately focused on his own breath, allowing it to come and go freely. Mary hummed, rocked her invisible baby, and stared toward the meadow only she could see.

Diana's Life

2005

near Toronto

Diana noticed how time rolled. If the days following her afternoon with Jake had shifted into slow gear, dragging into molasses minute by minute, she'd have known she was in deep trouble.

But time took its usual course. She had a phone call with Winona who wanted her to go dancing, "...you know, a night out, I really need it."

"Things tough right now?" Diana had known Winona was in trouble in her marriage, but she didn't want to pry. "Work?"

"No, of course not," Winona almost snorted, "It's Jeff."

"Ahhh," Diana let go a slow breath. "I don't know, Win..."

"Diana, you have been my friend for, what, over three decades..."

Diana stifled a desire to say 'so what?' She recognized her own cynicism and put it under wraps. She and Winona had been friends for a very long time.

"...and when you got back from India, who was here, waiting?"

"Oh good, guilt! The mark of a true friend is how swiftly they feel free to apply the pressure of guilt..."

Winona laughed, “But you know what I mean?”

“Where?” Diana already suspected the answer.

“Our favorite place...” Winona knew she had won and her voice rang in sunny tones.

“Oh, great...”

“David might be there...”

Diana knew David would be there. She knew because he had emailed her, he was back from his latest road trip, he’d be playing as usual on Wednesday night, ‘same place same time...famished!’ he’d written.

Like a teenager, still, Diana thought. Then to Winona, “Yeah, won’t that be fun? See you Wednesday night.”

Later that night Jake called. “You up for a long conversation?” his deep voice purred.

“Sure. How have you been?” Diana purred right back, expecting Jake to launch into talking about himself.

“I want to hear more about what happened...after.”

Surprised, Diana mused, “No one has ever asked for more about that.”

“Their loss. I’m in.”

“All right,” she said evenly, then chuckled through the phone, “You asked for it!

“Let’s see...after that day in the basement I was...different. I went to school, but my former personality, year book editor, athlete, first string trumpet in the school band, was being replaced by the wraith I was becoming, anorexic, empty, skinny, hollow. So I was in this change and there he was standing next to his locker, his guitar case right beside him, the new guy.

“He turned and just looked at me and I felt the air thrum, his blue eyes staring, meeting me somewhere inside, somewhere no one else knew about.

“When I heard there was a jam that day after school I decided to go. I was a loner and knew I’d have to face those pretty girls, the ones who knew how to dress and how to flirt.

What I knew was math and philosophy and poetry. Not much to use on a date!

"So it hurt, having to decide whether to go or not and believing I was somehow wrong for not being able to just make the decision. It shouldn't be that big a thing, I thought. Now I know it always is when we are young, when we first make these choices. But then it was one more proof to me that I didn't fit, couldn't fit." Diana paused briefly, then spoke again.

"I walked the long blocks to stand in the semi-dark basement of that upper middle class house, noticing the other girls standing together in their cool clothes, long straight hair, and their bored faces. I stood out, clumsy, awkward, dressed the wrong way, clearly alienated by the other girls who would not, did not talk to me and even he would not look at me, him with his guitar strapped on, notes coming through. Ignored me, I knew on purpose, until I gave up.

"I walked up that beautiful street in Toronto's East End..." Diana stopped as Jake said, "I know it well. Was born and raised right near there."

"Get out."

"True. Lived my life on Birchmount Road."

"You mean..."

"Yeah..." Jake's chuckle was rueful and warm. "We lived our lives separated by about twenty minutes of walking."

"Oh." Diana's brain came to a complete stop.

"That has meaning, you know...it's not coincidence." The certainty in Jake's voice sent goose flesh blossoming along Diana's arms and legs.

"I'm getting goose bumps."

"But go on...go on with your story."

Her brain kicked in again, "Those streets are lined with large mature trees and I was focusing on the trees, trying to get away from the inner collapse of my confidence...you know, teen trauma." Diana heard and enjoyed the sensation of feeling Jake almost smile.

"Then I heard a voice, 'Girl, girl wait up,' and there he was, David, trying to catch up to me, his ax knocking against his legs rushing up the hill. He walked me home, flirting, making jokes. I didn't know what to say so I said nothing.

"'What color are your eyes?' he demanded as we stood outside my house.

"'What?'

"'What color are your eyes?'

"'Brown.'

"'Nope.' He said this with great pleasure, contradicting me about something I ought to know. 'Nope. They're hazel. Your eyes have green flecks in them.'

"No one had ever noticed.

"I felt I had to put him out of my mind. You know this was a huge thing, to be so deeply attracted to him, and to believe I had no chance. Remember too, I did not recall one moment of what had happened in that basement. In the way of all trauma, it lay underneath, inside of me, controlling some things but not something I could get hold of.

"So I harangued myself, 'not possible, do not even begin to believe. He cannot like you, he is cool in blue jeans, his hair long, he plays guitar. He has cool girls, pretty girls after him. Many. Put it away. Do not think.' Yet I repeated every detail of that walk home for at least a week.

"I heard about him after that, learned he smoked grass."

Now Diana heard Jake laugh.

"Yeah, I know, it's nothing now but in those days that year in the late sixties it may have been all over California but here in Toronto it was still a huge thing. Reefer Madness, you know, blow a joint, tear your hair out, pull your clothes off, hump a hydrant..." The sound of Jake giggling slightly made Diana smile before she continued, "We all half-way believed it.

"So the memories of that basement sat inside me, coiled up, forgotten. Yet they controlled everything that started to happen. I refused...everything. I stopped being interested in school except to see how little I might do and still pass. Even passing didn't really matter. Nothing mattered. I stopped eating, stopped talking. The only point of life to me was David.

"I was seeing a psychiatrist, which in those days was rare. Now of course it's understood, high school years are so difficult but back then, I was the wrong one because I couldn't keep up, couldn't...be what everyone else wanted me to be, what everyone else it seemed to find it easy to be.

"I was in that state of madness, unable to sleep most nights, not eating, unable or unwilling to participate, and when I did open my mouth I said all the wrong things, talked about vibrations and energies and what I heard..." Diana stopped, suddenly aware she was saying things she had not even allowed herself to think about before.

Jake's warm voice brought her back, "I'm listening."

Diana gulped some air, carried on, "It was like that. Like standing outside a waterway where everyone else knew how to swim, and where I knew I was supposed to know how to swim, I had all the equipment to swim, but I couldn't. Failed every time I tried.

"I thought everyone else was just fine, getting along just fine. Then I met Winona.

"I met her in detention after class or one of those early morning things, you know..."

"Not me!" Jake's voice cut in, full of sarcasm. "I was an honours student."

"Yeah, right," Jake's delivery, his self-mockery made her laugh in spite of herself, "Yeah... I don't believe you!"

"Go on."

"Winona," Diana's voice grew soft, "a short girl with the largest brown eyes I'd ever seen...ever notice how you always met the best people in detention?"

“I never went to detention.”

“Come on.”

“No, I went to school, kept my mouth shut, my head down. I had no friends. Oh, yeah and that knife in my boot everyone knew about? Helped a lot.”

“What? You carried a knife? Back then, in Scarboro?”

“Yeah. My family...it was normal in my family. My dad gave me a knife, me and my brother. My parents survived the war in Europe. Carrying knives was nothing to them.”

“Oh.” Diana considered not for the first time how much of a bad boy Jake really was, and noticed how that thought made her lower belly churn.

“Go on with your story,” he said.

“Winona had these huge brown eyes behind huge glasses and black wavy hair, a nimbus, hanging to her waist. Her Native American blood made her exotic to me, romantic and when she smiled it was great.” Diana paused trying to pick her way through her thoughts.

“She didn’t smile much. Whatever sickness eats young girls’ minds and hearts, whatever disease takes all their joy away replacing it with grim despair, she had in the same way I did.

“Winona, knowing how I felt about David, arranged to buy some weed from him.

“I remember her saying, ‘You know, if we do this, there’s no going back.’ She had a way of pressing her lips lightly together. It was precise yet sensual. I knew no one else able to do this.

“‘Yes,’ I nodded seriously to her sense we were crossing a line. ‘Not ever.’

“‘We should consider. It’s our parents...’ she continued.

“‘I don’t care,’ I said to her. I was so defiant, thought of myself as a rebel.” Diana’s laugh was rueful.

“Yeah, such a rebel. Honours Student Goes Bad the headlines read.”

"For me it was a big step."

"I get that. Go on." Jake's sarcasm slowed Diana a little.

"Winona said she didn't care either, so anyway, we decided. It's pedestrian now but that event labelled us as outlaws. It was our initiation, a decision made consciously against whatever the rest of the world, those others who made no sense to us, believed.

"'I cared less about that, or about the weed, than having more time with David.

"'The tight circle of young bodies hovered in his small hallway, Winona, David, his friend, me, teen tension ricocheting off the walls, through the language and nervous laughter. All our lives we had waited for this moment, the possible forbidden entry into a darkness of living about to spill over.

"'His friend had a car. We climbed in, Winona and I in the back seat, David and his friend up front and we drove from his house in the East End to Cherry Beach.

"'To smoke up.' David said it casually from the front seat, the grand indifference of his language echoing the intensity and importance of the event.

"'We huddled together on the sand, stars everywhere above, even with the city lights.

"'Can go to jail for this,' his friend announced knowingly, scanning the beach, the bushes around it, as David opened the bag of weed.

"David glanced quickly at Winona and I, taking in our response.

"'I know,' Winona said in her precise way.

"David looked over his shoulders, saying, 'Doesn't look to me like anyone's around.' I thought he was profoundly smart, worldly.

"He lit the joint. We sucked on it according to his directions, trying hard not to cough.

"High, I walked a little way away and plopped down, crossed my legs, the sand under me. I looked up at the stars, hoping he would follow. It seemed like forever when he finally left them where they stood laughing and talking, walked over, saying, 'Hey, girl, come on, get up. It's time to go.'

"I looked up at him,"I feel like an Indian Princess."

"'You are a Princess,' he said pulling me to my feet. I could see in his eyes he meant it and when we were close I saw the hunger that stalks all young men. I thought it was personal.

"Through the short distance to his house I sat in the back seat obsessed with the idea the evening couldn't be over yet. In his house after the others left, he kissed me gently, then opened his front door.

"I walked out, crossed the porch, walked a couple of steps, and turned around. Knocked on his door.

"'Did you forget something?' he said lazily, standing aside so I entered that hallway again.

"'You're going to walk me home.'

"'What? No, I want to lie down on my couch, I'm stoned and real tired.'

"'I'm good enough to kiss, I'm good enough to walk home.'

"'I'm not going anywhere.'

"'Then I will stand here until your family return tomorrow night.'

"He looked into my eyes, grabbed his jean jacket, said, 'Come on, then.'

"We walked separately; all the way he kept saying, 'Good enough to kiss, good enough to walk home,' slinging the words through his mouth, small stones aimed at me.

"He will never see me again, will not ever want to see me again, I was sure. This thought argued with what I saw, that he was walking me home, giving me some show of caring.

"Instead of turning away at my house, stalking off in anger as I expected, he kissed me again. Kissed me over and over."

"'You're telling me you're a good kisser.'

Jake's voice brought Diana to an abrupt stop. "What? No, I didn't mean...I was just...I'm a story teller and I..."

"And you just told me you're good at kissing. It's fine, Diana. What else are you good at?"

"Oh, no, we're not going down that road, not tonight..."

"Does that mean some other night?"

"It means not tonight. It means I'm going to sleep now, Jake. Goodnight." Abruptly Diana hung up the phone, turned off the light and lay in the darkness, waiting for sleep.

Tahni's Life

1640's

Tonawanda

Watching Takoda's beautiful back slip out of their wigwam, Tahni felt all the warmth in the world leave with him. She remained sitting on the mat staring into the fire for a long time, going over and over in her mind what he had said, what she had said. Bewildered, she finally lay on the bear skins and fell asleep.

Next morning she awoke slowly, hoping to see his face when she opened her eyes. She stretched, pulled back the bear skin that covered her and walked around their wigwam, waking her body up. By the second circling, she was at the door, pushing back the flap. The village was alive and buzzing.

Everyone else it seemed was busy. She would have gone to the river to pull water, but did not know where the water bags were. She did not know where the food was kept, or she might have begun to prepare a meal for him. If he was coming!

If he was ever coming! Suddenly Tahni felt anger rise, its snakes whipping around inside her. All her people knew of these snakes, their dangerous venom. She began to run. Behind the village toward the trees where the horses and ponies were tied, she ran without thought as the anger within turned to heat and energy, an energy she pumped out through motion.

She found her pony, the one whose back had carried her out of her old life, slid herself across its warm back, grabbed the reins and with a soft cluck in its ear turned its head to face the open plain on the far side of her new village. Then she dug her heels into its fleshy sides.

Tahni relished the scent of warm horse and leather that wafted back into her nose as they raced across the flat land. She kept her hands on the horse's neck, her fingers laced in its mane, feeling the rhythmic pull of muscle as the animal ripped through the morning air. Finally she felt her stomach relax, her legs, gripping the pony's girth, let go just a little. Her mind was clear and her heart calm again. She slowed her mount to a walk.

She ambled along, paying full attention to the air on her skin, the animal beneath her and the flat plain dotted with many spring wild flowers she recognized, small holes where ground hogs, or chipmunks might live, birds above. Their sweet singing took her ears now the flush of wind from her ride had stopped. She looked up.

The river was to her left. To her right she saw a sweat lodge. Heat lines rose with a little smoke from the grandfathers, those rocks piled in front of the structure. A few men, she presumed from the Chief's village, stood around. She knew she was not supposed to see this. It was a man's ritual, one not necessary for women who had the honour and soul changing power to birth babies. Men had no such natural power. They needed sweat to cleanse their souls.

She dropped her eyes, turned her pony around in the opposite direction and urged it forward into a trot, then a canter toward the village.

The sound of horses' hooves pounding behind her came closer. For a small instant she wondered if another tribe, a hostile band lived close by. If so she would be a great prize for them. She urged her pony forward and again the small supple beast complied. Then she heard his voice, hailing her, "Tahni, slow down."

"You know how to ride!" He was smiling slightly and looking at her with that light in his eyes. The compliment sang in her ears and she glowed.

"I have, I always loved...horses and ponies mean so much!" she stammered.

His face opened into a wide grin, then he said seriously, "Would you like to come back to the village, or are you eager to ride more?"

She hesitated. She really did want to ride, to explore from the back of this sturdy beast this new area. "Let's ride, please," she said shyly.

They rode a steady pace toward the village until as they came through some birch trees Tahni saw they were at the lake.

"Little Bird brought me here yesterday," she said a bit surprised.

"I bet she told you all about Medicine Man. Tahni, you must not believe everything Little Bird says. She is known to..." Takoda turned towards Tahni, searching her eyes.

Then suddenly he grew playful again.

"Can you swim?"

Her answer was to strip her moccasins off, and wade in, her tunic floating around her. Takoda dove in behind her, splashed around, ducked under and used his hands as paddles to spray water on her. She laughed, but also noticed he did not touch her. Again her heart pulled.

Did she not excite him? Did he think she was a child? Why didn't he move towards her as she had been taught a man naturally would?

She lay beside him on the shore, her wet tunic cleaving to her voluptuous body's outline. She watched his chest rise and fall evenly with his deep breath. The spring sun was strong enough to warm them, then he stood, offered her his hand. As she leaned up, he brushed his lips across hers and turned toward the horses.

Suddenly, Tahni felt her skin tighten across her arms and chest, prickling with little bumps. Instinctively her head shifted toward the trees on the opposite shore. There, a distinct motion, shade and light to her right. A person. Her eyes steadied, but the outline kept still and blended with the shape of the trees.

She felt a shiver go through her body, a shiver that had nothing to do with the air on her skin. Again she saw the motion. This time the body came into full view, she knew on purpose. Anyone who could mask his body outline at will against the trees, that kind of shape-shifter would only be seen if he chose to be. He stood inside the grove of trees, away from the shore, but the angle of the sun revealed his eyes on her. She felt those eyes like another skin. She held her own eyes steady as she stood on the shore and waited.

Takoda's voice broke the spell, "Come, Tahni."

Now it was Takoda watching her.

Just as well, she thought, to have a Medicine Man know I am here, in case I have need of his medicine. Still she felt a strong difficult energy around her, a sense of foreboding in her chest.

As they walked their horses back toward the village, Tahni hesitated, then asked shyly, "Little Bird said Medicine Man was your cousin," she paused, "or brother."

"A long time ago."

They did not speak again, as though Medicine Man had put a spell on their tongues. When they reached home, he said, "I will go for food."

Takoda came back shortly with his hands full. She took the warm pot from him and gestured to him to sit, spooned the food into his basket, and sat herself down next to him to wait. Tahni felt empowered by this.

If she couldn't cook for him yet, she could serve him as a proper wife would.

She walked to the back of the wigwam where she stacked the dishes.

"I will wash them by the river tomorrow," she said. She wanted to support him, take care of him, be his woman.

He was lying on his side when she turned back. Their eyes locked. Tahni saw a stream of warmth, a river of fever slice through the room. She felt it enter her body, heating her. He patted the bearskin next to him twice. She lay down with her back to the warmth of the fire and her breasts near the warmth of his chest. He waited.

He turned to her steady gaze, smiled lazily then leaned up into a half sit. Disappointed, Tahni got up, followed his steps to the door of their wigwam.

"I will…"

"Be at your brother's wigwam. If I need anything…" she smiled. He kissed her lightly, turned and left.

Tahni lay down by the fire, the inner questions circling like hungry dogs, but soon she slept.

Light bounced through her eyelids, pushing her to wakefulness. She had been in a dream of some joy, in the meadow again, vague but beautiful. She sat slowly up and saw his graceful, solid body moving silently through their home.

"'Good morning," he said softly. Clearly he had been watching her, waiting for her to wake up. He slid through the air toward her, leaned in, kissed her cheek, then each eyelid.

"You slept well."

She pushed the bearskin back and sat up, noticing water skins leaning at the edge of the wigwam.

"I will be here this evening," he said. With a small smile at her he pulled back the flap and walked out.

Tahni took the water skins on each shoulder and moved through the village toward the stream. She knew she would be given one task after another, learning each one along the way until she was in charge of their home, their food, clothing and the children they would certainly have. Water essential for all life, the basis of all life, was first.

The backs of many women from the village bent and lifted over the flowing stream, their full water skins on the shore. Tahni thought the women looked like brown, tan and yellow river flowers, bending and swaying, river flowers with tongues of joy. Their sweet voices rose above the gurgling rush of water, seeming to welcome her. This she understood, she remembered and felt at home with, many women, working together, each for herself, for her family and for the village. She walked to the edge of the gathering. Everyone moved enough to give her space at the shore's edge without drawing undo notice to her.

Then she saw the beautiful older woman she had seen a few days ago in the wigwam where the women had greeted her. The woman saw Tahni. Everyone ignored Macawi as she glided toward Tahni.

Tahni felt more than her usual shyness around this warm, strong woman. She kept her head down, her eyes on the water and water skins until Macawi spoke.

"You have the look of a new bride," Macawi's strong voice, surprisingly deep for a woman, lay in Tahni's ears like a hug. Tahni laughed a little as, hoisting one full bag to the shore she looked into the older woman's eyes.

"I see," Macawi said, a little puzzled, "you are yet a maiden..."

Keeping her eyes on the flowing water in front of her, Tahni hid her shame. She felt the cool, refreshing water lapping around her legs, absorbed the deep green of the birch tree buds, dark shoots of fiddlehead ferns poking from the shoreline. She heard laughter and joy from the voices of the women and children so close by and knew they could not hear what she and Macawi said. Besides, it would be unspeakably rude for anyone to intrude upon a private talk.

Tahni turned back to the eyes of Macawi and said nothing, but her deep confusion about her husband rolled across her eyes like clouds.

"So you don't know," Macawi said very softly. The older woman waited a moment, deciding something, then said, "Takoda, your husband, disappears each day."

"I have seen his horse gone from the other horses."

"You don't know where he's going?"

As Tahni shook her head her lovely ebony hair fell across her shoulders.

"He goes to the Sweat Lodge, past the lake. Little Bird tells me you have been to the lake?"

Tahni nodded.

"Every morning your husband goes to the Sweat Lodge. The grandfathers glow very hot for him. That helps keep the heat in his blood from bursting."

Macawi waited. Tahni heard the words, then felt them come together in a different way. She looked, her eyes wide, at Macawi.

"Ah, so now you see. He is at war, with his blood."

"But if he…all he has to do...he is..." Tahni protested.

"No. This is our way. If he were chief of some other tribe, he would have already taken you, whether you were ready or not. He might have hurt you and you would become hard, tough like old skins that have not been properly treated. Your body would heal but your heart would grow old too quickly. This is what our people believe." Macawi paused. "Like all our warriors, he has been trained in love by the older women, trained to hold his desire until you are ready." Macawi paused. "We believe the union of man and woman to be the most healing and sacred of all healing rituals."

Tahni's eyes roved across the stream again. She thought, "He leaves at night because he believes…"

"You have not invited him. He believes you are not ready."

Relief poured through her body, loosening her shoulders, releasing tension from the back of her neck. Her beloved loved her, wanted her. He was waiting for her!

"Why," she asked the older woman, "did he not say something?"

"Then you would still be doing what he wants. He knows…he knows you..." Macawi stopped speaking in words. To speak the words of feelings, love, or yearning, or lust even, was to invite oneself into the experience. Macawi did not want to intrude.

Macawi led the way up the bank of the stream and over to join the other women. As Tahni followed she tried to keep her focus present.

"We are going now to gather food for this evening," one woman cast her eyes at Tahni as she said this, clearly inviting her.

Tahni found Macawi at her elbow, saying softly, "Just follow me."

Tahni with a skin full of water across each shoulder, walked with the group, listening, observing, but now waiting intensely for evening.

Tahni walked with the women past her wigwam, slipped inside momentarily to deposit her water bags, then joined this, the largest group of women, of people, she had ever known. Their sounds didn't stop, their voices tinkling over one another. They all spoke together but everyone seemed to know what was being said. It took Tahni by surprise. She thought she'd never be able to distill the words and speaker from the general throng of sound. Still they welcomed her with smiles of encouragement, to sit by the large pit where meat roasted, to dig in the ground for the tubers they had cooking, and when the time came, to take what she needed.

She sat inside the cool quiet of her home, resting. Half a day gone, half more to fill until she might have, and give, her heart's fulfillment. Her young strong body so used to hard work rebelled against the comparatively slow pace of this new life. She was restless.

She lifted the flap of the wigwam and walked strongly toward the lake, around the busy villagers in their lives. Past the ponies and horses, his gone.

She paused before stepping out of the forest onto the sand beach. She could feel, but not see Medicine Man. His sense was upon her skin, like a not unpleasant breeze except here, protected by the trees behind her, there was no breeze. The air seemed slightly different too, almost thick, as though an invisible robe lay upon her. She waited. A hawk flew from a treetop to her right, gracefully dove into the water, retreating with dinner firmly clasped in its beak. Gone. The signs, her skin, the air, everything back to what she knew as normal. She did not doubt he had been there. Her body had told her. Her body, she knew, did not lie.

She stripped, ran into the warm water. Using her arms like wings to push water cleanly in front and to her sides, kicking her legs like her friend Frog, she swam deliberately, focusing her mind on each motion, trying to escape the circle of joyful anticipation that made this day drag. She swam until she could swim no longer, then trolled her body along the lake's current, playing in circles, turning buoyant somersaults in the now refreshing wetness.

On the shore she lay her belly on the sand, felt the sun's slanting rays across her back. After a while she turned and let the sun dry her front. Relaxed and refreshed, she made her way back.

Inside their home, she warmed the food and waited, dogs of excitement leaping in her stomach, lurching against each moment.

Tahni lay on the bearskin rug, watching the fire. As Takoda walked silently to her side, his eyes catching something new in hers, she patted the place beside her.

"Come here, my husband," she said a little shyly.

His eyes lit up and his body emitted a warmth that felt to her like a warm fur on a cold winter's night. He sat beside her very still.

"I do want..." she began.

"Yes," Takoda turned to look into her eyes, "yes, and I am eager. First, we blend our breath," and he waited until her breath matched his.

All through the night as they made love, he slowed down to find her breath, to match their inhales and exhales. Tahni didn't know what it meant beyond a joy of wreathing herself with her own inner vitality to him, her husband in soul and now in body.

Finally, exhausted, they slept curled in each other's body, their hunger satisfied for now.

Night sky spilled into her eyes, slowly the stars she knew, had known from earliest childhood arranged themselves in her still sleepy brain through the small hole above the fire. A waft of the food she had brought it in earlier greeted her nostrils and she pulled back the covers, his hand on her arm sudden in its grip, holding her, letting her know he was aware of her.

"I'm hungry," she smiled at him.

She ladled stew into a pot and handed it to him with a piece of bread, coarse, dark brown, his mouth folding over it, slack with pleasure.

When the meat met her tongue, its flavor broke open, dark layers tripping each other across her mouth. The intensity stung her mind until she half believed her husband was shaman.

By and by he put his hand out on the small patch of ground between them. Slowly she reached her own hand over. She placed it on his. Warmth spread between her legs and into her belly, a small volcano of fire again.

In the morning Tahni opened her eyes to his smiling face, his warm arms. He said her name again into the light;

last night's dream vanished. She reached for him.

"You..." she began, but his eyes told her he knew the invisible cocoon held them both, safely alone, together. Again the hunger rose in her, again his gentle, restrained and disciplined approach reached the deepest parts of her, body and soul.

Satisfied by each other, they needed more food.

"But first," he said gently, "we need to bathe."

He took her hand and helped her to her feet. Tahni felt herself flowing, aware of a new lightness in her body.

She stood still at the open door of their home, taking in warm, even breaths. The same sights greeted her, women, children, the familiar noises of village life, the known scent of spring air, wet and wild with promise, but something caught her mind.

Underneath the talk, bark, caw, and laughter, below the surface of faces and bodies, she felt viscerally, almost saw, an energy, a force of life that united each one with the other, into a totality of everything, everywhere pulsing also in each one. Her body recognized this Greater Body, part of her belonging, her being, as much a part of her now as her own breath.

What surprised and thrilled her was her new ability to sense this pulse below the surface of everything: this living, breathing vibration pulsing beneath all she saw, heard, touched, tasted or smelled. Everything rose from this field of intelligent, loving strength. That pulse sustained her own body, the bodies of all the people, and more: all animals, insects, fish and birds, that wild pulse emanated life, was the source of life and in the end all would return to it.

She knew this as the Soul of the Village. She knew this energy as the part of Great Spirit infusing her new life, her new companions, two-legged and four-legged in this village. Tahni was struck still by the thrust of its power.

"It is natural," he said, reading her mind. "When the great storm is met with welcome all the world rejoices. Our senses wake up to greet the real physical world. In this way, loving heals."

She listened, focusing on that living presence, Great Spirit.

Mary's Life

1883

London, England

Two years and some months before the day Mipham walked into Benham House For the Indigent and Insane to find one Mary Eagleton, Lady Agnes Fieldworth discovered a way to satisfy her desire to enjoy the vast material wealth of her own life with less of the accompanying guilt, through a philosophy known as Fabianism. This stream of thought encouraged Lady Fieldworth, widow and owner of the most expensive estate in London, to believe no distinction, except through dress and housing for example, existed between persons of what was termed the lower classes and those of her own extremely upper class.

To prove to herself she was a good Fabian, dedicated to the Fabian beliefs in action and not simply words, each year she extended invitations to one or two people from a different social strata, an invitation to attend her own storied social gala of the season.

This year Agnes Fieldworth's largesse had landed on one Beatrice Eagleton and her daughter Mary. Known to Agnes Fieldworth as the dressmaker, a superb seamstress, really, Beatrice Eagleton received the verbal invitation in a manner typical to the personality of her would be hostess.

In the elaborately decorated bedroom of Agnes Fieldworth, as the seamstress on her knees attempted to pin an unruly hem of voile, the generous Lady trilled, "What would you think, Beatrice, what would you think, if I..." Lady Fieldworth, anticipating a declaration of delight, a thrum of excitement from the woman at her feet, paused dramatically, "...if I invited you..."

Beatrice, her face to the floor, felt her cheeks reddening, and her temper rising.

"...if I invited you..." she repeated, "...and your daughter, Mary I believe her name is, yes? You and your daughter Mary..."

Invisible still, Beatrice's face lost its flush and her mind snapped to genuine interest. Mary?

Beatrice saw the beautiful face of her young daughter. Beatrice had kept Mary close to her, not allowing time to chat with the local boys, suspicious of everything Mary said or did. She knew Mary would beam, that all of her sixteen year old heart would delight in such an opportunity. 'That's the problem with her,' Beatrice's thoughts continued. 'She's all impulse and no thought.' As much as Beatrice tried to make Mary wake up to this world, a world that could be so cruel, Mary insisted on returning to some land where fairy tales come true, a place she believed the world to be. 'Child lives in a fantasy. It'll lead to no good,' Beatrice, her mouth full of pins, heard her own thoughts. Still, a chance like this? Once in a lifetime? Perhaps some good man of breeding might be taken with her daughter's beauty, fall in love, overlook the child's flightiness.

"...you and your daughter Mary to this year's gala?" Lady Fieldworth waited, gazing upon the head of greying hair at her feet, waited for the face below the hair to look up with joy and gratitude.

Beatrice Eagleton, her eyes as remote as they'd been since the moment her heart had first been broken, looked up at Lady Agnes Fieldworth who, seeing neither joy nor gratitude, felt her own cheeks flushing in embarrassment. Such was the effect Beatrice had on many people.

Removing the pins from her thinly set mouth, Beatrice continued to gaze at Lady Fieldworth, then said, "Thank you. Mary will attend," in a most curt tone before returning her focus to turning, pinning and stabilizing the frothy material at the bottom of Lady Fieldworth's ankles.

Thus it was Lady Fieldworth now scanned the room quickly filling with beautiful young woman, tuned her ears for the name Mary Eagleton to issue from the door man's nasal voice, heard it and rushed forward.

"Mary, my dear," she punctuated her words with a kiss on each of Mary's glowing cheeks. "How beautiful you look! I'm sure you are the most dazzling young beauty here!"

Mary blushed under the genuine warmth of her host's comments.

"But come with me. I must introduce you to some of the young people." Lady Fieldworth led Mary, her senses basking, her mind dazed, toward a cluster of young women about her own age, all beautifully dressed, all looking confident, exuding the easy happiness of youth who have lived untouched by life's harshness.

Among these young women Brigitte was royalty. Despite a short, stocky body, currently swathed in expensive material that had been coaxed by none other than Mary's mother to show off the best features of her body, regardless of eyes set a little too closely in her face and a slightly large nose, she was their leader. To avoid being the target of her deeply jealous and intently ambitious verbal cruelty, the other young women agreed with her in all things.

Brigitte spotted Mary, a stranger, gliding across the floor on the arm of Lady Fieldworth. In an instant Brigitte absorbed Mary's voluptuous shape, tiny waist and abundance of auburn hair looking in the gas lamp light as fine as spun gold.

"Mary Eagleton," Lady Fieldworth introduced Mary first

to Beatrice.

As she reached her hand limply to hold Mary's fingers in greeting, Brigitte took in the dark blue eyes, almost violet, lit from the inside with excitement. She assessed Mary's dark brown eyebrows and full soft pink lips. The final, agonizing detail was Mary's flawlessly smooth pink skin.

Brigitte purred as she clasped Mary's hand in both of hers. "And what," she murmured so those in the immediate crowd might hear, "does your father do, Miss Eagleton?"

"I...I have no father." Mary felt blood clawing up her throat, laying siege to her face in a rouge of feelings she tried desperately to handle properly. "My mother...," she continued, confusion compelling a belief that saying something would be better than saying nothing, "is a seamstress."

Lady Fieldworth, oblivious to Mary's precarious social position, had melted into the whirl of color and sound outside this small circle of faces, abandoning her young charge to the very snobbery the Lady herself hoped to extinguish.

Mary felt her fingers dropped, suddenly, as Brigitte turned with a triumphant smirk on her face to the others.

"Oh, really?" she sneered, turning eyes full of ice back on Mary. "How nice for you and your mother." The words had the effect Brigitte desired. Like a garden of flower blossoms reaching toward the sun, the small clique leaned their shoulders together, excluding Mary and began to talk all at once.

Flames burned Mary's cheeks. Slightly bewildered, she moved quietly away from the row of shoulders, and stood by a wall. The acute sting of her embarrassment quickly dissolved as her young senses turned outward to absorb the ballroom scene she witnessed.

Such refined clothes, colors, shapes, each woman curtsying, each man bowing, the room itself bulging it seemed with freshly cut flowers. Exquisite music from the orchestra laced the air. Perfumes she had never imagined filled her head. She stood, quietly dazzled, a little giddy, just watching.

She eased her way past some potted plants and casement windows to a large pair of French doors and slipped out into the night. On the stone balcony, geraniums bloomed in urns, lilacs from the garden beyond scented the air and overhead a sliver crescent of waxing moon brightened the night sky to a dark blue.

She rested against the cold granite balustrade, which glittered as though with diamonds in the light from inside the house. Grateful for this moment of quiet in an evening of sensual excess, she breathed in deeply, wanting to capture all the details she might.

She closed her eyes for a moment then suddenly felt another presence on the balcony. Opening her eyes she saw the most dazzling young man she had ever seen.

He was of medium height and build, perfectly proportioned but it was his face that drew her in. Handsome, even features and large hazel eyes reminded her of something warm and intimate, something she instantly knew she had forgotten and now wanted to remember. Across his features played a clarity of feeling, a mix of emotions she watched with a sudden hunger she felt she had always known. She wanted to be the reason for those feelings.

She understood before he spoke what he was feeling, although she could hardly believe he felt this because of her. He was attracted and the attraction shone with a touch of humour from his eyes.

"A beautiful evening, my Lady," he began.

"Yes. A wonderful night for the ball."

"I don't know how mother manages it, but every year she chooses a different date and every year the weather is perfect."

"Oh, so this is your…" Mary felt suddenly confused and embarrassed. He was Lady Fieldworth's son, one of the wealthiest young men in London.

"I'm afraid so. It has terrible drafts, I must apologize. I'm sure you've noticed." His warm voice was full of humour.

Gaining emotional balance, she quipped, "Do you refer to the house or the party?"

His eyes lit up at this and his mouth, which had been in a slight smile, the smile of a host, widened over even white teeth until his whole face reflected her humour. Two deep dimples appeared in his checks.

Mary found herself staring into his eyes as unfamiliar emotions and sensations begin to roil inside her. At sixteen she still possessed the impulsive nature, the unthinking enthusiasm of a child. Indeed, where many her age had already developed insight about the nature of men and women, social status and the potential pitfalls of life, Mary's imagination and idealism protected her from taking in harsher aspects. She gave herself fully to each moment, without thought, convinced that was all that was required of her.

As she stared she realized he was staring back as intently, and it seemed to her in as much bewilderment. She felt her lower belly churn, rolling and burning.

"The house, of course," he murmured, still smiling. Recovering himself a little he offered his hand. "I am Theodore Fieldworth, son of the owners of this Drafty Hall. And you are…?"

"Mary. Mary Eagleton…" Mary blushed.

"Well, Mary, Mary Eagleton, anyone as beautiful as you deserves to have two first names. Would you do me the honour of the next dance?"

As Theodore offered Mary his arm she felt fire licking up from her stomach, under her ribs. Her thighs grew warm and she heard herself thinking perhaps she was coming down with an illness. The thought melted as she glanced up at her host and recognized on his face a look of delight and appreciation.

They walked together through the French doors onto the ballroom floor, where for Mary everything dissolved in a delicious swirl of motion, color, sound and the touch of Theodore Fieldworth's body, strong and gentle, holding her, turning her in the fast paced waltz.

Exquisite music from the orchestra reverberated through the air as Theodore Fieldworth's expert moves guided her through the spins of the waltz. The long frilled gowns with tight bodices covered in trilled lace, gathered silk, sheered satin, the plummeting necklines revealing creamy upper half-moons of beautiful breasts heaving faster and faster, bright colors twirling round and round called upon Mary's senses in a dizzying manner until her fingers clutched Theodore's arm. His eyes, having never left her face, lit up at the pressure. Her world narrowed suddenly to one person and one person only.

The music ended and Mary, panting slightly, reminded herself he was the host, obligated to be charming and attentive to all his guests.

"He is," she struggled to use her reason, "only being a proper host. The dance has ended and that will be that."

Theodore looked down at her. He saw her flushed face, pink under the flawless skin, her dark and serious blue eyes, half-opened mouth gasping a little against the tight stays which offered her swelling breasts, rising and falling hard on her breathing, up to the soft gas light. He couldn't take his eyes away. Instead of leaving to offer his arm to another partner, he found himself holding his arm to her for a second dance. The quadrille involving four pairs of partners, kept Theodore and Mary looking at others as often as each other and so was more socially appropriate.

However, Theodore's slightly rash move in asking Mary for a second dance had not gone undetected. Matrons who believed the purpose of their invitation was to compare this ball unfavorably with others from the past, and to comment upon the flagging moral standards since those earlier fetes, lined the walls in small clusters. Like border plants guarding the soil from weeds and providing delineation between one riotous spring flower and another, these matrons sat squarely on their chairs, commenting behind their hands and fans and between delicious bites of delectable morsels, on who was dancing with whom, the personal history and possibly suspect morality of same, and whether said morality had been inherited. "His mother, my dear, was exactly the same at that age," one of them might say.

"And with such a father, who can expect more?" another might add.

Through raised eyebrows they signaled to each other they had noticed the flushed faces and probable raised pulses of the eligible young host and his partner.

One other person noticed. Brigitte, from her bevy of young beauties and behind her mask of angelic serenity and pleasure was mentally embroiled in a temper tantrum. She saw Theodore Fieldworth as hers; their parents had practically arranged their marriage since childhood. She had welcomed this ball, had looked eagerly forward to making a display of their affection, although Theodore had given her nothing to hang this desire upon. She simply took it as her right, given their equal social status and their parents' enduring friendship. She deserved to be on his arm! Now that little snippet of a nobody, Mary Seamstress, was spoiling everything.

When their dance ended, Mary looked up seriously into Theodore's face, knowing this time she must let him go.

"Thank you, Mr. Fieldworth." Mary curtsied quickly, in part to hide the feelings consuming her. "You have been most kind."

She glided back to her position at the wall, content with having glimpsed paradise. She did not for one instant believe herself a member of that blessed crowd, nor had she any conviction that Theodore Fieldworth thought of her as other than one of many guests so her surprise was genuine when after a few more dances, during which Mary kept careful if furtive note of where he was, she saw him walking again towards her.

"Would you," he seemed a little unsure of himself, "would you accompany me to the balcony?" Almost whispered, his words yet thundered through her blood.

"Surely," she murmured, already following him. The power of her inner feelings made her believe she need do no more than follow those same feelings and all would be well. The grip of lilac scent fell upon her again and the air, now cooler than before, made her gasp a little, as she entered the night through the French doors.

"You're too cold. I shouldn't have…" Theodore began.

"No, I'm fine. It's just a little air," Mary's hands instinctively rubbed her upper arms as she said this. Theodore took each hand, pulled her gently away from the light of the room inside, and into his body. She felt his warmth through the clothing, and since he held her so close, felt something firm, through the layers of her skirt, against her.

She was swimming in an airless space, with light all through the darkness and his face, Theodore's handsome face, swimming in this air toward her, "Mary, I …" he moaned, before kissing her softly on the mouth.

Mary felt her body relax in the warmth of the fire, now flaming against her upper legs, her belly, her breasts. She knew nothing but him and the heat his mouth awakened in her.

She pulled away from him to catch her breath.

"Mary, the guests are almost ready to leave. Stay with me. Wait for me down there. There is a coach house. Please…"

He took her by the hand and led her, half running, down the stone balcony steps and out to the back of the garden. There, a tiny house, one room really, stood. He opened the door and drawing her inside, held her firmly against him again. His fingers twined through her hair, one hand strayed along her bosom; her eyes met his and "yes" escaped her mouth before his mouth landed once more on her soft lips.

"Oh, Mary, I won't be long." His voice was husky.

Her voice broke softly as she whispered, "I'll wait." Then he was gone, the air closing behind him.

Diana's Life

2005

near Toronto

Winona pushed open the door, slid her small frame through while Diana spread the door wide to allow her own tall body into the outer recess. It was all the same, the pale green paint peeling even more than before at the corners of the walls, the ceiling missing a few cardboard tiles, the front area where a couple of guys in black jeans, logo-ed t-shirts past their best-before date, hair pulled back into grey streaked pony tails, leaned their white skinned beer bellies billowing out beneath the t-shirts above the low belted jeans, leaned those fleshy parts against the green felt of the slightly off kilter pool table. Posters on the wall announced a gig that had happened so long ago the musicians' grown children barely recognized in them their own parents.

Up one more step past the pool table area, Diana noticed to her right the same waitress, forever just past middle age, dyed blonde hair turning grey, rounding her large circular tray against her comfortably padded hip, ready for the first table of the night.

Diana glanced to her left and saw the owner's son, Kenny, working the restaurant area. Or so it was called. The food was always as greasy as any belly wrung with too much booze might want, served in scarce portions on white paper plates so a customer even a little high might believe herself at an indoor picnic.

Winona raised her arm to Diana, signaling which table she'd chosen, then disappeared into the Women's. It was behind what passed as a stage, beyond a towering stack of mostly unused old speakers, to the right. Two wooden door framed cubicles displayed enough graffiti scrawled in every imaginable color and pen, pencil, magic marker, indelible ink shooter to satisfy any street artist. The words amounted to the usual collection of cleverness "Kant says 'to do is to be', Sartre says 'to be is to do', Sinatra says 'do be do be do'," as well as measurements of various men's bits and some girls parts. Scribbled in one corner, a piece of hate against David, citing his size and the inverse proportions of his intelligence. Diana read it, tossed it in her mental bin, marked "trash."

Outside in the small passage, David stood unwinding some cords. He smiled before he turned to hold open his arms as she came into them.

"Oooh..." he said, all sexy and warm.

"Uh, huh..." Diana responded, her body registering his warmth, his need, the way all boundaries seemed to dissolve so their flesh became one, even in a hug.

"Winona is here."

"I know. Already saw her." David's prim tone told her he understood. She would be leaving with Winona.

"Just hafta wait, I guess." David chuckled.

Diana and Winona danced, so much and so long that the more boisterous drunks started hollering after them, "you two lesbos? dyke dames?" They ignored this, as they ignored the wallpaper, streams of browning, fading line drawings of women with naked breasts of various sizes and shapes, a throwback to the sixties when tastelessness flourished in the name of freedom. Ignored everything, everyone except the music and the glorious joy in movement.

At the break, David stood near the back of the room, surrounded by members of the band and a variety of musicians who clung to the notion of their turn on stage. It was an open mic during the second set. David stood there, taking names and organizing these wannabes as he called them, and off to the left sat a woman Diana noticed. She was short, plumpish, and obviously taken with David who spoke with her a few times.

The alarm in Diana's stomach flipped on as she watched that, a fluttery, 'I'm not going to like this' feeling brought on by roller coasters, natural disasters and every time David strayed.

Stay, Diana, she thought. You are here to clear this out, once and for all. No more! No more believing him, if he's lying, just stay, watch it all, wait and see.

Two nights later, Diana answered the phone to Jake's warm deep voice.

"How's your week been?"

"Good," she said truthfully. "And you?"

"About as good as a retired gunslinger's can be."

"So, if you had such a hot shot job, what happened?" Diana's natural bluntness was softened by her easy going tone.

"Politics. I wasn't well liked. The suits wanted someone they could control and that wasn't me. So I took early leave. Got a large package and left."

"Hmmm that simple, huh?"

"For tonight, yes."

"What did you do with the money?"

"Just like a woman, wanting to know about the money..."

"Whoa buddy, remember this is an old feminist you're talking to so don't bring all that 'woman' stereotyping to..."

"All right, then. I took the money and supported my brother who had MS. He was dying. I couldn't do anything to change that but I could buy him a first rate hospital bed, get him a private room, all the bells and whistles that money would buy while I supported myself. I visited him almost every day for the last two years of his life."

"Oh, Jake...I don't know what to say...that's so sad but it was so loving of you to care for him that way."

"That's what you do." Diana heard the verbal shrug in Jake's voice, a shrug that was sincere. It really was just what Jake did.

"Anyway, I want to know more about you, Diana."

"You haven't had enough yet? I have...the best way for me to talk then, is to keep the story going. You all right with that?" Diana hesitated for a moment, then began again. "David walked me home..."

"I like that part. Tell me that part again."

Diana was quiet for a long moment.

"I'm sorry, Diana. That was childish of me. I do want to listen. And..."

Diana knew he meant he wanted her. Diana realized with a start she knew or felt Jake's thoughts in the same way she had known David's. The understanding chilled her momentarily.

"It's okay. Let's just continue. I'll keep talking, something I'm good at." The weak joke eased the slight tension.

"The next day I told Winona what had happened. I thought her quiet response meant she was concerned David was not committed to me yet. It took some time before I recognized she wanted David for herself. Still, she and I understood each other in some way that mattered greatly.

"You understand, she was just as close to... she was just as depressed as I was. She too hung by a precarious balance, any hour being the one in which the final act would take place. People think suicide happens with great drama inside the person. Not my experience. For me and I believe for her it was the inner silence, the death of any emotion, feeling, anything at all. That inner death signaled a need in me to end my physical life. We hung on to each other, knowing without speaking about it, we were each other's life line.

"Winona and I begged our parents, received permission and money to attend a Donovan Concert. In the huge stadium, no chairs on the floor, but large floor cloths topped with various rugs and carpets and pillows where people were meant to sit, cross legged if they chose, our silent looks to each other meant we believed this was to be a superlative spiritual experience.

"Dwarfed in the crater size space, one small raised platform held the thin young man. Dressed in flower child white cotton pants, long sleeved colorfully embroidered shirt, a variety of musical instruments around him, Donovan sat, tuning his guitar and watching as the crowd streamed in.

"Winona and I moved directly in front of him. He looked at me, straight into my eyes and I felt a connection that thrilled some place deep within. Everything felt smooth, simple and clear. It was all right now, going to be all right. I felt strong enough to accept what had to be done.

"As we filed out afterwards, Winona said, her eyes flashing up at me, 'What did you think?' I saw her catch the void inside me.

"'It's all right now,' I repeated. She held my arm, used my elbow to steer me. Winona, this tiny girl, my dark haired angel, guided me to the street car.

"'It's not all right,' she insisted, concern smearing her dark eyes. 'Everything is just like it was before.'

"Her eyes searched mine for contact. I had to respond to their frantic laser focus, had to force myself out of that wonderful, limitless place where no pain ever existed, ever would exist, had to because she loved me.

"'Yes,' I said finally.

"She turned to me again, her black eyes flaming each with a single yellow point of focus, 'You must come back. I know it's difficult,' her smooth full lips moved only enough to allow each syllable its due.

"'Yes,' I said.

"She heard me, turned to leave, said, 'I will call you when you get in.'

"'It's all right, I mean I'm okay,' I said.

"'No. I'll call you.'

"I stayed by the phone, and when she called admitted I had had a blissful feeling of the next reasonable step.

"'I know,' she said. 'I feel that way, too sometimes.' We said nothing more but held onto the phone for many minutes, breathing, staying close in our hearts, our minds in some blank, peaceful place we both knew, knowing that without the other, that place would compel, magnetize, force us into its seductive peace.

"She said good night and hung up only when I had promised I would not try to kill myself.

"If she felt I was unhappy, or 'in trouble' was how we put it, when each sensed the other was again falling into that dark empty place, we threw out life lines and quickly saw we hit target far more than mere coincidence allowed. Then we began to practice consciously.

"'Are you all right?'

"'I thought I felt you.'

"'What number am I holding in my head?'

"'What object in this room am I focused on?'

"Our meetings had always had the feel of meditation, few words, long pauses, sometimes punctuated by music, usually Leonard Cohen. I tried to meditate, alone, but then the phone would ring. Sometimes it was David because he also had it. He'd 'send' to me, and I knew what he was feeling, thinking but more often Winona, phoning because she sensed me close to an edge she shared. Or I felt her falling away, her silence losing itself in the immensity of that place. I knew my words wound like a rope bringing her back. Without each other, an unbearable vulnerability prevailed, like the unfurled wetness of a butterfly's wing exposed prematurely to air, light, too weak to fly.

"Phone call by phone call, hand over hand she and I kept each other from what mesmerized us both. Gradually we three saw we were bound to each other, so strongly, but they both said it was strongest with me.

"I knew my body had scars, physical ones, temporary scars that had to heal before I let him see me. He would have asked. I kept the scars to myself, the burn marks and bruises until they healed.

"That was how I fell in love with David. It felt like fate. He used to rock me in his arms, the scent of him comforting and exciting, through his jacket as we huddled together, cuddling, next to the concrete walls of a Catholic schoolyard up the street from my parents' house, where we necked our angst into a deeper thrust, more profound need. He'd rock me and say, 'We are star crossed lovers, can't you feel it?'"

"How romantic!" said Jake.

"I guess it does seem syrupy now, but we were kids, you know first love. What was first love like for you?" Diana heard the slight demand, tiny defensiveness in her voice, wondered if Jake would respond to that.

"No, I'm sorry Diana. I'm a cynical bastard sometimes."

Diana paused, "Yeah, that was pretty cynical. Now I'll hold you to listening to the rest of it."

Jake groaned loudly into the phone, "Penance."

"How Catholic of you!"

"Go on," he growled playfully.

"Our first time...The first time I told my parents I was going to a school dance, would meet up with some kids when I got there.

"His basement room held that soft smell of dampness. He was playing his guitar, unplugged and kept right at it until several minutes after I arrived. Teen cool.

"'Are you sure?' he asked. Then, 'Take off your clothes.'

"So I did. No strip or anything, just took them off. We lay on the lower bunk, his bed. I'm sure we necked, since we'd been meeting and making out, like I said, for a couple of weeks."

Diana felt, more than heard a question from Jake, so she said, "That school yard was the only place we had. We'd say, I'd say I was going for a walk, with David, and we'd walk but we always landed at the school yard, protected by the cement walls of the church, the rectory and the school."

Jake was silent, attentive.

"After, he asked me how it was for me. I answered honestly, told him I didn't know how it was supposed to be, but I was happy.

"Next week at school he told me his family would be gone to the cottage on the weekend, the side door left open. I forgot and banged at the front door. His irritation with this landed like a slap. He'd had to get up when he'd been up late Friday night, wasn't I thinking? I think now he didn't want the neighbors to see.

"I woke up early on Saturday mornings after that, sometimes walking barefoot on cement sidewalks warmed by the September sun, the few blocks to David's house.

"I'd open the side door quietly, slip down the stairs noiselessly, take off my clothes and climb into bed with him, where the damp, warm smell of his body filled me with an ease and comfort I found nowhere else.

"At first, he turned away from me afterward to sleep, but when I had visited him this way for a few weeks, one morning he pulled my arm across to the front of his body.

"I did not sleep, but measured my incoming and outgoing breath to match his. As I lay beside him in that tiny basement on the single bed, crunched into his back listening to his breath come and go, I smelled the dampness and the sweat of his young man body. I paced my breath to glide in and out with his, or sometimes to syncopate. Somewhere in my heart I believed this would join us, be an invisible thread that would keep us linked throughout lifetimes, an umbilical cord I might hold.

"I learned many years later that breathing with someone or in opposition to their breath is considered by Tantric practitioners, healers, as a way to link lives through death and beyond. Back then I was relying on a memory I did not know I possessed. It just made me happy to think about each breath wreathing itself with the last, spinning their union between us.

"I would rather have died than leave him. I told him so. He was my body. My brain, overstuffed with Greek philosophers, eastern religions, Camus, Sartre, Nietzsche, already outstretched my body, this body that had suffered more imbalance through the shutdown in sensation, the almost total numbness coming from what I did not remember.

"I felt nothing in sex with David, nothing physical, but the sense of being in my body by being close to his set the world right. The satisfaction I gained was what he called a spiritual orgasm. And it was. His release was enough for me.

"David thought it all through. He was more intense about never having sex without a condom than I. Secretly, the thought of having his baby drew me mostly because I believed David would then truly be mine.

"'I know you want a baby,' he said one morning after sex. 'But there is no way. I'm... we're not ready.' He kissed the top of my head and I felt good because he was not saying we would never have one, just that it wasn't right, right now. He continued in his disciplined way to avoid love with no glove. I confess, once or twice I tried to entice him, but it never worked.

"Then he asked me what I wanted in sex, so I told him, 'Lie inside me. Don't move. Stay as still as you can for as long as you can.' He did.

"Again I had no way of knowing this was tantra. I just knew it was a chance to draw out our union so I could have more time completely joined to him, time when he was completely and only mine.

"Sometimes when he lay still deep inside me, he put his hand on my back, a signal not to move because he was close to going over. Then I held still also, pushed my breath up into the highest part of my lungs, made the slow air flow softly in and out, a tiny sip at a time.

"If he spilled, he apologized. 'I'm sorry,' he'd say smiling 'but that was so good, I couldn't help it.' Then he'd wrap his arms around me and squeeze. This was when I was happy. The only time.

"We lay on his bed. One morning as I lay next to him my fingers found a long hardened ridge of skin just below his groin.

"'What's this?'

"He sighed deeply. 'My mother...my mother is schizophrenic.'

"This came as such a shock to me, I was only sixteen at the time recall so I waited many minutes before gathering the strength to ask, 'What would happen, when your mother, I mean how did you know...when did you find out she was...schizophrenic?'

"His response relieved me. 'I'd come home from school, and she'd be gone.'

"'That was it? What about your brothers and sister?'

"'She left them alone in the house. The house was turned upside down. She was looking for something, in all the drawers and all the closets. I learned the pattern. The kids were alone. I learned what to do.'

"'How old were you?'

"'Twelve. Started when I was twelve.'

"I saw the scene as he described it. He's about twelve years old, comes home from school and she's gone again. He's already seasoned in the salt of her wounds, knows to call the police, the social worker, the hospitals, yes, she's gone, she's turned all the drawers inside out, everything strewn around, looking for whatever part of her she knew was missing, that golden piece that might make the world make sense, might make her roving husband love her, make her head stop churning through its piles of memory garbage, all littered and decaying, thoughts spewed against the walls of unfelt emotions, unceasing sound of their cries through her head.

"Time to go, get out now, maybe go the distance of her sea roving husband, home long enough to drop another child on her, maybe go the distance from the long lineage of women behind her, consigned to poverty, too many children, until the DNA rags thin out where the strength to handle life should be.

"'That was it?' I asked him.

"'She was getting stranger as time went by, but this one day...there was no coming back.'

"'What was it?'

"He paused and sighed lightly, then said, 'I came home one day in time to see her holding my brother by the shoulder. She had a butcher knife in her hand. He was already cut in a couple of places, bleeding. She was looking at his throat.I called out to her, yelled her name. It startled her.'

"'And?'

"He paused. 'She threw the knife.'

"'She threw the knife and then?'

"'It landed just below my groin. Here.' He placed my fingers on the long ridge of tough flesh, bunched up like the thoughts in his mother's tormented mind.

"'Good thing,' he continued, in a light, playful voice, 'it didn't land any higher up or you,' he gave me a squeeze, 'would not be enjoying what you enjoy.'

"He didn't want to talk any more about his mother, his suffering, but I knew. The insanity just below my surface, emotional disturbances so like his mother's, called to him but with a caveat: I leaned on him, I looked to him, I ran to him to fix my shakings, to be my inner balance. Something he couldn't have with her.

"I learned in time to recognize her in him, to see in his absences her leaving, to find in his need to hurt me emotionally a symbol of her urgent requirement for knife, for blood.

"That Christmas his mother, often in hospital, joined his family at his grandmother's house. She stood by the dining room windows in that small space, barely any sunshine getting in. I registered her jaw working overtime, her face slightly plump with edema from the drugs, her eyes, almost colorless upon me lightly as though one of us was a butterfly about to fly away at any moment.

"She handed me a package. David stood while I opened it. A tam, in the most garish colors imaginable, bright reds, blues and purples. I put it on immediately, told her I was so happy to have it.

"At the door, David said, 'Are you really going to wear it?'

"'Yes, I am going to wear it home. That way I can tell her I have worn it.' To his surprised eyes, I continued, 'I may never wear it again, but I'll wear it once.'

"David smiled, kissed me lightly.

"Winona was jealous of my need for David. Her need for him matched mine. She withdrew as I made my way straight toward him. She withdrew into a silence I was unwilling to penetrate, unwilling to care take, a silence I still believed was about her wanting more time with me.

"Whatever he offered, whatever it was in his body, I needed in a way that depleted other loyalties. His mind union with mine, his telepathy matched the outline in my psyche where an antique man remained, one upon whom my life depended. David was that antique man, or as close as I could get."

Diana had gone so far into her own reverie, Jake's voice startled her. "Some people believe we come into this life with an imprint from other lives of what person or people we'll meet, the ones that will have significance in our lives..."

"Yes, yes, I totally believe that's true..." Diana blushed on her end of the phone, realizing what she had just said.

As though he had seen her, Jake said playfully, "Or maybe it's all just random..."

Diana's response was to return to her storytelling, shelving her comments about imprints, archetypes, many lives, for a later date. "He was gone, playing with his band, or with drugs, or other girls. Small rumors fell on my ears, dust devils, bits of dirt biting at my heart but he protested, he convinced and I was so willing."

"Young men are self-centered..." Jake said. "Did you try to tell him, let him know you felt ignored?"

"I did complain to him, complained I was tired of not seeing him on the weekends, and barely seeing him through the week, except when I came to his house for sex.

"So he took me out to the Bluffs with the drummer from his band, Tom, the three of us walking around Scarboro Bluffs in late autumn. We must have passed right by the street where you lived..."

"Yes, you had to if you came along Kingston Road. Did you ever hear of the Bluff Boys?"

Diana's mouth dropped open on her end of the line. Recovering she said slowly, "Yeah, David told me about them. A band of bad guys. All their members had to let their leader hang them over the edge of the cliffs by their ankles...You knew them?" Diana tried to keep her voice from a screech.

"I knew them."

"What? You were one of..."

"I was their leader."

Diana took a deep breath and let go. "I'm not sure what to..."

"Go on with your story."

Diana was used to being in control of conversations but found herself at the receiving end of Jake's signals. She registered this as a good change, if a bit uncomfortable.

"I remember the brown and barren bushes, long grass already light yellow, and hardly anyone else around. David ran out on one of those fingers of cliff that spike a couple of hundred feet above the water," Diana couldn't resist, "the ones I guess where you hung those young men." Diana paused as a new thought crossed her lips, "Were you ever hung over the edge?"

"No."

She could hear the lightness, a kind of silent laughter, in Jake's voice.

"You mean they let YOU hang them by the ankles, but they never got to hang you?" Diana gave an exasperated laugh, "So why did they let you hang them by their ankles over those long drops if you weren't...?"

"I couldn't tell you."

"Men! Especially young men!" Diana sighed. "David ran out on one of those cliffs and yelled at the top of his lungs, 'I am the God of Hell Fire!'

"Yeah, it was kind of cool..." Diana said to Jake's laughter. "Kind of cool but I was scared. It made Tom laugh, while my nerves strummed tight with fear David would fall and I'd lose him. I still get dizzy thinking about that narrow ledge, the deep cleft on either side, the water and the rocks below. It's got to be at least two hundred feet, right?"

"Yeah, at least in some places..."

Jake's confirmation of her worst fears increased Diana's confidence. "There you were living on Birchmount Road, being the leader of the Bluff Boys and there I was...Funny, isn't it? Strange how we circle back and around as though things were destined."

"Maybe they are."

Diana purposely turned away from that line of thought, a line that pulled at too many of her already churning emotions.

Diana continued, "So yes, I knew about you and your Bluff Boys. What did they do, once you belonged to their club?"

"Not much. Nothing, really."

Diana blurted loudly, "You mean they let you hang them over the edge of a two hundred foot cliff to join in a club that didn't do anything?"

"Uh, huh. And you women look to us as leaders!" Jake almost snorted a laugh.

Ignoring his last comment, Diana went on, "I asked Tom and David the same question. Really I wanted to know the purpose of the club but they changed the subject. Much later in life I learned men do that when they don't have the answer to your question. At the time I just thought I'd asked a stupid question."

Diana paused for a moment, "I thought about leaving him, cried a lot, but then he'd ask me out. 'Let's go to see 2001, A Space Odyssey, you have to see it, you'll like it. Get some money, I can't take you because I don't have any.'

"'How do you know I'll like it?'

"'I saw it on Friday night and I know you'd want to see it. You'll like it.'

"'How come you had money on Friday night to go, and didn't take me but now you have money again to go?' I didn't really ask this question with words, but it hung about in my mind, in the silence I gave him and he always heard me.

"He grew angry and said out loud, 'Do you want to go or not? I'm not here to get cross examined.'

"I remember that conversation because I felt as if a string hung too tautly between us, a string that if followed would lead somewhere I didn't want to go.

"He brought me the song Age of Aquarius, someone had given it to him, probably...yes, likely another girl gave it to him but because he knew I was into astrology he gave it to me. See? I'd just be getting ready to leave him and as though he knew the thread that bound me to him was fraying, he'd weave it up again with a gift, or something so romantic I'd fall right back.

"In his bedroom after we made love, he strummed his unplugged guitar, sang 'And I love her' to me. What every woman wants. Made a believer out of me. Or because he knew I was writing poetry, mailed me a three page letter saying, 'Due to circumstances beyond my control, I Love You.' Three pages of I love you. He understood the way I value words. He got it.

"'I want to drop acid,' I told him one night.

"His long eye lashes flickered. 'You don't need it.'

"'Then why do you do it?'

"Silence. 'You don't need it,' he repeated, 'because you are already high. You are already in another place. Like some straights are freaky. That's you.' He sounded satisfied with this.

"'Are you sure?'

"'Look, you have trouble staying grounded. Acid's not going to help that.'

"He took care of me that way. Surely that meant, to me that meant he loved me.

"Another time he took me to the Rock Pile to see Howling Wolf and Ten Years After. Well, he took me in that he knew which streetcars and buses to get, but I had to beg for the money from my mother. She barely glanced at me, just flung the tenner down. She knew about David, knew what was going on and hated it."

Diana stopped for a beat here, "It felt like she hated me."

Jake said nothing.

"Our sex grew into something that moved us deeply.

"'Do you feel that?' he asked me one time. 'Do you feel how we are so connected?' He was genuinely surprised.

"'Yes. I feel it. I believe this is what love is supposed to feel like.' He just pulled his arms more tightly around me as though to keep the world away. I was happy.

"Then, in his basement room all those afternoons after sex, he'd play music. I was jealous of individual songs. If he played Hendrix 'Foxy Lady' I felt him move away from me in his thoughts, like he had someone else on his mind. I'd sit by him, waiting, knowing I was not good enough to be that kind of woman.

"'You getting all insecure?' he'd sneer.

"'No,' I'd lie.

"He was right. I was insecure. I hated that I was insecure, but also hated I had not known that until he spoke. Part of his magic to me was how he knew about and named what I was feeling. That brought the feelings to the surface where I could learn, too.

I also knew he had the power to change all the bad feelings in an instant, by putting his arms around me. It seemed in those moments I might move more permanently off the dark planet where I spent the rest of my time.

"I was driven. An addiction deeper than any of the other dangers, weed, hash, booze, psychotropics, sister morphine, junk, I already had my drug. When you are on your knees you don't question. Too busy looking at the floor, I guess.

"Then one morning he started to undress like he'd been doing for so many weeks. It may have been something in the dusky light in his bedroom or something, my head flushed with memories of being in that first basement.

"I just started crying and couldn't stop." Diana recalled the instant, David in his underwear turning back to the lower bunk bed where she lay, sobbing, his face full of concern and her own unending grief spilling over.

"You want to keep talking?"

Roused from her reverie Diana spoke again, "He, David hugged me and comforted as best he could while I told him, told myself really, the truth of that horrible day and night in that...in that basement...then my rage rose and the sobs changed and I began pacing around his room, flinging words like knives of revenge in all directions.

"When I was finished, David looked crumpled in some way, all fallen in on himself." Again Diana remembered her young love, his shoulders fallen in towards his chest, his face long, arms dangling between his legs.

"What did he say?"

"'You have to leave now.'"

"That was it?"

"Yeah, Jake, that's all he had," Diana almost whispered. "I worried for the next week. Actually, I was completely sure he was leaving me. I couldn't feel him, he didn't knock on my door, he didn't call, nothing. Empty."

"What did you do?"

"I was a mess. Rage, beyond anything I'd ever felt marked every day. I stormed up and down on the boardwalk, trying to release myself of those ugly memories, trying to convince myself David still cared, trying to figure out why I cared if he cared since all men were scum. I skipped school, disappeared regularly from home. My parents knew at my age none of the social agencies would bring me back or help them, so they stuck it out. My mother went on anti-depressants, my father...I don't know what he did.

"'Finally after a few months I ran into him at a local pub, one on Kingston Rd.

"'It was like it always was. As soon as I saw him I wanted him. He was carting a couple of drinks, holding them above the crowd on his way over to another girl, a short blonde thing with a good body who looked about the place like she hadn't a thought in her head."

"Your cat claws are showing."

Diana laughed in spite of herself. "Yeah, you're right. I was not kind to her in my thoughts. I still felt, always felt that David belonged to me. And right there in that moment, he flashed his eyes at mine, asked how I was doing and I sent back to him that I was fine. Fine and I wanted to see him.

"He delivered the drinks, and came back to find me standing at the back of the smoke filled room, listening to the music. Listening, yeah sure and looking for him, waiting for him.

"It is sad how much power young women have in their sexuality. I put my hand on his arm in just such a way, and looked into his eyes in just such a way..."

"Stop. You're hurting me," Jake's humour again startled Diana into the present.

"Oh, come on, Jake," she said laughing.

"I like it when you say my name," he said simply and Diana felt her heart shift its rhythm.

Whoa girl,' she thought, You know you can't go there.

Out loud she said, "I phoned him a couple of days later and offered him a massage."

"You do massage?"

"I have given massage, have studied it mostly out of books, but I don't do it anymore."

"Sigh."

Again Diana smiled before continuing, "It was our generation's way of contracting for the possibility of sex."

"Still is, I believe."

"Yes." Diana giggled in spite of herself then quickly carried on, "In the upstairs bedroom of that house, trucks whizzing by outside but warm on the carpeted floor where his body glistened with the oil, I rolled my fingers over his body.

"Finally he said, 'I can't help but be aroused.' He began apologetically, like a shy dog knows sometimes this is the way toward the master's favor.

"'I've done everything I can think of.'

"'Then get over here,' he said, his voice all husky.

"At the door, I kissed his face, his nose, mouth, he kissed my cheeks, neck, over and over, not able to leave, lit with this warmth, that aura between us, solid, someplace to fall into.

"'I've got a gig. I have to go. I'll call you'," he said.

"'Yes, yes, you do that, yes.' Long hug, kiss, entwined. I shut the door tightly behind him, stood in the living room, everything quiet, stood still in the waves of energy after he left.

"When he did call, I didn't answer. It has taken me years to understand the volley between us, between David and I was power. Whenever he had the power, he left me and vice versa. Years of repetition, but I'll get to that."

"The shortened version, I hope..." Jake's voice traced the joke.

Diana bristled, "Hey, you have something else you want to talk about?"

"It was a joke, Diana," Jake's voice was soft.

"Anytime you want to change the subject, you just let me know." To herself Diana thought, 'No joke to me, mister. You ask for my life story then cut into it with that sarcasm? Get back.'

Out loud she said, "I next ran into him at a local restaurant. I saw him as I came in, saw him sitting with that girl, his live-in girlfriend. Oh yeah, he'd been with me, at my house that night all the while he was already living with her. I knew and I didn't care. It always seemed to me that he and I...somehow we were above the rules, the rules didn't apply, like we were outlaws, or adrift from the culture, the rest of the world. It felt powerful, meaningful, almost life and death in its intensity but never within the confines of how you might live a life. Nothing like 'let's get an apartment and stay together.' Always a feeling of being on the run with this immense energy between us.

"It felt like he loved me, like our love was so strong..."

Diana took in a sharp breath. "Anyway, he waved me over in that restaurant, a glint of cold fire in his eyes.

"I tried to call you the other day," he started.

I watched his live-in, who batted her eyes, looked out the window, as though she knew she was intruding, or hearing something that might have implied something she would not like. I recognized those signals.

"'You weren't home,' he continued.

"'I was home,' I insisted. I had played him, made a fool of him. He stood in a huff, grabbed the blind girl's hand, and dragged her out the door."

Tahni's Life

1640's

Tonawanda

Tahni stood at the door of their home, her body still thrumming from the oceanic experience of bliss Takoda's loving had compelled inside her. She saw the pulse of energy, vibrant, warm, intelligent and just below the life that teemed around her. As she waited for Takoda to join her, she sensed her mind open to new understanding.

Her senses twined with her thoughts as she realized how her people behaved so often in ways to support this vital underlying force. When times were very tough, the elders walked into the forest, to become food for animals so more animal food fell to the young. In this way the elders fulfilled their belief that the Soul of the Village, the survival of all, was more important than their own, tiny life.

If this seemed harsh the rewards were great. No one felt alone, or alienated, no one suffered from feeling friendless or abandoned. Although much teasing took place around the campfires about this one's temper, or that one's greed, all were equally accepted. If any were sick, the entire village knew and participated in whatever way Medicine Woman required. No medicine was kept away from the one who was ill. If any were unhappy everyone in the village also knew, and in small ways and big, responded until that person's right relationship within the village was restored.

For the belief was that right relationship within the village matched right relationship with Great Spirit. Nothing was more important than this: that the village and its collective Soul match in a positive and loving way all the signs and gifts from Great Spirit.

When it came to dying, each villager knew they belonged to the Soul of the village, at one with Great Spirit. They died knowing they would journey directly toward Great Spirit, guided by the chants and rhythms from the rattles of those chosen to help the dying cross. None were left to wander in the damp and terrifying Between Worlds, but all would travel directly under the Soul of the village to the Great Spirit's welcome home.

What was most important was that in death, each tiny person would journey directly to Great Spirit. They could do this because Medicine Men and Women knew the songs and dances to lead any part of the village Soul directly home to Great Spirit. During life everyone followed Medicine Women and Men as they performed the songs and dances that took the souls of others in the village to their final resting place. Each knew when their time came, they too would be led directly home.

The Between Worlds were spoken of around the Campfires during important ceremonies. Every child knew the stories of those caught in this terrifying place. Endless, bleak darkness, despair and loneliness waited for any soul unlucky enough to go there. Only a Medicine Woman or Man might find that soul and bring it back to the loving place of Great Spirit.

All this crowded in upon her in an instant, and stayed for too brief a moment. Tahni marked the insight clearly as it occurred and tucked it away inside her, next to the place where she kept her unspoken night dreams, the ones she had had since youth.

She felt Takoda take her arm.

He smiled, very slightly. He knew some of what she was experiencing.

"It will never go back," he said.

For many days and nights, Tahni knew a union with Takoda that went beyond anything she had ever imagined about love. They were joined, one person. He spent some time in other activities with other men, and she with the women of the village who teased her now freely on her new status as married woman, but she and Takoda experienced the truth that they belonged as if of one body.

The ceremony of their union before the village was a matter of great joy to everyone. The marriage would have been enjoyable no matter who was involved; that it was their Chief and his beautiful young wife added energy to anticipation. The whole village assembled in the meadow she had stepped around the first time Takoda had led her home. As she stood to its side, she recognized with a small start this meadow and the village were home, more deeply than any she had belonged to before.

The meadow fire had been stoked all night. A large spit held the slowly roasting body of the young stag Takoda had taken with proper prayers and thankfulness to the spirit of the animal. Its pungent smell wafted throughout the autumn meadow.

As Tahni stood on the edge of the dark forest, still hugged by the trees, she looked on the scene of the village, her village, playing, laughing, talking, waiting excitedly for today's events. Her heart opened in warmth.

Then suddenly the air turned thick, as another layer opened. Her eyes shot instinctively around the edges of the forest, and there, just on the other side a barely visible figure wavered. She knew he wanted her to see him there. She let her eyes stay on him, as he gradually moved ever so slightly toward the meadow. She saw his outline clearly once, then he melted away, a single cloud evaporating in a sun filled sky.

The air returned to early autumn warmth and she focused on the scene before her.

Even the youngest children stopped in respect when she emerged, flanked by the women she now thought of as her family. Stepping out of the forest, dressed in her white buckskin bride's tunic embroidered in greens, blues, purples, she made her way in silence up to side of the meadow where Takoda, dressed in his wedding pants and beautifully decorated shirt stood waiting for her.

As he stepped up to take her hand, hc held her eyes and whispered, "Your beauty sings the sun into morning."

They stood quietly side by side throughout the short, formal ceremony. Macawi spoke of Great Spirit and its loving embrace, and the blessing from Great Spirit upon their village that their Chief had chosen such a beautiful and healthy young bride. Tahni and Takoda stated their desire to participate as loving people in the village, and then the ceremony was over.

Next, while Takoda held the large basket with its aromatic pieces of deer meat for each villager, Tahni spoke a few words to each person. In this way they enacted the truth of their status as servants to the greater village, to its Soul to which everyone belonged, and to Great Spirit.

Takoda stepped aside preparing to go for more food, when Tahni spoke softly to him. Keeping a smile on her face, she covered the concern in her voice as she said, "Medicine Man was here."

Takoda kept his eyes on the ground, "Yes?"

"He was at the rim of the meadow, just beyond where others might see. I...I ... he wanted me to see him, to know he was there."

"He enjoys frightening people with his presence. It makes him feel powerful."

Takoda looked into her eyes, "You are my wife." Tahni felt a thrill go through her body at his words.

"You do not need to be concerned about him."

After their wedding, Takoda let his seed flow into her and soon she was with child. Through their love Tahni knew a life few ever experience: the simple joy of a deep passion with her husband, health for her and the baby growing inside her, much companionship and affection with all the lives of her village.

Yet one morning Tahni's skin prickled with goose bumps as she spoke to Takoda about a dream. "I was in a place I do not know and I could not find you. You were gone." She brought her arms around his body, trying to tell herself it was not a future dream, but her heart felt heavy.

"I am here with you now," he said softly, cradling her and stroking her hair.

"Yes."

"You know I am going to the hunt. Your dream speaks of this leaving. Nothing more." Takoda held her more tightly, hoping his words assured her more than they did him.

"And now," he said, "we must eat."

His ever present focus on the next practical task grounded her. Her feelings about the dream dissipated as she rose, prepared food for them and for the baby growing inside her.

He would be gone, today, this morning! The thought rose like a whip on her heart, which sank like a dog, whining about her feet. She regarded that cur, then held her head high and said, "There is much to do."

She put her hand on his shoulder, then wrapped herself around him. He brushed his hand lightly across her belly.

"I will be back. For you and our child," he said, smiling slightly. "If not in winter, then look for me by spring. By spring at the latest. Wait for me." He smiled and she knew she would wait until whatever spring returned him to her.

Tahni's young heart lifted. Of course he would return, he would come back and they would have many, many years, if Great Spirit allowed, they would grow old together...but as she looked back into the fire, she could see only a wall of darkness. Tahni felt a shudder but decided this must be natural. He was going into danger, as he had many times before.

Takoda lifted the flap of the wigwam, inviting her to follow him into daylight.

Outside, the village rhythm had ramped up to fulfill the necessary preparations. So many hunters readying to leave for a month, two, maybe much longer.

The custom was to allow small groups to splay out across the fields and forests, to creep stealthily upon their prey. With Great Spirit's power they would return with many deer, beaver, skunk, rabbits, to provide for the women, children and old men at home, and perhaps to sell, to use as barter. Takoda's group planned to travel farthest, to take the most dangerous animals, including the two-leggeds, onto themselves.

Tahni focused on the sight of the women before her, Macawi and Little Bird among them, and on what she had to say to them. She stepped forward and heard them speaking softly about their husbands and sons who must leave. These women rallied their courage with stories of previous hunts, many much more dangerous than the one facing them now.

"Yes, it's true," she began. "My husband also leaves, but I know the child in my womb calls to him and he will return soon."

"Ahhh, eeee ya," the women let out whoops of delight at this inspiring news. "Ah, our Chief is mighty in all ways," said one.

Suddenly it seemed from the middle of the circle of joy appeared a headdress of large Eagle feathers sticking out at odd angles above a head and its shoulders.

The apparition drew the whole village, who witnessed the vest of bearskin, naked legs, streaks of red and black trailed across the face and upper chest in zigzag patterns. The rest of his body where visible was caked with mud and dirt, whether for ceremonial purposes, or from daily living it was hard to tell.

"Go on." He said slowly turning in a circle, "Speak of victory in the hunt but I tell you, the snake is upon the ground, the White Snake which brings the end of the world writhes now upon you. You will not turn it back."

Tahni's head turned upward. Her inner vision filled with a huge white snake, whipping its tail ferociously back and forth across a midnight sky. She felt Takoda's arm at her back, comforting, strengthening her. The vision faded, and her breath, gasping at the fading sight of the serpent, returned to normal. By the time she had returned fully to this world, Medicine Man had evaporated into the forest.

A chill went through the group.

Macawi was the first to speak. "Well, if we had to rely on him to be a hunter, we would starve before any white man arrived." Uneasy laughter rose around the camp.

Tahni felt Takoda take her hand. She followed him to where his horse stood.

In the chaos of last minute preparations, they had this one last moment together.

She took in her husband's eyes, warm, steady and strong. She felt his lips graze hers, and his arms enfold her body, gently, firmly. She received all his longing, tenderness and sorrow at leaving.

She looked at him, gathering strength from his and shining that back to him, said, "I am proud of you, my Chief." He slipped onto his horse, took his hunting bow and arrows decorated with brightly colored feathers from her hands. The Chief's headdress rose like a spine along the top of his head, a brilliant red ridge declaring his status. Then he and Tahni began to walk slowly, she at the flank of his horse, through the length of the village.

Tahni stood for as long as she could, straining to see the last glimpse of him. He neither looked back nor waved but she felt his thoughts were of her and their baby. She knew too, once the hunters had cleared sight of the village, his mind would be focused only on the hunt.

Finally the hunters appeared as only small specks in the distance. Her eyes clear in spite of the darkness in her heart, Tahni turned back toward the others, women, children and a few old men. She was their leader now. Eighteen years old, married, pregnant, until the hunters returned she was leader of her people.

"I have also wanted to be Medicine Woman," Little Bird said, her round eyes facing Tahni. The two young women lay on the narrow strip of beach by the lake taking in the weak warmth of the late autumn sun. Soon the days would shorten and the sun be even less warm.

Little Bird watched her friend's belly rise and fall.

"Beautiful," she said, lightly tracing with one finger the swelling, letting her finger trail a small distance down. She held Tahni's eyes while she did this, watching. Tahni saw the greed, an animal sense of desire in her friend's eyes, not for the first time.

Tahni felt below her own body into the sand. She tossed her mind up into the sky so her mind encompassed this physical world, even while she probed below its surface. Everything was quiet. She had no words for Little Bird about that greedy animal. There was nothing to do. She took her friend's fingers and laid them gently back on the sand.

"Then we will go to Macawi and ask her. Come on." Tahni, still agile, rolled on her knees and rose, placing her hand on her four month pregnant belly.

"You still wait for him?" Little Bird's eyes slanted slightly as she looked at Tahni.

"Of course. He is my husband."

"You have the last one worthy. All the others are boys." Little Bird tossed her hair as she said this.

"Iron Tail looks for you."

"Ah, he is small, too small for me. I want a tall husband, with big shoulders, and legs long enough to wrap around me when we rock in our sweat." Tahni shook her head and laughed.

She and Little Bird approached Macawi, who sat with the women by the fire. The weak sun of late autumn on her back, Tahni noticed the first trees emptied completely of leaves. She wanted winter. After winter comes spring, she thought. He said he'd be back by spring at the latest.

"Yes." Macawi looked up at both young women. "Yes, to you both," she said.

Now Tahni's days filled with endless information from her teacher. She watched as Macawi helped birth a baby who was turned backwards, easing the tiny form around so its head came first. She learned to dress a wound properly, which herbs for pain relief, which for fever, what to do for toothache, extracting a tooth, Tahni observed, absorbed and remembered, especially the prayers to Great Spirit, asking for help, or offering gratitude. Little Bird was her constant companion during the lessons, as Little Bird repeated she wanted to be Medicine Woman.

"Come." Macawi's back was to the winter sun as she pulled open the flap of the wigwam. Inside, Tahni saw the old woman, the oldest in the village, Eyes with Song, her breath now coming in long pauses at the bottom, then sudden, sharp short intake.

Macawi unrolled her blanket of items: cloth bound bundles of dried herbs, sticks whittled to animal shapes, sacred stones, a tassel of sweet grass to lighten the air, and rattles. Three or four rattles, each one more elaborately decorated than the last. Tahni and Little Bird stood respectfully watching in the silent room.

"Which one?" Macawi pointed to her rattles, asking Little Bird. She hesitated, confusion in her eyes, for a moment.

"No," Macawi said and turned her back so she covered her sacred items from Little Bird's sight. The sound of that labored breathing, short inhale, longer out breath followed by a deep space of no breath at all, filled the room.

"Which one?" This time Macawi turned to Tahni who without hesitation put her hand on the smallest, most delicate of the rattles. Macawi nodded, so Tahni picked up the rattle and began to chant. Macawi swayed slightly, stood over the dying woman, adding her chants to Tahni's. The rattle shook in Tahni's hand with the exact amount of energy needed to support this dying one, giving the comfort of sound but not disturbing the progress of Death.

Neither woman noticed Little Bird's flushed, angry face.

It took a few hours more. Under Macawi's supervision, Tahni performed much of the Death Ritual, choosing each chant accompanied by the small rattle, until grandmother's eyes opened, her lips pulled back in a grin exposing toothless, pale gums and her chest at the top of what would have been her next breath, stopped.

Little Bird expressed a small 'O' sound, then she covered her mouth with her hand.

Slowly Tahni lay the rattle back in its nest among Macawi's things.

"You," Macawi pointed to Little Bird, indicating she was to leave. This time both women saw Little Bird flush.

"Now," Macawi said to Tahni, "which chants?" Tahni began the chants herself, while Macawi focused on the dying woman, bathing her, brushing her hair, preparing her body for its last ceremony.

This would have been Tahni's natural place, to take care of the body while Macawi held the sacred energy in tones of chanting. Tahni knew she had done well.

"Now you must learn," Macawi began this evening's lesson. Little Bird and Tahni sat comfortably in Macawi's wigwam, ready to hear the precious words of their teacher.

"Anyone can learn how to fix a bandage on a wound. Anyone can learn which herbs help take down the swelling from poison, or which one helps a pregnant woman have much milk for her baby, anyone can learn these things.

"It is only possible to be born with such power, such vital energy that dreams and experiences tell a person she is chosen by Great Spirit to do more than that. To be Medicine for someone means entering the Soul of the Village. The Soul of the Village must invite the person. The person receives this invitation, and responds.

"It is a responsibility that has life and death consequences, for it is the Medicine Woman who requests Great Spirit bring life to the village. It is the Medicine Woman who through prayers and intense concentration, shows the departing spirits of each person born to the village how to move through the Between Worlds and arrive at the Land of the Ancestors, where all our departed have gone before.

"Without the Medicine Woman or the Medicine Man, or if their medicine is not strong enough, the spirits of the dead roam this world, neither flesh nor soul, wander forever without reaching Soul's Land. Such spirits make easy prey for evil.

"Since every spirit in the village belongs to the one Soul, if one is lost, all feel the loss. The Village Soul is weakened by the loss of any one soul to the Between Worlds.

"A strong Medicine Woman also dreams. She dreams at night and sometimes she dreams in the day. If she dreams in daytime it is stronger than this world because it breaks the barriers. Most of us in this world usually cannot access that world except at night."

"I have had dreams, since childhood," Tahni began. "I dreamed of the meadow, the one where…where Takoda and I…where Takoda and I were married. I dreamed that meadow from childhood." Tahni felt the pain of separation from him cut through her.

Macawi asked "Who did you take this dream to?"

"No one."

"What other dreams have you had?"

"I saw, clearly but inside of me, I knew it was not in this world, the white snake Medicine Man described when he joined..." Tahni stopped, unsure of what Medicine Man had done.

"Yes, you saw what he described," Macawi said.

Tahni nodded her head.

"That is the day dream bleeding from the dream world into this one. Little Bird?" Macawi turned to her.

But Little Bird had no dreams to offer, neither night dreams nor these day dreams.

She wasn't sure she even believed in the daydreams but she knew who she would ask.

"No," was all she said.

Macawi told them each Medicine Woman or Man has a force, a genuine power that is personal. That power opens most deeply toward one aspect of healing, whether herbs or birthing, cleaning wounds or in escorting the dead to the Land Beyond.

"For you," she indicated Tahni, "it is the rattle and chant to accompany those on their way to Great Spirit. You are marked to work with Death. Your gift comes from Death and will be given to many. That is all for now."

The two young women left. They did not see the sorrow on Macawi's face before she gave over to Great Spirit and began her evening chants to protect the village.

A measure of warmth, of genuine pleasure, small but clear swept through Tahni's chest.

"Oh Little Bird," she sighed.

"What?" The tone of her friend's voice brought Tahni back to the present moment.

"You are not happy with what Macawi says?" she asked.

"It isn't about happiness. It's about whether she tells truth." Tahni registered a bitterness rising from deep, wounded pride in Little Bird.

Tahni sucked in air and waited.

"I know someone else," Little Bird went on. "I'll ask that person about this day dream and night dream stuff. Then I'll know for sure." She strode quickly away from Tahni, anger in every step.

Tahni looked up to the vast stars winking off and on in the endless dark cool of night sky. "If Takoda is able to hear, take this message to him that I love him. Tell him I, we," she put her hand on her belly, "wait for him."

Mary's Life

1882

London, England

"Everything here is beautiful," Mary said to herself, looking around the small room. It seemed protected, a cocoon away from the harsh poverty and struggle she knew with her mother. Surely nothing ugly or difficult could ever happen in this magical place! And he, Theodore Fieldworth, due to be Lord of this estate, wanted her.

She felt again that knot of excitement in her belly, a feeling that had risen when he'd kissed her. She was sure the torment of this sensation was one of the signs, the most important sign, of true love. I am already in love, Mary thought, how simple, how sweet and how suddenly, easily this has happened. That he returned her affection she had no doubt.

For the passionate heart, such intensity believes always in itself so fully it sees the same everywhere it looks.

Mary glanced around. The single room was twice the size of the living room she shared with her mother but furnished so well. She took her shoes off, crossed the small entrance mat and stood on the Persian carpet, wiggling her toes in the deep plush pile.

Her toes registered the soft, supple caress of the finely made floor covering. The sensation sent a wave of breath up through her chest and she giggled to herself as she looked around the room.

The large carpet with its sensuous blossoms completely covered most of the floor. On it stood a couch and chair set, upholstered in light cream and pinks, luscious roses, that set off the carpet perfectly. The couch to her left faced a stone fireplace on her right, now blazing with a lovely fire, warming and high, like nothing she had ever seen.

She recalled her mother's biting tone, "No more coals, girl. You think they come like rain drops from the sky?" when Mary had reached to build their fire.

Circumstances dictated a few coals at a time, meagrely stretched across the winter months to provide just enough distraction from total chill to prevent illness.

Everything, Mary shuddered at this new thought, in her life had been dedicated to necessity, to just keeping alive.

Her next step took her toward the couch. She turned left behind the couch, ignoring for the moment a large armoire and walked two steps toward a large four poster bed. And what a bed! The largest she had ever seen, it was draped with the most magnificent covers, splashed with a design of roses to match the carpet and furniture. Soft, inviting pillows lay scattered across the large frame so "I might lie down with my back on the back wall and watch the fire, and still feel the comfort of those…" she mused, delightedly.

Mary now looked at the dark, intricately patterned wood on each door of the armoire. She couldn't resist. She lifted the latch and was about to peer inside when she heard the door at the other end of the room open.

"Well, do you like what you see?" The warm chuckle in his voice told her she had done nothing wrong, yet she flushed in embarrassment and in the intensity of what else she was feeling. At the sound of his voice a sudden surge of warmth and moistness rose between her legs, her nipples tingled as though the body she had always called her own already belonged to him.

He strode across the room and with one gesture embraced her waist and began to undo the stays in her dress. Instinctively she pushed against him but his yearning was too strong and he ignored her feeble protests. What she felt destroyed all thought and sent a shock through her that immediately settled into a warmth and desire that left her mind in tatters. She wanted more.

He removed her bodice, leaving her white slip as the only barrier between them, then said huskily, "Step out of it."

Languidly Mary responded to his commands and stepped away from the silken yards of her mother's hope.

With her nearly naked body before him he lifted her easily onto the bed. The pain of his next swift move knifed through her body and sent her into spasms. To stop herself from shouting out, she clamped down hard on her lower lip and tasted the sweet and salt flavor of her blood; she focused her mind on how he was enjoying himself. She looked up to look into his eyes but they were closed.

It was over in a few minutes. Mary felt a sense of disappointment, a sense that something else was meant to have happened, but hadn't. Then her mother's voice reached her mind, "Stop asking for more than what you've got in front of you," and she put the sad, small feeling away.

This is how it's supposed to be, how it must be when one loves, she thought and reached out then to have his arms around her. He lay on his side, just out of reach and leaned one hand on her belly.

"What happened to you?" Theodore gently ran his finger on the corner of her mouth and his words filled her with disappointment although she couldn't say why.

"I…I don't know. I guess it happened…before, when we…when you…"

He laughed, "It's all right. I see it's only a small wound and will mend quickly. Now, let's get the rest of this cleaned up."

Mary looked to where he pointed and saw what appeared to her as a massive pool of blood staining the bed's beautiful cover.

"What? I am so sorry…" Embarrassed, she began again to stammer, but he hushed her with one finger to her mouth, gently so not to hurt her lip.

Mary drank in each gentle gesture like a hungry colt sucking from its mother's warm milk. The warmth and affection he showed her in these tiny moments felt to her love-starved heart like a geyser of nourishment. She relaxed, with the exuberance of the child she was, into trusting him.

When daylight spilled again across the room, Theodore stood with her, walked her to the door, held her once more before finally letting go. "I'll see you soon," he said huskily. She nodded, delirious with a sense of belonging.

Fix everything, she thought to herself, the dream of this night still filling her young mind as she sat in the plushly cushioned carriage clattering through the back streets of London.

My body feels like a pulsing peach, she giggled to herself.

As long as she was in the carriage, heavy blinds kept the earliest rays of morning out of her eyes but now, stepping down, hearing the coach man click the horses away, as she walked slowly up the side alley to her door, she was aware of dawn's first light.

She turned the door handle softly, but her mother, with her back to Mary, was already awake, preparing a kettle for tea. The room, as usual when her mother was around, was silent, but into the silence suddenly Mary remembered singing as a child. She recalled how she had hummed or sung tunes from the street, from the hawkers and barkers who filled those dark streets, who roamed past their house now and then, dressed in bright blues and yellows, reds and royal purples, singing and performing a moment for the little girl who sat by the window, or stood in the doorway. Delighted with some attention, Mary had hummed or sung in return what she could recall of those brightly dressed, daring men and women. That is, until her mother's voice poked through the child's moment of happiness, "Stop it right now."

Her mother's rebuke had stung and Mary's small body had slumped over in her corner. She had not sung, at least in her mother's company, since. As a child Mary had believed the music made her mother sad. As years passed, in angrier moments, she believed her mother's envy of anyone's happiness, especially her own daughter's, was behind the command.

On this morning Mary's unusual arrival at this time of day did nothing to break the routine rhythm of life for Beatrice, who looked at her once and lifted her eyebrows.

Instantly, Mary felt as though she must explain. That feeling was followed just as quickly by a flash of resentment flooding her mind.

"Why must you spoil it?" she demanded, then defiantly, "He said he'll call on me." Her desperate words melted in air. With them went Mary's confidence.

Beatrice shrugged slightly and turning toward the fire said clearly, "You may need herbs."

"Oh, you and those stupid herbs! I'm all right! He's going to call for me, I'm to wait outside and he's sending the carriage and, and…" Mary's words fell on the ground, useless against the shawl of silence Beatrice pulled around her own worn body.

Mary stepped toward the bedroom she had shared all her life with her mother. Those steps were stopped by the grate of her mother's voice.

"Night is for sleeping. There's work."

Mary stood, trembling, took another step toward the inner chamber as with one hand she began to unfasten her gown. Her shoulders slumped as she said softly, "Yes, ma'am."

For the next few days, Mary's inner world sang with the memories of that night, that ball, and the handsome Theodore. He'd said, she reminded herself over and over, he said in the little cottage he would send the carriage around for her. Her ears strained constantly for the sound of carriage wheels in the alley, but all that rose was the usual noise of daytime, hawkers pushing their wares, the gentry talking of grand things, the wheels of carts loaded with vegetables, breads, wine, whatever might be purchased through the shops on the street. These sounds blended over the background of pigeons cooing, dogs barking, children running, screaming, and the occasional raucous laughter booming from the nearby tavern. No whirring of wheels chattered against the cobblestones.

As day three slid into four, Mary began to think. I have no more beautiful clothes and no money to buy any. She knew asking her mother to sew for her again was out of the question. Her mother's silence had grown deeper, even more disapproving in the last few days.

On day four, Mary suddenly heard the carriage wheels! She dropped the broom, and held herself back from rushing to the side door. Instead she willed herself to walk slowly and slowly open the door.

The coach man from the night of the ball stood erect, dressed in a fine suit of black. As she opened the door, he said without smiling, "A note, m'lady, from Sir Theodore Fieldworth."

There on a filigree silver platter lay a piece of heavy, embossed, folded paper, the color of fresh cream.

Standing in her work dress, with her hair tied back in a rag, Mary drew herself up to her full height, picked up the paper with trembling fingers. As she read, color rose into her cheeks, bringing the beauty of her blue eyes, their dark brows, to attention. Her hand flew automatically to her throat. She smiled slightly at the coach man, nodded and tucked the paper into her bosom as she slowly closed the door.

Theodore was sending the carriage around for her at 10pm this very evening! She was to meet him in the little cottage!

By the time the sun had set, Mary felt exhausted from the excitement of seeing Theodore again and from doing battle with her despair over having nothing fit to wear. She knew she must appear before him in the only clothes she had. She had washed carefully, thoroughly, the best underwear she owned and had set them in front of their tiny coal fire.She washed her body with care in the porcelain bowl in her room, the cold water dimpling her young firm skin. She brushed her hair until it shone and finally began to dress in the clean work shirt and the least patched of her skirts.

She sighed, her lower lip trembling. Her dream, she was sure, was over. One last time, she told herself, one last time I'll see him, before he laughs at me and returns to the young women who always dress in beautiful clothes.

Mary walked into their living room where her mother sat by the window hacking into a piece of linen. The habitual silence of life had recently been broken by the cough that seemed to accompany her mother's every move.

Right at the stroke of ten the carriage pulled up. Beatrice knew without words what was going on. She sat as always in the dark of night by the window, but her eyes instead of gazing out into the alley and the sky beyond, followed Mary around their tiny home.

Silence remained until Mary in a moment of confusion, with desire, fear, embarrassment and excitement all yapping at once in her heart and throat like a pack of unruly hounds, whispered out to her mother, "Good night, Mamma."

Mary's mother nodded and the girl, disappointed as always when her tender, warm heart yearned after her mother, closed the door quietly but Beatrice's cough struck as her daughter left. It hung onto Mary's heels as she took the coach man's hand and he lifted her into the carriage. "What can I do about it?" Mary thought.

Beasts of emotion raced along the wheels of the carriage as Mary's disappointment climbed in her heart. She believed he would leave her, after tonight, after seeing the poverty she could not conceal. Yet within a few moments of being inside the beautiful carriage, of feeling again the soft brocade interior, of realizing that now, again, in the same week, she would see her beloved, Mary's heart lifted with the unflagging optimism of youth. She would see him tonight. Tonight was what mattered. He was what mattered. She turned her mind willfully toward the memories of the one night she had shared with him.

Had Mary been aware of her inner being, she may have noticed one particularly large, unusually vocal hound of the heart cut free from the rest, racing fiercely off. She may have, had she been listening for it, heard his loud howling echo off the high hill outside of town, a sound of loneliness, fear and warning.

Instead she was aware of nothing but the growing pound of her heart and sweat of her palms as the carriage wheels rattled their way through the dark night.

Mary peeked out as the carriage came to a full stop, the driver already on the ground, where he opened the gate in a high stone wall which Mary recognized as the back entrance to the garden where the cottage stood. This was the door she had used only a few brief mornings ago. She felt relief to realize she did not have to appear at the front door. The coach man held the gate for her and she glided quietly, murmuring thanks to him, over the garden path and up to the cottage. Its door was open so she stepped inside.

The one room was as she had first seen it. Curtains hung cheerfully from the window which faced the main house. Beneath that stood the brass bed, remade since last she saw it, a new but equally beautiful bedspread flowing with another abundant rose pattern across its ample size.

A new addition, a table, stood between the couch and fireplace. On it she saw cheeses, a variety of white and orange triangles and squares, lying against crackers, sumptuous, abundant.

Fresh fruit, apples without rot spots, clear in their cheery redness such as she had seen in the finer stores, but never believed she would have, along with oranges still firm to the touch, and cherries, ripe, red and full of their own juice, graced a beautiful bowl in the center of the table.

These simple, high quality items made Mary's mouth water. An opened bottle of red wine stood between the plate of food and a multitude of candles, lighting every corner of the room.

"He must," Mary thought, "have prepared everything so beautifully, for our time together." The thought made her knees sag. "And now," she thought sadly, "he will see what I really am."

Then she noticed one of the doors to the armoire was open. She walked over to close it, when her glance took in several pieces of beautiful lace, panties and slips, corsets and garter belts, along with three of the most gorgeous gowns she had ever seen. She pulled the green one from the closet. Inside the door was a mirror so she held the dress up and gazed. In the warm light, the green accented her eyes and auburn hair to perfection.

She slid into a slip and panty set, noticing the sensual feel of silk across her skin, then reached for the gown. Instead of pulling it over her head, she held it up to her body as she turned at the sound of the door opening and saw him standing in the doorway.

"Mary! I was afraid you would not come…" he started toward her.

Why would he think that, the thought crossed her mind before she felt his arms gather her and his mouth press deeply, his tongue searching for her answer.

Answer she did, with her body arching toward him, her arms reaching across his back and holding him tightly to her, her mouth pulsing in his, then sliding across his cheeks, his jaw, his throat. Her ardor surprised him slightly but the thrust of his hips took most of his attention.

"I'm so glad you are here," he murmured into her hair.

Why on earth would he be so glad? Didn't he know that now they were one, now until the earth ended? Didn't he know she would cover that earth on her hands and knees to see him, to be with him?

Mary did not recognize it was not sex but the sense of a body, his body, to which she might cling. His body, its smell next to her, the warmth of it, provided her with something she hadn't known she was missing. Lying next to him before sleep, her hand on his back or shoulder, her legs lined up and touching his, she felt she belonged.

When he was finished she ran her hands along his thighs, feeling every curve, every hair. She put her hands gently between his legs, running them softly across his skin. At the top of his left thigh she felt a ridge, where the skin thickened.

"What's this?" she asked timidly, afraid she had intruded.

"An accident, from my younger days," he said, rolling onto his back and pulling her closer until she lay half across his body.

"May I look...?" she asked shyly. He smiled, indicated with the slightest shrug he didn't mind. Mary lifted herself up and looked at his genitals.

Hair covered most of what she could see. But she put her fingers again where she had felt the thickening. There, just at the join of his hip and leg, a ridge of white, tough skin. She played her index finger along its length. This sight made her almost dizzy with an unexpected sense of familiarity, She shook her head to clear the feeling.

"How did you...?" she asked.

"A stupid child's game. Nothing," he pulled her back on top of him, "that interferes with what is important."

His mouth on hers stopped any further conversation. The need to touch him, to be touched by him dominated all others. His body was her anchor to the world.

For many weeks this was the pattern. His carriage arrived for her, they met in the cottage, she left again in the morning by the back gate. Mary had, she believed, everything she wanted and much more than most people ever get in life.

Beatrice endured the nocturnal departures and returns of her daughter in silence. She sat coughing in their flat, her stiff shoulders ratcheting up and down as she watched darkness fall upon the street she had known for most of her life. If she thought of better days, if a time of sunshine appeared in her mind from the past, nothing showed upon the thin lips, the slightly frowning brow.

One evening after Mary had left and Beatrice prepared to take up her vigil, she heard for a second time the clatter of horses' hooves nearby. She peered out the window and saw the coach man rapping on their door. She opened the door and stared silently at the driver who presented her with a silver plate, upon which sat a small bulging purse and a white, beautifully embossed slip of paper. Beatrice looked at the coach man.

"Sorry ma'am," he began in a serious tone, more than a little unnerved by Beatrice's unyielding expression, "I beg pardon but I am to await m'lady's response."

"She has already gone."

"Yes, ma'am. I am to await your ladyship's, that is, your reply, if you please."

The coach man noted Beatrice looked no more pleased at this moment than she had a moment before. She took the purse in her hand, carefully lifting its weight. Coins. Then she gently replaced it on the silver plate and took up the note. In the darkening dusk she read:

> *Please forgive my directness in this matter. I wonder if you would consider tailoring for Mary some gowns? Anticipating your approval of this plan, I have enclosed payment. Please indicate your response to the coach man.*
>
> *Yours truly,*
> *Theodore Fieldworth.*

Diana's Life

2005

near Toronto

Trouble doesn't really describe it, Diana thought as she drove towards the home where the meditation meetings took place. Being what amounts to evicted for no apparent reason, she mused, after you've lived and raised your kids in the place. And all the meditations that have gone on there. She wondered, not for the first time, if all that meditation softens the mind toward the harsher parts of this life.

The meditation hosts, Wayne and Andrea, had requested this day's meditation be about their land, to see what information might be gleaned to help them in their fight to stay on and although Diana had willingly agreed, part of her wasn't sure this would help. Especially since the landlord in question was the Provincial government.

The small group of five sat close enough on their chairs they were able to hold hands in the large, parquet floored room. Lovely sunlight softened the stark white walls and warmed Diana's shoulders. She was also warmed internally by seeing Jake, loose and comfortable in his body as ever, sitting opposite her.

In addition to Jake, Wayne, a large man with a soft round belly, and Andrea, his plump wife, sat with the hands of people on either side of them held lightly in their palms.

Finally, still beautiful into her fifties, her flaming mane of hair softly curling down to her shoulders was Hazel. Her dark eyes lingered slightly longer on Jake as they swept the faces of each in their group.

Diana noticed. No doubt Hazel was interested in him. No doubt she doesn't know about the strengthening bond between Jake and I, Diana thought, a little surprised at how clearly she felt Jake was already hers.

The meditation technique was called Star Group. Developed in Western Europe by a secret society called the White Lodge, a branch of the Western Mysteries, their teacher Rinpoche had explained the White Lodge had used Star Group through the darkest days of the Second World War. When Hitler threatened England with invasion from France, Star Groups had been set up all along the eastern coast of England day and night, synchronized so there were always people building mental walls of energy to keep Hitler and his powerful army off the shores of English land.

This meditation involved creating a space platform above the heads of the meditators. Diana had already experienced how, from that space platform, it was possible for one or more of the participants to leap off, into space travel. And, as she had said to Jake, space travel means time travel.

As the minutes progressed, Diana felt herself being pulled into the ground beneath them. She also sensed death, all around her so she stopped her focus for a moment, pulled herself back into the room by focusing on the sunlight, felt the palms within her hands and asked silently, "Is this safe?"

She felt a warm glow in her chest and above her head, a glow she recognized as the Angels. It was safe for her to go on. Not pleasant, but safe.

Now she followed the pull towards the ground and found herself below the earth, in a damp, dank place. Diana almost smelled the stench of rotting meat, and her nose wrinkled reflexively. She followed her eyes around the space, but those corpses were all she saw, chaotically strewn about, clearly the remains of a bloody battle.

Many people, Natives and Whites alike had lost their lives and many more had been wounded badly whenever this deadly skirmish had taken place. When, she couldn't determine but where was very clear: right here beneath them.

Soon the soft bell sounded, signaling the end of the session. Diana mentally thanked, as she so often did, her Teacher for having taught her so well. "Calm first and then insight," he had stated many times. Had he not taught her to go for calm first, this kind of insight would have knocked her over.

After a few minutes of stretching limbs, toes, fingers, everyone began their report. As her eyes opened Diana noted Jake's on her. She saw a question in his, and sent him a reassuring warmth through her eyes.

Wayne began, revealing he had felt calm and extremely present, listening to the birds and sounds from outside. Andrea smiled that warm smile of hers and said she had nodded off lightly for most of the time.

Then it was Jake's turn. He said, "I believe Diana was into something, I could feel something as though our group, our circle, tilted in her direction. She was...are you all right?"

Diana flushed, "Yes, I'm fine. Thanks for asking. Yes, I was into 'something.' I experienced the remains of a slaughter."

"I hope you made yourself safe. That was potentially very dangerous work." This was from Hazel who understood the dangers associated with meditations on death. "You know what you experienced," she continued, "was a Chod meditation and that can be very dangerous."

Diana sat still and looked back kindly into Hazel's eyes. "I know," she said finally, "I understand. Thank you for being concerned. I did ask, permission you know..." Diana pointed upward, over her head and realized again this level of meditation needed a new kind of language.

Hazel's eyes softened, "I'm glad. Obviously you handled it well." Hazel gave her own report, about feeling a kind of death energy all about them, but not feeling threatened by it.

Diana nodded. "Yes, that's it. It was a Chod, a cemetery meditation, as you say Hazel, but it happened spontaneously, so I went with it. You obviously felt it as well." Diana turned her eyes to Hazel's.

"Yes." The word came from Hazel's mouth but the thoughts she sent to Diana contained more, much more. Hazel had seen the corpses, if those immaterial appearances may be called that, but from a distance. She had felt the intensity of the experience and had stayed calm within it, without going toward the scene.

She wondered again if Diana, who had been in the thick of it, was alright?

"I'm fine but thank you, thank you all," Diana looked around the group of concerned faces, "for caring." She took a breath, "Now, the corpses mean some horrible conflict took place right here, on this land."

Wayne, a history buff, added, "All up and down the St. Lawrence River, including this land our home is on, many great battles were fought."

"Between White people and Natives?" Hazel asked.

"With White people against Natives and Natives against Natives."

"So the land here has been fought over before and we now are re-experiencing these battles but on a much lighter scale," Diana concluded.

"Easy for you to say that, Diana," Andrea Wayne's wife lamented. "You don't have to leave your home."

"I'm sure," Diana spoke softly, "that's true. And yes, it's not my home being taken, but then, you still have your lives. Those folks I saw a little while ago don't even have that. They can't rebuild."

"At least, not in this lifetime!" someone quipped.

"Or that one."

Andrea walked down the hall to get tea ready. They all stood, stretching out from the hour of sitting still. Diana watched as Jake complimented Hazel on her hair, then walked to the kitchen behind Andrea.

Hazel strode in two steps over to Diana, "Jake noticed my hair! Did you hear that?"

As Diana nodded, Jake returned with slices of the carrot cake he had brought, and offered them around, before sitting down next to Diana and putting his arm around her shoulders.

Clearly a little flustered, Hazel asked Diana, "So it's arms around the shoulders already?" who could only nod and smile and try not to blush.

Jake drove behind her to her house, as they had done the last several Sundays. She climbed from her car and as he had before he asked to sit on the dock for a bit.

"Yours was the only meditation with anything happening," he began.

"Jake, you have to understand, meditation is a group activity. I may have been the one in the action, but everyone supplied the energy. Without their energy, it would not have happened."

"And without your skills it wouldn't have happened either, Diana. How are you? That was some heavy stuff..." Jake noticed Diana's gooseflesh in spite of the warm sun.

"Now it comes," she said softly. "Now my body speaks of how difficult it was, it's like this whenever I go...when it's cemetery meditations." Diana's teeth chattered slightly, then stopped as she rubbed her arms.

"Why do it, then?"

"Because..." Diana paused, again wondering how much truth to risk with Jake, "Because I am their only hope."

Jake shook his head, a quizzical look on his face.

"Jake, those bodies, those...corpses, they will stay for all eternity in that suffering, the same agony as at the moment of their death, unless released."

"So it's up to you? Why? Why risk it for people you have never met?"

Diana heard this harshness came out of caring for her. "Jake, the truth is, I...I'm sure I have met 'those people' as you call them. I believe," she took a breath, "I believe I was one of them."

Diana was not expecting the smile that rose warm and clear across Jake's face.

"So when do you think you were a Native?"

"First, I'll tell you what led me to this, besides what Rinpoche tried to teach us." Diana's eyes skimmed the water's surface. "I spent some time with Native elders when I lived out West. They taught me to build a sweat lodge. What happened was I had held back, wanting the guys to get to our meeting place first so they could set it up. I figured that's how it would go. When I got to the land belonging to one of the men he pointed out a structure about quarter mile away, down a little hill and close to the stream that ran through their property.

"Now this was in the West, the real West where wild Sage grows everywhere in clumps, clusters flowering all over the place. The man who was directing the sweat, his name was Garn, had been taught by the Lakota people, whom he had lived among for two years. Every day of those two years, so I was told, he had been in or led sweat.

"He pointed to the structure and said, 'A woman has to build the sweat lodge. We got the poles up, which is kind of breaking the rules...' then he grinned at me, you know, because Garn, a White man, was already breaking the rules by holding the sweat in the first place, 'but we need you to go and place the canvas all around the poles. A woman has to do that much.'

"I grabbed the canvas sheets they had piled up by the round triangle of poles and draped them as best I could to keep out all the light. Since it was a sunny day at that point, there was a lot of light so I had to keep at it until inside the tepee was dark.

"Finally it came together.

"I looked up and Garn was suddenly right there, beside me.

"He told me now I had to go and gather the sage. I argued, 'I'm just a dumb White woman,' but he insisted since I was the only woman present it was up to me.

"So I walked among the Sage Grandfathers, as he called them, walked trying to feel my way among the plants to the one that was the strongest, oldest, most powerful.

"I walked for a long time, feeling as though I was trying to knit a pair of socks while I had mittens on, you know. Feel for the Grandfather? What did I know? Who was I to be deciding? How would I know which plant to approach?

"Garn had assured me I would know the Grandfather when I found it, so I kept on.

"Suddenly I stopped. I didn't make myself stop or come to a stop you see, I just...as if my body responded to something and stopped of its own will. And I turned slowly in a circle, very slowly, listening and looking at each plant and then I saw it.

"It stood among the others, so much like them you wouldn't notice unless you...unless something told you. But once you saw it, once I saw it, it was obvious. This plant was at its stem larger, thicker than the others. The green along its leaves just a slight pitch brighter in tone...and the plant itself seemed to glow. Yes, it did! It seemed to glow with what I thought of as strong life force.

"The glow is what made it stand out. None of the other plants around it had this light, this visible energy stretching along their stems and leaves.

"So I bent over, my hands in prayer, and asked the Grandfather to let me know which plants I might use for ceremony, because we two-leggeds wished to cleanse our souls and become more worthy of sharing the earth with all the Grandfathers, all the four-leggeds and all the winged friends...this was as Garn had instructed me but the prayer went on for some time, which did surprise me."

Jake raised an eyebrow and Diana grew a bit flustered, "Oh, all right, so I talk. But I don't spontaneously babble prayers, at least...not every day, I mean..."

"Diana, I'm kidding. Breaking up the tension, you know? But I am following you, deeply, and," Jake reached his hand out to cover hers resting on the arm of the lawn chair, "I want to hear more."

Diana glanced at him and continued, "When I felt, when I saw the energy begin to dissipate, I stood and began. It was like my hands had a secret language I'd never heard. They knew which plants to take from and which to leave behind. Once I tried to play with it, tried to direct it and my shirt got caught on one of the branches, snagged up so I had to untangle myself. Metaphor, indeed!

"Finally with enough sage in my arms, I staggered back to the tepee and placed the sage inside, noticing where Garn had put tobacco, cedar and sweet grass inside. The medicine plants had to be at the four corners, in line with the four directions.

"Garn had the rocks, the grandfathers, hot and ready and we began. He conducted four rounds, with prayers and songs in each round. In the last round we each were encouraged to give sound or words to our inner wishes and prayers."

"What did you pray for?" Jake asked.

"Can't tell, not fair to ask me! Later, the weather changed. It was hailing in one place from a really dark cloud to the East; rain soft and light fell on us for a while from other clouds, grey ones that floated in and then away and at the same time part of the sky was sunny so a rainbow shone down across the shadow studded plains. It was beautiful.

Garn noted it for us all, saying four different weather patterns in one sky.

"We walked away from the sweat lodge up the small hill to the stream. Each of us stripped and walked in but as I did I almost shouted. I saw suddenly many corpses twisted and bruised lying on the shore, so close I felt I would stumble over them."

Diana stopped for a moment.

"Garn saw something about me and put his hand on my arm. As he did, it all fell away and there was just the stream, the guys in the water and me about to walk in.

Garn asked what had happened so I told him what I saw. He looked at me for a long time, then said, you were here, then. That's all. That's what he said but I have never forgotten seeing the bodies, or the way he told me I had been there. It made something fall into place, something inside."

Jake was quiet, his eyes looking out on the water's still surface.

Diana sat still, trying unsuccessfully to feel his thoughts, wondering if this was it, she had gone too far and now he would leave her.

At last he spoke again, "Let's go up..."

"Here," Diana tossed him the synthetic shirt, a Chicago Black Hawks emblem emblazoned on its front. "Your security blanket."

"It's my shirt," he responded in a simple voice.

"Yeah, I know but you wear it all the time."

"Does that offend you, Madam? Does it smell?"

"No," Diana giggled, then paused, "I like the face, the Native man with his strong nose."

"Probably not PC."

"Probably not."

Tahni's Life

1640's

Tonawanda

Takoda and his party hid behind the dark green pine limbs hanging low in front of his eyes. His bow and arrow taut, Takoda watched from inside the cover of the forest. He registered the smell of a late winter melt, dank and wet in his nostrils, welcoming what it meant—the hunt had been successful and was nearing its end. Soon he would be home with Tahni.

The doe stood easily close enough for a full shot. Takoda steadied his arm, silently drew back the bow but a sliver of light sliced the air, a sharp sound like a dog in pain hit his ears, and the doe staggered, a spurt of blood splaying across the air. A second later the smell of burnt flesh like meat left too long on the spit scraped in the back of his nostrils.

He lowered his bow and arrow watching as men from another tribe, a fierce, warlike people, gathered in, exclaiming and shouting to each other about the kill.

Kill? It did not seem to Takoda there was anything for these hunters to brag about. The doe had been cut down with no chance, by something that looked like lightning.

So this, Takoda thought, is the lightning from the sticks of White Men.

Takoda peered through the trees, saw Iron Tail's eyes

staring at the sight. The intensity of Takoda's gaze turned Iron Tail's eyes to him. The two men signaled stay put, stay silent. Iron Tail turned to send the message along the line of their hunters ringing the forest when they heard war cries behind them.

Takoda saw the same staggering, but this time it was one of his men. The crack in air, the split second delay and then again the acid smell. Takoda's eyes found the ground as his feet shot through the dense underbrush.

He ran, separated from his men, keeping himself straight along the bottom of the rock cliff their party had followed into this new territory. Finally the rocks seemed to afford a place of shelter, a place where the rocks melted into the trees and bush. He lay on the ground panting.

No one had pursued him. There was no need. Instinctively Takoda reached across his chest where blood dripped from the stinging bite of the lightning stick. The smell wafted up. Pain announced itself with each breath. He settled his back against the rock warmed by a shaft of sun beaming through the trees, his bow and arrow across his lap, and waited.

He sat watching the night sky fold in. In its dusk he saw again the many enemy braves he'd sent to the other side. They rose now strong as ever and he again took them down, one by one, until below his feet he saw the earth thick with blood. It was warrior blood, an honour in the taking. Gratitude slid through his chest to Great Spirit for these deaths. He watched the cloud bank darken outside, smelled the first stirrings of night wind begin to blow, then the warmth of that other place called him.

He recalled the women, their warmth and curves spreading around him like a comforting blanket. His mother's arms, her strong body and soft voice came with the blanket and on the blanket were stars and suns and moons, and the seasons passing until as he stood up, stretching and feeling completely healed, he saw Tahni come toward him, her beauty and the depth of her eyes filling him with everything he would ever need. She held out her hand and as he touched hers he felt himself washed away as though he had always been a darker shade on an endless sea of color, now peaceful, content to fade.

When the enemy found him next day they saw first the colorful feathers on his arrows and the distinctive headdress of a Chief. One young warrior, high with blood and death, put the headdress on.

"Aihhhyiii, no, that is sacred." His companion started with fear.

"What? He's dead. He's dead and we found him and this and this," he picked up the weapons along with Takoda's roach cap, saying triumphantly, "are mine."

"If you want his spirit to follow you, go ahead."

"Nayee, here you take this, hold it, go on." The young man with the headdress on poked Takoda's bow and arrow at his companion.

"Not me! I'm not touching it." He moved away from the other's taunts.

Later that day the young warrior braced the top of the rock cliffs, shaking his new Chief's arrows at the sun, laughing, taunting and challenging his enemies to come back, take back what had been won from them.

Below, stealthily moving through the forest the small band of Takoda's men who remained alive looked up at the sound and saw their Chief wave to them. His headdress blazed in the sun which shone directly behind him, showing his body as an outline, his voice strong and happy.

Bewildered, Red Fox looked at Iron Tail. Their leader was too far away for the words to be clear.

"We must go back for him," Iron Tail said.

"No. He wants us to return, give the meat we have to the village and come back with a larger party. The enemy are all through these forests. They know this place."

So Red Fox and Iron Tail along with their few men stole through the dark of night and dark of the forest weaving carefully away from the enemy toward home.

One sunny day with new snow in patches on the ground, Tahni, intent upon her task of searching the ground for herbs and grasses, was startled by the sight of a few straggly men emerging from the forest.

She stood fixed, watching as they walked toward her slowly.

"Iron Tail? Red Fox?" she could hardly believe they were real.

"We are glad to be back," Red Fox said.

Tahni threw the question, "Others? Our Chief? What of him?"

"Others, yes, there are a few more. Have they not made it home already?"

"You are the first to return. Our Chief?" Tahni demanded this time.

The warriors grew quiet for a long moment gathering their thoughts. Tahni's heart sank a little more with each second. Finally anger took her tongue, "Did he die with honour?"

One man tried to describe how they had seen their Chief, his headdress on, his arrow in the air, exclaiming, cheering them on, from the top of a cliff. How he then disappeared. Like smoke.

"Now," Iron Tail said, "we must get ponies and go back for him."

Tahni's heart pounded. He is alive! He is alive! O Great Spirit thank you for protecting my husband! she thought.

What she said was, "No, you are needed here. We must wait until the warm season." She was now their leader and although deep in her Tahni wanted these men to turn around, right then, go back for Takoda, rumors of war with strange sticks of lightning, sticks that killed with a speed and force she could only imagine had come to her ears. Her body knew this enemy was like no other. Deep snow may still come any day. The way through to that far forest was long and difficult. Chances of them all returning safely would be much greater in spring. Besides, they had lost a number of their best hunters, warriors, without whom the women and children would be defenseless should the rumored war spread to them.

The men walked into the village. Tahni watched one of the women drop the basket she was weaving and run toward them, watched as Red Fox and Badger Woman reunited. Her heart warmed. Not long now, she would be running for Takoda! She felt her strength, her will for life surge, and instinctively she placed her hand on her large, round belly.

As she moved toward the villagers now crowding around their returned hunters, she said, “You must rest.” Her tone was strong, her voice direct, the kind of speaking she had often heard from Takoda. “You must rest, gain your strength, then return later for our Chief.”

She withdrew into her home, where she lay on the bed near the fire. He was alive, and for this she gave thanks. He would return to her in spring, as he had promised.

Throughout the night, restlessness tore across her dreams, dreams of loss, of rivers overflowing their banks, of trees tossed in huge winds. She was still tired before she opened her eyes and her body hurt. Then she felt a warmth between her legs. Glancing down she saw the blood, strong enough she identified an ugly pulse in its rhythm.

“No, Great Spirit, no, no... I must...” she stood gathering her skirt, a pitiful blanket against the tide of blood carrying her baby, hers and Takoda’s, from this world. Unconsciously she clenched her thighs.

Staggering to the door of her home, she walked out, blinking strangely and calling, “Macawi, Macawi, help...”

Macawi stood, turning away from the morning fire where prayers had already been said. She saw Tahni walking forward, her arms gathered around her skirt, blood spattering down the young woman's legs.

Macawi moved against heavy air, as though she had no strength, yelling for help. Little Bird and two other women assisted Macawi in carrying Tahni into the medicine hut. They felt the heat through her tunic, the fever already raging as she writhed on the floor, gripping her belly with both arms.

Heavy warm clots slid between Tahni's legs, a pungent odor filled her nostrils. Her mind fought against this. She focused her breath, trying to will her blood to stop, stop taking her baby.

Tahni's eyes roamed the room. Over there, by the fire in the darkness she saw the White Snake Medicine Man had spoken of. Or was it a man, yes, it was a thin man who rose up slithering, his shadow dancing against the wall. Tahni tried to say, "Look, look it's there, he's there" but her thick tongue did not obey.

Macawi laid her fingers lightly across the bulging belly just in time to feel the swelling give way. Tahni slid back, whimpering as eight months of deformed baby boy leaked into the world.

"Boil water," Macawi said softly to the others in the wigwam. She wrapped the stillborn in cloth, said a prayer and handed it over to one of them. "Bury this. With prayers."

Chanting and praying, Macawi forced herself to focus her breath and begin. She bathed Tahni's legs and belly, her mind a trance of dedication and determination. Her rattle convulsed up and down to split the evil spirit in its ears, so its head would spill open. She sang, telling it what would happen if it did not leave Tahni's body.

Her own heart would bleed to lose Tahni, but Macawi knew the villagers, especially the women, needed her. They needed the Chief's wife with them through the long days and nights ahead. She was their sign Great Spirit had not deserted them, that their Chief might yet return.

Macawi watched, sliding sips of water through Tahni's parched lips, applying herbs she knew would help fever and infection, the infection that boiled through Tahni's skin in tiny pustules, as she slept fitfully through the day. Macawi continually washed the young woman's body, taking care around several red spots on Tahni's face, arms and legs.

Tahni settled late that night into a deep sleep. Macawi opened the hut flap, stood and stretched. Stars, brilliant, in every direction. Macawi walked wearily to her own home, lay down and slept.

Tahni, her body sleeping fitfully on her bed, walks in dream toward a rock wall, *rocks on either side of her. Then, suddenly, Takoda is there, his back to her. She tries to call but her voice does not sound. He reaches his hand for a figure in front of him, a woman. Tahni can't see who she is, just that he reaches his hand for her.*

Now he walks toward this woman. Tossing and moaning in her sleep, Tahni frantically scratches at her throat. He will turn, she knows this, he will turn if he hears her, he will see her and reach for her but Tahni can only watch in anguished silence as he takes the woman's hand. Then they both, Takoda and the woman, disappear. Tahni's heart knots, then breaks. He has left her.

Tahni had never experienced such a clear dream. He would not be back. A well of grief and anguish opened. He would not be back and her baby was gone, taken. What had she done that Great Spirit punished her like this?

She woke, sweat dripping, alone. Still sobbing, she rose into the dark night. Her limbs weighed against motion, yet she felt a curious lightness, as though her legs and arms belonged to someone else. She pushed against the air. That was why he had not returned, because of another.

She came to at the lake, up to her knees in the chill water. She cupped her hands to splash water on her face and looked at the waves her body made.

No more fire, no more, no more... she thought, before a dark, cold peacefulness welcomed her and she pitched forward.

Then the sound, a voice, parted the pulsing thick stillness she craved.

"That water is not good for you. Here, sip this."

Liquid bliss fell across her mouth, dripped down her throat. Liquid bliss refreshing, then opening her body to sensations of natural warmth, ease, a feeling of fullness. Her pain about Takoda was not forgotten, but seemed far away, maybe across the other side of the lake.

Then the ground turned dizzily under her, she felt her waist stretch across a rock, limbs dangling. Not a rock, a man's shoulder, jagged rocks cutting into her bones, no, dragged across a field of rocks. Her mouth filled with thickness, her throat refused to open. A sound like an animal crying met her ears. Someone should help... she thought before she fell again into a place of nothing.

He ignored her incoherent pleadings to be left in her icy grave and focused on getting her back to his medicine tent where he placed her gently on the thick skins he had prepared. A hot fire spit to his right. Water buckets emptied as he gently wet and pulled her clothing away.

Tahni's eyes, opened the slightest bit, watched everything from her bed.

He began. He taunted the Evil Spirit, "Do you fear me, a small human?" His rattle shook, its feathers bouncing as he swayed over her, incanting, intoning, "Are you so cowardly you do not come out and meet me, face to face? My medicine must be very strong. With my strong medicine I will bring you great ransom. More than one soul for this useless, stupid girl. I will bring you Wolf. You are great and powerful. You do not need such a puny human being."

He hummed and sang, the grainy sound of his rattle matching beads of sweat that worked their way across his face, chest, down his belly as he bent over the small, red pustules, naming and calling each one, daring them, "Bring me your maker. I am just a small human here, bring me your Strong Leader. "

Then between where he knelt and the far wall of the tent, she saw the Dark One, its rank odor filling the tight space.

Chaytan, Medicine Man, contracted his nostrils involuntarily, but he cooed like a child, "O, come to me, I have a great ransom for you." With his mind, Chaytan shaped Raccoon, sent it sniffing, curious and intent, its black mask searching for the source of the smell.

The Dark One dissolved the image of the small creature before it had taken two steps.

Now Chaytan produced Beaver, fine and heavy, its luscious coat gleaming in the firelight. The picture of Beaver chattered its teeth as it approached the far wall. Dark One scooped this image up, too.

Unwavering Chaytan next created Wolf, large limbed, young and healthy. This he sent across the floor, its tail straight out behind so one or two steps brought it to the Dark One's side. The smell in the small space intensified.

"I will do slaughter to tribute your great power," Chaytan intoned, "Take these powerful animals, all three, leave the worthless human here..." He sprinkled herbs between them, inviting the Spirit.

Chaytan's nostrils widened, then narrowed against the gamy smell. His stomach contracted, nausea starting. He forced his mind into a smaller tunnel, turned it away from his body, toward the enemy. A wall of solid evil met his force.

He felt himself weaken, then he blew a long, slow breath out, sucked in a long, full breath laden with the deadly scent. With his mind he reached down into his lower belly, to the base of his spine, compelling a column of fire. Its intensity lit the room, white heat. He sent this through his mind toward the evil one, who this time, swayed slightly. Chaytan's quick senses captured the subtle sign. He knew the Spirit had weakened.

Lighting sweet grass, Chaytan held the smoking braid toward the Dark One. He watched the Spirit lean forward until it and the smoke from the offering were one. Chaytan continued, his rattle and song softly piercing the space, until the last of the smoke cleared.

The Dark One was no longer present.

All through this, Tahni watched, her mind alternately in the room and skimming across an endless field of loss, barren lands, winter trees.

Then she dimly saw the outline of a human standing over her. He knelt down, making sounds. She tried to speak but her dried, cracked lips hurt. The human smeared oil on her lips, held a water pouch up, dripped a few drops into her parched throat. Each drop felt like liquid air, pure and refreshing as it slid across her tongue, down her throat. He crouched by her, holding a bowl in his hands. Tahni noticed his hands, slightly gnarled but not yet old.

He pushed the bowl towards her so she knew to open her mouth slowly, carefully. He dripped thin gruel into her. She was ravenous.

"A good sign, you are so hungry," he said clearly. She looked into his eyes and with a start found her body coursing with another kind of hunger. His eyes picked up her widening pupils, the slightly quickened breath.

"For all things," he said, wryly. "You must rest." He laid his hand across hers for a brief moment. A strong current, a warm river of life flowed into her, lit her from inside. Instinctively she searched for his eyes. He looked into hers, but she could not read them. Then he left.

She was inside the Shaman's tent. Through the opening at the top she made out the dark inky sky and a few stars.

Then she is walking back toward the village. She has been away too long. All the children run to greet her, tug at her hands, pull at her skirt calling Grandmother, Grandmother. The children lead, then some adults also come to meet her, worry and sorrow in their eyes, they say hurry just as she falls on her knees to ask Great Spirit for guidance.

"Wake up" she heard clearly, but when her eyes opened she was alone. A tunic of fine leather, a large coat of fur, a pair of moccasins lay at the bottom of the bed. She rose, dressed, flipped the patch of skin at the opening of the tent aside to breathe in air. Sharp and cold it flooded into her lungs but what her eyes took in stung her mind.

He was sitting across from her, a fire between them. To his left lay carefully arranged carrion, raccoon, beaver. In his hand he waved a skinned rabbit, back and forth. Wolf stood looking away, then back, watching the man who chucked and cooed to him, held out on his hand the scintillating smell of fresh meat. It had been an unforgiving winter, with little food. Wolf wanted. The fire, the man's proximity confused him.

Starvation's pangs won. Wolf took a step. Chaytan cooed, half mother, half animal, so rhythmically Tahni felt dazed by the enticing notes. Wolf took another step, lunging its beautiful neck toward what it so needed. Chaytan rasped one stroke through the heavy fur, blood spurting as the animal attempted to leap away. Another quick slash into its neck with the blade, and Wolf was a corpse, warm, still bleeding.

"Why?" The word fell loudly out of her.

Splattered with warm blood, Chaytan intoned, his rattle now appearing where the blade had been. He continued chanting as though he had not heard her, his frozen breath puffing in small white clouds on the dark night air.

She stood silently for a long while, then turned, slipped back into the Shaman's tent, under the bed skins, her mind tumbling around, why did he not make offerings to Great Spirit for the animals he killed? None of his chants declared gratitude to Great Spirit for the souls he had taken, especially for Wolf.

As she focused on Chaytan she found the warmth of sex moving in her for him again, but now her mind argued with what her body wanted. He hadn't even expressed humility before Great Spirit when killing the Wolf.

How could she feel desire for someone so soon after Takoda, especially this man? Takoda! He had left her for another. With that thought, the emptiness inside opened again.

For the first time in her life, Tahni felt anxiety, as her mind argued against what her body felt. Bitterness followed: Takoda had left her for another. Some part of her heart, cornered, cowering, held out its hand for her to recall the love she and Takoda had shared, how good he had been to her, how...but her mind, temporarily free of the shackles of her lifelong discipline, spent itself wildly against her.

Finally she heard herself, "He's gone. His choice. Why should I worry about him?" This grey snake slithered through her and in her weakened state, she did not have the energy needed to dismiss it.

"Wake up." The determined command tore her from the welcome oblivion of sleep, hauled her unwillingly back to her empty world. Chaytan, his sinewy body, strong shoulders and hawk-like features, was standing above her. She felt the sweat of sleep on her skin and smelled a faint odor.

"Can you walk? Put this on." He handed her the tunic. Tahni pulled it on over her head, leaning into it as she stood up. She took a step, faltered, he caught her arm and she felt again the pulse of sexual heat for him.

"We must move," he said. Outside they walked side by side. Although their bodies did not touch she felt his energy support her, as though he walked for her. He lifted the entrance flap of his home. She walked in ahead of him, aware of this as a signal of how ill she was, or had been. When she turned around, he was gone.

She saw in this bigger space two separate piles of skins for sleeping, a large fire in the center and a pot of food sitting next to the fire. Something glittered next to the fire. It was a necklace, a woman's necklace of shells and stones.

Her nose filled with the scent of meat. Ravenous, she tore into it with her fingers. When he returned she had washed, was dressed and sitting up. Again Tahni felt the heat of sex rise in her body followed by confusion. Her love was Takoda. Takoda, who had taken another woman! How easily he had forgotten her. Tahni found now whenever she thought of Takoda the grey, slithering snakes of bitterness trailed right behind.

"So be it," Tahni agreed to the strokes of anger firing inside her, anger turning again to sexual heat as she watched this man glide through the space, muscles on his back rippling slightly in the golden firelight.

He sat and stared at the fire as though she was not there. Desire for a man who ignored her, as though he did not like the sight of her face. Her face...gingerly she put her fingers up to touch her face. The signal they returned told her of pocks.

"Perhaps it is better Takoda not return," she thought sadly. The thought of him made her heart twist.

He placed the pot of stew in front of them. She waited, keeping her face down, convinced she was ugly. He ate in silence.

Tahni watched the orange firelight dance and flicker. Gratitude for her life rose in her, a habit, followed by thoughts from her newly unquiet mind. What does this mean, being alive, without Takoda...or my baby? Everything's gone. Great Spirit and Chaytan have spared my life. Why didn't they just let me die?

Pain sliced through her belly before she tried again to gain some clarity, some sense of calm. She fought against one side, telling herself, Contain that inner demon of bitterness and despair. It is not yours to argue, but to have faith in Great Spirit who, in sparing you, indicated some purpose yet exists. Then she thought, Medicine Man does not look at me. My face must be very bad. Her fingers rose again to her scarred face. She pulled her hand away.

He said nothing but sat by the fire, ignoring her. By and by he wordlessly took up his pipe, lit it, sucked hard through the narrow tube and handed it to her. She took the warm bowl in one hand, placing the mouthpiece to her lips with the other. The first puff coughed up out of her chest, harsh and hot.

"Hold the smoke in your mouth, then take it slowly into your lungs."

She puffed again, and again a few more times, noticing him inhaling as she did, pulling in air as she pulled in smoke. Tahni thought, He's trying to teach me how. Then she began to see thoughts, opening like dreams. In the smoke rising from the firelight she saw her parents, then Takoda. Pain hovering now on the other side of the fire, present but away from her, replaced the warm love she had known. Pocks. Just as well he would never see her like this...no more love...she saw her pride, felt it fill her, stiffen her back, knew she would never settle for the desperate men who would love her in spite of her ugly, scarred face.

Again she sighed, the fire, vague awareness of her companion, a growing sense of the heaviness that sometimes comes before sleep. Then her village, Macawi, a large grave, all the people fall in, calling her, it seemed, as though it mattered very much but she is tired, so tired, that heaviness weighing her down.

"I will go with you as far as the lake," he said.

She rose at his words without thinking, stepped outside and found the sun of a new day on her skin. Her habit of mind, if not her heart, reflexed in gratitude to Great Spirit for another night and another day.

At the edge of the lake he said, "You must go back."

Tahni felt a flash of contempt, how dare he tell her, when he disobeyed the laws...

"Of Great Spirit," he finished her thought out loud.

She faced him, Why? No word was said, the thought itself flowed through her dark eyes into his.

He looked directly into her. She heard his thoughts, although he did not move his lips. Ransom. A very big spirit. And... She knew he meant she had been a prize for either of them, this Medicine Man of this forest, or for the powerful black Spirit that had tried to take her life.

"What is your name?" she asked suddenly.

Silence. After a long pause he said, "Chaytan." Hawk.

"I want to thank you for your kindness."

"Oh, you will." A slight mocking tone in his voice, his eyes laughing at her, whether in kindness or not she couldn't tell. Then he melted back into the forest.

Mary's Life

1883

London, England

It took a brief flash for Beatrice, standing at the door, the coachman waiting for her reply, to calculate: Mary would continue to see Theodore no matter what. If so, the payment for gowns might be set aside, for the day when he no longer cared.

Beatrice took the purse, nodding her head slightly toward the man who retracted the silver plate, bowed and withdrew. If Beatrice smiled slightly after his departure, if those thin lips curved into the unpracticed shape of a bow, if any suggestion of hope crossed her mind or heart, it was not seen by any in the growing dark. She coughed heavily, and went to bed.

The following morning as Mary rose preparing mentally to sweep, clean, go to market that day and wait, wait again for the carriage to arrive, wait until this evening, or the next or the next, when she might be summoned to his side, her mother called softly to her.

"Yes."

"I have received a commission from...from Theodore Fieldworth. It's for gowns for you."

Mary's face showed her surprise. "I said nothing...I didn't know..."

"I know child." Beatrice interrupted. "It came with the coachman last evening. If we are to make something, we must get to it. Hand me my shawl."

Mary grabbed her mother's shawl from the peg near the door, her excitement building as she realized what this meant. A trip to the dry goods store, to buy material, buttons, clasps, lace! What love he must have for her. He was indeed the most kind, caring, considerate man in the whole world, and he was hers!

They walked the familiar streets in silence, Mary's heart nearly bursting with joy. Only when they crossed the door of the shop filled with laces, buttons, hooks and eyes, mounds of the most fashionable, and most exquisite materials, did Mary let out a small gasp. She had been in the shop and seen the items a hundred times, but never had she dreamed one day their tantalizing luxury would be for her.

Her mother nodded to the small, brown-haired woman behind the counter. The woman smiled warmly in return. It was well known that Mrs. Sweeney, this petite woman with the curved shoulders and thin portions, was a kind, sweet woman, whose husband did well by staying in the back room all day, as he was usually drunk, so she might attend to customers. She was an excellent business woman, by nature caring and attentive to details including those of the ledger. Even when the babies she had so longed for did not make it through the first trimester, nothing persuaded Tilly Sweeney the world was anything but well-intentioned.

Beatrice had some of the coins from Theodore's small purse in her pocket. She fingered a fine brocade, a deep yellow shade. That would work for the blouse. The skirt? Her eye caught a salmon colored silk, thick and luxurious.

Mary stood patiently, knowing her mother's expert eye in such matters.

"Oh, for your customers, I see," Mrs. Tilley Sweeney smiled from behind the counter. "Some that want what only you can create."

"Yes, of course," Beatrice tried to smile in return but the gesture was more grotesque than affective.

With the parcels under her arm, Mary, barely able to breathe in case this dream came undone, opened the door for her mother. On the street, Beatrice turned to the right which signaled their shopping was not over. She walked slightly ahead of her daughter, her stiff gait getting them both quickly around the puddles and pools, and into the door of the Milliner's.

In the window, Mary's eye fell on a feathered, silk-beribboned hat, with flowers and flares like wings that rose on either side; her mother's sight moved instantly towards a small hat, almost a cap.

The Milliner was one Mr. Axle. A bachelor, he had loved deeply in his early life one Beatrice Eagleton who had rejected him. Steady and even-tempered, to say he was plain was to flatter him. His nose spread across his face and hung almost to his oversized chin. As though pressured by the size of both nose and chin, his lips slipped across his face, thin as spring ice. Pox had marked his skin. His eyes were the one feature true to his nature; large, dark brown and warm, at the sight of Beatrice Eagleton, they displayed his warm generous heart.

He stood now dressed in shirt and suit, with a complexion as clear as a winter snowstorm, if marked with potholes. He came out from behind the counter, his large hook nose almost swallowing the wide, uneven smile. His warmth was genuine. He bowed and had she given any sign, would have taken the hand of the woman, stern and stiff who stood before him. He saw the wild, dark-haired beauty of his youth, a sight that never failed to move his devoted heart.

"Madam Eagleton, what a pleasure…" Beatrice began coughing and could not stop, all through his lengthy welcome of her and her daughter, his profuse offerings of help, whatever he might do, she coughed. At last the coughing stopped. Mr. Axle stood quietly to his full height and swept his arm out before the two women, announcing succinctly, "At your service."

They moved instantly in opposite directions, Mary toward the feathered creation she had spied in the window, Beatrice toward the small cap which her years of experience dressing others told her would frame her daughter's shock of auburn curls and set off her eyes to their best. That the cap would be much less expensive than the feathers and flowers was not lost on her either.

Mary was trying on the feathered glory. She saw Mr. Axle quickly suppress a smile, whether from amusement or delight she could not tell. She didn't intend to take any chances with Theodore. He must be swept away, without hesitation.

"Mary, come here. You are about the same size as…" Beatrice muttered just loudly enough that Mr. Axle might overhear. If he had any impression his love's statement was less than sincere, his demeanor did not betray. He acted as though they shopped, as usual, for another.

Mary walked to where her mother held out the small cap then fitted it on her head. A hand mirror appeared from the ubiquitous Mr. Axle and as Mary looked at herself it was her turn to smile.

Watching her daughter, Beatrice thought, It will not be seen by anyone but him, and probably won't be on for long. Mary turned to her mother, whose stern eyes flashed a warning and her daughter, used to this signal, understood to suppress her smile and say nothing.

"This one will do," Beatrice stated firmly. Behind the counter Mr. Axle carefully tallied the bill and took the coins from Beatrice's hand, without touching her skin. He felt it would have been impolite. Besides he did not trust his already overwrought emotions with so close a connection.

"Good day, Madam Eagleton, Miss Eagleton," he held the door out for them and bowed as each walked past him, only a murmur from Mary in return. His heart thumping with joy and grief, he closed the door.

This time Beatrice turned toward the left, which Mary believed signaled their way home.

"No gloves?" Mary asked, her excitement spilling into courage.

"What for?" her mother's eyes slapped Mary's request down. Mary understood gloves were seen by others, those in the public.

Mary ventured one more brave gesture. When they entered their home with the parcels and put them down, Beatrice began to unravel the string.

Mary began, "Mother, I..." Beatrice looked up and into those eyes, those beautiful eyes of her daughter that every day reminded her of her loss.

"Mother, thank you!" Mary tried.

"What for?" her mother almost sneered. "I did nothing. It comes from him." Mary blushed and held quiet for the rest of the evening while her mother fussed, cut, and sewed the first of many outfits.

Occasional trips to the Milliner's were required, to gather the wire and trims necessary. At each venture, Mr. Axle found his heart warming and uplifted, then deflated when the latch came down again on his door.

On the nights when Mary, dressed in one of her mother's finest creations, answered the door for the coach man and with a quick nod in her mother's direction, set sail to the night world she inhabited with her lover, Beatrice sewed until the light failed. She coughed, increasingly tormented, into a rag which was always present now, to prevent the drops of blood from spilling on her creations, spoiling her work. When the light gave out, she sat, staring through the window, her night time reflections punctuated by the argument from her lungs.

On such evenings her heart opened a little. She saw again the girl she had been, leaning into her mother's arm as Mama had sewn beautiful little dolls with big glass bead eyes and lovely dresses gleaned from bits of leftover material. Her beloved mother had died when Beatrice was eleven. She took over care for her younger siblings and sewed by night to help augment her father's income.

Then a stop at the milliner's changed her life. The wild dark eyes, chestnut hair and full curves of her young body seized the eyes of a Duke, passing at the same moment in front of the store.

"Excuse me, I'm new to town..." he bowed low before Beatrice, his eyes caressing the curves in her body as he stood again.

Beatrice saw the handsome face, hazel eyes piercing into her, and the slow smile along the sensual mouth. She knew without thinking his clothes meant nobility, so she felt fine in answering, "How can I help you, sir?"

"I'm afraid," he continued, staring into her with such intensity she thought his eyes might burn clear through her, "I have lost my heart."

The sudden declaration made her laugh spontaneously, showing even white teeth and sweet dimples. "Then, sir, you had best see a surgeon." Her wit enticed him beyond where her body had led.

In the dark of her night now, she recalled how he had protested her refusals, how he had sworn, this handsome, rich man, he loved her and would forever…With a heart full of love she had opened herself to him, and his promises.

Her father had only snarled at her, "You made your bed. Now lie in it," when she came to him with her trouble. Her bed was shards of glass, slicing into her flesh no matter which way she turned. She took herself to a home for pregnant women, had her baby, and against all advice and custom, kept her. She worked her way back into the world by sewing. Eventually she had this small place, a rented home for herself and her tiny child.

Mary had been too young to remember the dingy one room dwellings where Beatrice had nursed her, sewed desperately and kept the rats away, in the hours when the baby slept.

Too young to remember and just as well, Beatrice thought. All in the past now, and what I was able to do this life, I have done. There was nothing, she knew, she could do to stop her daughter from living out what seemed certain to be a dark fate. Yet, her mother's love rose again and she determined to at least say something. Then a cough racked her chest, rumbled across her throat and Beatrice went to bed.

Their new pattern of life had become so smooth Mary was startled when one evening a week or so later, as Mary crossed their tiny second room, kitchen, living and dining room in one, and whispered "Good night," in the usual way, her mother stated flatly, "He will never marry you."

Mary felt the words enter her body like driven snow, cold, bright and cutting. She swayed slightly under their thrust, then straightened her body.

"You don't know that. You don't even know him." Her voice was barely a whisper but the anger in it flew through the dark room, hitting Beatrice, who turned away.

Her joy shaken, Mary climbed into the carriage. She's jealous, Mary thought as the carriage tumbled toward her destination. She doesn't want to believe he loves me. I know he does. I know it! Yet Mary's heart trembled.

From that moment on the perfect bubble of happiness which had surrounded Mary was marred by a tiny hard seed of doubt in her heart. From this seed grew limbs reaching into her brain. Eventually those roots took hold and she came to conscious understanding. Her power in Theo's life was her sexual attraction. To ensure that power she must somehow ensure the sexual fire between them.

Mary waited with her eyes open. She sensed it would be a mistake to say anything directly to Theodore and she felt the vulnerability of her position keenly enough to want to prevent mistakes.

One evening as she arrived for their rendezvous she saw the lights on in the main house. Music and voices floated across the dark garden toward her. She raised her eyebrows, half-consciously and pursed her lips for a moment. Then she opened the cottage door and let herself in.

On the arm of the chair was a large book. No new clothes or any of the signs he usually left for their games. Only this book stood out as a signal to her. The flutter in her stomach told her she didn't much like this change.

She went to the book and ran her fingers over the cover. Although she knew how to read a little, she knew this book, with its oddly shaped letters, was different.

"Mary, you're here! All right then, grab it and let's go." Theodore's voice filled her with warmth and her hands reacted to his wishes. She grabbed the book and his hand as they walked toward the main house.

"We'll go round front and enter the main lobby like everyone else." Theodore's face was lit up, so when he dropped her hand as they rounded to the front of the house and the main doors, she believed it was because he was so excited.

"What is it? What's going on?"

"You'll soon see. Mary, this man is amazing..." but Theodore would tell her no more.

Her heart raced wildly as she stood at the front of his mansion, remembering her first visit here. Now she walked beside him toward the imposing front doors, her stomach twirling in excitement. She saw the front doors thrown open to greet the still arriving guests.

Her dress was perfect for this sudden change: a dark rose-coloured skirt fanned around her feet encased in soft gold slippers. A creamy blouse showed delicate embroidered pink flowers, and lay beneath a jacket of plush dark rose velvet. Mary's mother had chosen the colors to fully exploit her daughter's beauty.

The door man nodded formally, "Sir Theodore, and guest," as Theodore barely nodded before moving toward the large hall inside where guests were gathering.

"Look, Mother, look who I just ran into, and she has time to stay with us through this evening's program." Mrs. Agnes Fieldworth eyed her son with the edges of her mouth pursed in a smile. Mary caught the glance and understood Agnes Fieldworth knew what was going on between Mary and Theo, and did not disapprove. Mary's confidence grew a little.

"Yes, timing is everything, isn't it? How wonderful to see you again, my dear." Her hands reached out and clasped Mary's. "How is your mother?"

Before Mary could respond, a man appeared at the door of one of the side rooms and announced "It's time, now, everyone, right now."

Mrs. Fieldworth, and her son Theodore, with Mary trailing, turned immediately and walked quickly toward the side parlour where the few remaining guests not already seated sat quickly.

"Whatever is going on," Mary thought, "has everyone moving in quick step."

About thirty people sat around the lushly furnished room, on velvet chairs, satin settees, and brocade couches. At the front of the room, on a slightly raised dais covered with the whitest cloth Mary had ever seen, sitting in a manner of ease and authority, a small, brown-skinned man, his legs crossed up in front of him smiled benignly at the room.

Theodore ushered Mary, still holding the book, to a seat at the front of the room. The room grew eerily silent, a silence containing a strange energy, a pulse of interest as though something momentous was about to happen. More importantly to Mary she recognized this silence felt good, inviting and warm.

"Good evening," the small man began and Mary felt herself encased in a delicious sense of well-being. "We have come together to speak about important and joyful matters."

She heard very little else, at least that she registered consciously until, almost an hour later she felt Theodore's hand shaking her arm. "Take the book to him." He smiled into her eyes as he said this.

Mary blushed and rose, walked two steps to give the strange book over to the equally strange but welcoming man. As she handed the book down to him, he looked up at her. His hands briefly brushed hers and an exquisite sensation like liquid velvet filled her body. She felt this man knew her, loved her unconditionally and, she saw as an odd tingle rose in her spine, without sexual wanting.

"Like a father," she thought to herself, "like a very wise, loving father." She returned to her seat feeling wrapped in a cloud.

At the end of the lecture Mary stood to the side of the room, watching as people came up and knelt down in front of the dias to receive his hand on top of their head. Each one seemed special to him; to each his reception was warm, filled with kindness and joy. She saw him say a few words to some, laugh with others, simply place his palm on the heads of others. After this blessing, each person looked changed, charged with a slight inner light not visible before.

She watched as Theodore came forward. She noticed Brigitte from the evening of the gala standing beside him, then kneeling beside him as he received the hand of this teacher on his head. It looked to Mary as though Theodore was oblivious to Brigitte, but just as they stood again, suddenly Brigitte's face turned to where Mary sat and her eyes shot triumph and derision straight to Mary. Theodore stood then and turned to Brigitte, his back to Mary.

Mary's belly roiled with fear, insecurity, tension. When Theodore nodded his head slightly toward Brigitte, Mary felt the tension flare, but then Theo turned, smiling toward her. Reassured by having him at her side again, she knew better than to ask questions about Brigitte, or any woman.

"Well, Mary, what did you think of him?" Theodore gushed.

"Amazing," Mary's response was sincere. "Where did you come across such a person?"

"His name is Mipham, he's from India obviously, and Mother found him speaking at a Theosophical Society event last month…excuse me, Mary, I think he's leaving now." Theodore moved toward the crowd around the Teacher as he stood up and started to walk for the door.

In spite of herself Mary was drawn into the group of people who trailed after this Mipham, through the lobby, out the front door and down the steps until he stepped up into his carriage. He leaned back out of the carriage window, said a few words to those closest to him, then swept his eyes up and into hers. She felt her body come alive, as though she had been made of cardboard and now was flesh. It was a sensation without sexual desire, yet full of sensation. As she struggled with this, he suddenly turned away and tapped the door for the driver to spur the horses on their way.

Mary was left in a warm ray of sunshine. She stood very still, but soon overheard passing conversations, "Did you hear what he said to me? At the last there, just before he left, he said…"

This man, this small dark skinned man turned people into rivers of gushing language, thought Mary.

Theodore swept through the crowd then leaned into her when he came by, his eyes lit with warmth and desire. "Mary, my sweet, will you meet me still?"

She didn't know how he could think she might leave

without being with him, but she smiled demurely and gave the slightest nod of her head. Theodore's smile lit slightly wider with her agreement, then he slid into the group past her and stood beside Brigitte, just long enough for them to be swept up together by the crowd, now eager to return to the lights and warmth inside the grand house.

Watching this, Mary felt her stomach drop, her heart thump loudly. She stood very still as all the others flowed by totally unaware of her.

"Like a ghost," she thought, and shivered, "I might as well be a ghost to these people." She drew her jacket more closely around her, turned and walked slowly around the grand house towards the back of the garden, to the small room in which all of her love and joy took place.

Half way down the garden, Mary stopped. She turned to look at the house, the bright lights still shining from what she knew was the room the Teacher had occupied. Then she looked ahead to the small place, the room where she shared whatever Theodore was willing to give. The view from this point sent a chill through her.

Then she brushed those thoughts away with a shake of her head.

No, Mary thought to herself. Don't give in to bitterness and doubts. Too much like Mother. Theodore loves me. I'm sure he means to marry me. He just hasn't had the time or...or...No, I know he loves me. Mary pulled up a recent memory of Theodore. He had left for her a piece of clothing she had never seen before. A bustier, he had called it. Theodore had ordered the garment from France where, as far as he knew, everyone enjoyed sex freely and openly.

"Whatever they do," he had told her, "they know how to make sexy clothes. Go on, put it on." His voice had crooned in that sing-song way she had come to know meant he was happy and was going to be happier. "Yes, now turn around. Slowly!" He had chuckled at her eagerness to please by turning too quickly.

Theodore had seen the hair of spun amber, tucked up now so the curls fell gently to both sides of her beautiful face. Her eyes, open and willing, still shone with an innocent sincerity that never failed to move him.

"Mary, Mary, now" he had whispered. Mary remembered all this in detail and felt her confidence return. No, he must love her, or those feelings, those powerful emotions she felt from him would not, simply would not be.

Mary walked in the night air slowly, deliberately, considering Theo. She believed he loved her, had to love her. Confident in his love, she nonetheless wanted something…something from him to signal to the world that she was his. He was hers! Yes, she saw clearly what she wanted now was to show the world, everyone in that big house with its fancy lights and beautiful furniture that she, Mary Eagleton now belonged to Theodore Fieldworth. He had wooed and won her, fairly. She wanted everyone, especially Brigitte, to know.

Something stopped her. How to express this to him? Much depended on how she approached him. Was tonight the right time? Focussed on her inner world, Mary felt a bit strange. Then a more startling thought came to her. I've become a woman.

She entered their room, crossed to the wooden armoire with its beautifully carved doors and pulled out the bustier. She touched the silk frills, the black and pink lace. Then she took the lingerie from the hanger, laid it on the bed and began to unbutton her jacket.

Diana's Life

2005

near Toronto

They sat on the couch. Diana watched Jake's eyes rove out the window, then turn to her as he asked, "How did you meet this Rinpoche, your teacher?"

"After David, I...I was suicidal, but soon recognized a coward. Instead of a quick dramatic exit, I opted for the slow route, one to which I am inherently well suited: a life with no direction, no attempts, a life already dead."

Jake's blue eyes flashed out the windows. Diana waited for his thoughts to settle then began again, "I kept to my quest. In those days, you know it was 1969 or 1970 everyone it seemed was on a journey, questing for deeper meaning, as trite as that may sound now. It mattered then.

"Besides, I was unable to function, couldn't go to school, hold a job for more than a few months at the very most. I knew my insides lay in tattered shreds and I knew no one in our culture was going to be able to put me back together, or help, or understand, I knew...because of all that, I kept searching. That experience of sweat lodge had been a beginning."

"That came much later."

"Yeah, it was the beginning of an answer to my life questions. I lived out west during the 1980's. Now, back then in the last year of the '60's I was searching.

"I chanced on a White man, friends of mine who had heard him speak, who went by the name of Rinpoche, some kind of caste of high teacher according to the Tibetans. Rumors that he had been recognized by another high muckity-muck in the Tibetan hierarchy circulated and that recognition was meant to indicate Rinpoche's vast awakening, his intense...something. The people around him seemed intent on an experience called Enlightenment, one meant to...well, listen." Diana stopped talking, aware of Jake's sudden shift in interest. "You were at the meditations, you told me you studied Buddhism, but let me go over this a little, for myself if not for you."

Jake shrugged, "I'm not going anywhere."

"You know how in Tibetan Buddhism there's something called the Four Noble Truths? The first is that there is suffering, the second involves the causes of suffering, the third the ways to end suffering and the fourth, the path to the cessation. At least this is sort of close. I was always terrible at memorizing the enormous lists of things, like the Seven Factors of Enlightenment etc. All those lists seemed unimportant, almost obliterating what I was after, some truth way down deep. But the third on this list captured me.

"It was already clear to me life is suffering. No surprise there. But here was a religion, or way of life boldly saying there was a way to end the suffering. That caught me. What if it was true? What if the suffering, *my* suffering, might end?

"So after a couple of classes in Rinpoche's house, classes about which I remember little except that I felt slightly better when I left than when he began, when he announced a possibility for retreat, I was open to it.

"He had many demands. First, he demanded we ask personal permission to travel to India with him. Then he would put our name on his list. Then...it went on.

"So I stood before him in his living room, courage gathered and focussed through a tiny point of determination. As I looked up into his brown eyes, his six foot four frame, I felt suddenly very small and saw him as being about ten feet high. An acid flashback?" Diana noticed Jake's eyebrows rise a little and she responded, "Yes, of course I had taken acid. After leaving David I tried almost everything."

"Yup." Jake nodded, "And more..."

Diana went on, "So in this living room, a really lush space down in the Annex, his house, I saw him soar above me.

"'Yeeeesss?' he deliberately toyed with the word, his voice moving through at least four tones.

"'Seeking permission, Sir, to come to India.' I dropped personal pronouns, since no one else in this Buddhist group used them for reasons I never understood.

"'You? You want to come to India?' He was playing me.

"I nodded.

"'Yes.' And he turned away.

"That's how I found myself on an airplane, headed for India and months of strict meditation with Rinpoche.

"The first signal I had arrived in India was the storied stench. My nostrils tried to contract against the overlay of urine and feces, but no way. This was, recall, over thirty years ago.

"In those days the airport was a Quansa Hut. We disembarked down the portable stairs, walked across the blistering tarmac and into the milling crowds thronging everywhere in this country of sacred sadhus and holy cows. I was surprised by the roughness of the customs officers, their tone of voice and apparent unhappiness with our arrival. They pulled us from the crowd, made us stand against the side, while they conferred. We upset them in some way, all forty of us arriving like that literally out of the blue. Then they waved us through, all without changing the intensely stern, self-important look on their brown faces.

"The traditional three-wheeled public cars lined up outside, their festive greens, reds, yellows, in the swirling shapes so common to India looked like child's toys. We hired some to take us to the destination point Rinpoche had arranged, the Empress Hotel in downtown New Delhi, one of the few very British hotels of its class in all of that sprawling city.

"White linen on every table in the discreetly decorated, dark wood walled restaurant, beautiful rooms appointed with the best bedding, and everywhere dark, dark wood, real mahogany as the backdrop to soothe the eyes, mind and heart after the intense light and pervasive heat outside.

"I felt cheered by these surroundings after the long flight and further encouraged by the extremely small price. Such luxury has always appealed to me. Although I have steadfastly refused to make life decisions based on how much money I might earn, have instead stubbornly and sometimes you might say stupidly clung to the belief that learning about Soul while I am here is the best use of my time, I am a wimp for the finer things of life.

"A bath and a good pot of rich tea poured from a real silver tea pot, joined by the best cream, with small, heavy shortbread cookies on a tiny silver dish to the side, courtesy of hotel management buoyed my spirits fully. I felt ready to listen and learn.

"In a beautiful side room off the main lobby he met with the forty or so followers who were game for retreat, where he revealed more of his demands. Before we might have his permission to enter full retreat we had to complete the Ngon Drol, a practice of 100,000 prostrations..." Diana quickly brought her hands up over her head, then lowered them to touch her forehead, throat and heart center,

"See, you put your hands like this, then go down on your knees and slide along the floor until your hands are out in front of you, fully."

Jake nodded.

"One hundred thousand times! Impossible! or so I thought at the time." Diana laughed. "Then he wanted the same number of mantras, a kind of short spoken word uttered while holding one of the beads of the mala, the Tibetan name for a rosary, in your hand. 108,000 each of Chen Rezig for the practice of Compassion, Guru Rinpoche for the practice of awakening the higher teacher within, Vajra Sattva short form for purification and Vajra Sattva, the one hundred syllable version for more intense purification. Each of these meditations with their distinct mantras had to be practiced with complete visualization of the deity, so Chen Rezig with his four arms and peaceful face, Guru Rinpoche with his staff and slightly wrathful face and so on. Full visualization, 108,000 repetitions of each mantra.

"Right. I already felt defeated, but had nowhere to run! Had I been here, in Canada, I would have headed to the nearest bar and oh how I wanted that! Wanted but had already shut the door on the possibility.

"Next morning we boarded a couple of Indian buses, replete with those swirling designs in bright colors, to make the journey for what was to be our home for the next several months.

"We swayed and jerked, the engine stumbled and it looked like we would all fall over the cliffs, down the gorges, around the cows that wandered freely onto the road, away from the cliff rising steeply on the other side, for over twelve hours. I had retreated already, into a sullen, miserable silence.

"Others on that journey smiled, joked, seemed to enjoy themselves. The grime up my nose, the discomfort in my jostled body, negative thoughts in my head conspired to form a frown on my face that worked as a warning. Everyone carefully refused my company.

"It is no wonder then that when it came to picking out who would bunk in with whom, I was left out. I took it as normal. Others seemed possessed of a secret ability to be chosen. I alone, it seemed, was excluded.

"I had my almost-two-room home to myself, then. I tell you honestly: I had scoped it out and none of the men around looked interesting enough for me to even bother having sex with." She watched Jake's face, but no particular emotion ran under the skin, just those accepting eyes, that non-judgmental attention she was growing to need.

"As I stepped across the cabin door, I realized I had been holding my breath against the prevalent smell of burning dung. Here in the mountains the air was greatly improved or at least the smell was. The air felt better, lighter, more clear, the smell of dung lay lighter on it.

"Rinpoche held evening classes. He spoke about so many things and spoke about them all so eloquently I believe to this minute it is a shame I was such a poor student. I took notes, then lost them. I tried to write then got caught up in his words, his language. He was a great story teller! I tried to recall the important parts of what he said and could not. I resigned myself to simply being present, hoping my cells, simple beleaguered creatures as they are, might soak up something of the gems he scattered continually.

"He held the classes in the living room of the large house in which he and a few attendants lived. He never lived alone. Always young men filtered through his house, opening the door before class, directing us out afterward.

"The room had windows almost as high as the ceiling, and a large beautiful wooden floor. On its expanse, bright colored pillows splayed out under the stunning tangkas, pictures of different Tibetan deities hanging from every wall.

"The warmth of candlelight completed a mystical feeling as Rinpoche's voice rang with the opening invocation of protection or ended with traditional prayers.

"All these customs as well as the prostrations themselves and mantras I was to complete were totally new to me. I was compelled, fascinated and repulsed.

"As I said, we were not supposed to write letters, but I did. For the first several weeks my need for David increased to a level... I felt I would burst my body. I was still in withdrawal. It was painful. I wrote and wrote, I walked the distance to mail the letters, knowing I was contravening the rules, but rules have never mattered much to me."

"Another thing we have in common."

Diana paused a beat before resuming, "No reply came, although I begged for even the most terse response. I believed he hated me." Diana stopped.

"What was retreat like?"

"What was it like? I hated it, everything about it. The smell of dung paddies in the air, their smoke carving outlines up from the village and from the dingy houses of the few neighbors who lived across the valley, the pervasive dirt, the sounds of the tongues of those impoverished people smiling their broken toothed smiles as their hands reached out for whatever pennies foreigners might give, their crippled legs smashed at birth by parents intent to provide a successful life as a beggar, and their laughter. Most of all I hated their laughter. They laughed all the time as though none of this mattered.

"I hated the crowded streets, flooded with dirty people everywhere and the honking horns of those three-wheeled vehicles painted garishly with colors that swirled past as they raced and pushed through the hordes of cattle, children, dogs, beggars, rushed over cow dung patties, human excrement, dead dogs that filled the streets, raced and pushed as though within their tiny seats sat the only possible purpose in this smutty world.

"I hated being there, getting up every day to see the stupid sun rising over the same degraded valley, knowing these people had nothing to look forward to in their lives, knowing they were doomed. I did not feel compassion for them. I felt contempt. I felt rage at the social forces including their own ignorance which shackled them.

"Every morning I watched a young boy climb the torturous trail to my place, the memory of my crumpled rupees in his hand no doubt fueling his way. He held across his shoulders a large stick on which hung from either side red clay cones. He steadied the stick with one hand and used the other to hold a large kettle of chai, the ubiquitous milky tea.

"Every day he arrived with a large smile, set the kettle down and jabbered at me as though some miracle overnight had opened my ears to his language. Every day I sat on the front step watching him pour the steaming liquid into one of the red clay cones. Every day I paid him more than a month's worth of his usual salary before he hoisted his load back on his shoulders and returned to the place below.

"I sat, contemplating all the lousy lives of lousy people on this lousy planet, while I sipped the first hot tastes of the tea and sucked on a harsh local cigarette. When the chai was gone, I smashed the clay cone against the step, its soft crunching sound very satisfying.

"Breakfast completed, I walked inside and sat. I did not sit on a cushion, although one was there. I sat on the battered wooden chair and let my mind have its way.

"The onslaught of negativity and hatred now turned inward. I was unable to meditate, and uninterested. What was the point? Deprived of my addictions, those patterns of destruction I had used to keep myself away from what I felt, the basic wiring of my inner circuits lit up, their unmedicated message singing ferociously inside my head.

"'No point, no use, don't try, useless, give up,' an example from an easy day, a day when my hatred and negativity were not too pointed. Other days, the voice turned against me.

"'Why are you even alive? You along with all these other useless, stupid and depraved beings crawling along the planet like lice. Why not just out, now?'

"Rinpoche in his wisdom had mentioned in one of the talks before the retreat that in the Buddhist view, those who suicide set themselves up for at least 47 lifetimes of the same suffering. I'm not saying I believed this, but what if?

"It was enough to keep me from it. Instead I endured the torment of my inner world, crooked, black, reeling through its uneven rotations, cranking absonant, grating inner sounds that raked against my nerves.

"Nowhere to go; nothing to do. Every day. The meditation beads lay beside the pretty pillow, flaunting my inadequacy. Every night, when Rinpoche gave class and students gathered in the large, beautiful room, I scanned their faces. They looked relaxed, contented, happy. I alone seemed destined to this pattern of morbid narcissism.

"It would be many years before realization dawned of what had occurred: the meditation had taken place, I had seen the contents of my consciousness. By removing the patterns of daily life, the activities I hid behind, I was left to hear, feel and see the bottom.

"This made eating very difficult, not just because I had to haul food up from the village, almost every day or else partake of the local restaurants, with their dishes of colored, spiced slop but because I didn't want to eat. Anything. Nothing appealed, and I felt no hunger, only a slowly growing sense of being lighter, and lighter, of fading. This, the perception of fading was infinitely soothing. I recognized what I was in although in those days it wasn't called anorexia. I forced myself to eat at least a bowl of rice, three times a day. Well, sometimes twice.

"Then gradually, slowly over a few months I began to notice other things, moments for instance when nothing went on, but the pleasant in and out sensation of my breath. This was not, I'm telling you, meditation! I was not able to meditate and probably never have since. It was just something that happened after many days of sitting in that two room house and letting my mind go.

"After that I learned to stay gently with this pleasant

feeling until it whispered through my body. Nothing was happening at all during such moments, the most pleasant and easy nothing I had ever experienced. I began to anticipate the possibility of this ease even through the negativity that was never far away.

"I also began to notice threads of air changing with the mood of whoever was next to me in class. I learned to identify those threads, as though seeing colors, by paying attention. In this way I learned to know what another feels, or is sensing. Sometimes I almost can hear another think.

"This is different from what David, Winona and I practiced but only by degree. With those two the inner connections were up and running from the moment when we stumbled on each other. I have learned with most other people I am also accurate, but it upsets them that I know what their truth may be."

"Must be helpful in your work."

"Yes, yes it is..." Diana mused softly.

"Go on, I'm enjoying...hearing you talk."

Diana blinked once and went on, "One night I crawled from the warmth of my sleeping bag to make the journey to the outhouse. I slipped into my white clogs and recognized, as I stepped out of the cabin I felt no chill despite the cool temperatures. I saw at my feet the outline and shining light of millions of stars upon which I had to walk! The beauty of the vision held my gaze on the ground both there and back and to this minute I can feel the wonder of it. It was a layer of frost, but without the usual mind filters, it looked exactly like a carpet of stars! That is one result of retreat." Diana flipped her hand open as she said this then saw Jake's eyes on her wrist, felt the want in him. She felt heat rise in her body; her face colored slightly.

Diana, you know you are not ready...you know you must... she heard her own thoughts ride the top of all those feelings, his, hers, theirs and went on with her mind focused on what she was saying.

"As I said, what Rinpoche spoke about I never could follow or recall. But feelings were there, large and buoyant, fierce and warning, simple and straight, the feeling tones he created in that room fell around me like a shawl. The words themselves often had the effect of a spring rain, gentle. My body began to respond. The black planet, the one with no feeling, started to recede.

"One night I could take no more, negativity won out: no more of the uselessness of sitting, repeating dumb syllables in a stupid foreign language, might as well be intoning Latin for the Catholic Church, no more of listening, of sitting, repeating, hearing the drone inside my head, 'Why do this? You're no good, never have been, never will be, no point in this, it's for others, those who are not scarred, damaged, deformed, and deranged like you. Give it up!' The ugly voice was never far from my inner ear.

"I walked that night out into the dusk of my hillside home, down the dirt path lined with trees whose names I never learned, green, living things harmlessly hanging their arms above my moving body. I walked through their darkness, their embrace and into the smoke laced air of the dingy town where people spent their whole lives patting dung for the fires whose smoke and acrid smell permeated everything.

"If I could have found a bar, I would have lived through such a night into an alcohol softened dawn. But if a single woman drinking by herself is dangerous here, it was twice so there. Even I knew that. So I walked, walked and gradually returned to my solitary rooms.

"The only other memory I have of that time involves a wolf. It might have been. At least, it looked like a wolf, large, silver coated, staring at me through the window near the puny fireplace. It sat there for what seemed like a long time. I felt no fear and just stared back. When it turned to leave a sharp spike of loneliness flooded me and I wept, hard.

"After that I noticed it was easier to eat, easier to live, really. That was it.

"I had confronted the depths of pain in myself and without knowing it, had awakened something from other lives."

"Your other lives?"

"It isn't like that. It's more that there are these other lives, other people who lived those lives and you or I come along, get born and we walk in their shoes. The shoes are already made from what happened in those lifetimes, so if bad things happened..."

"If the shoe fits..." Jake's eyes lit with warm humour.

"Yeah," Diana's face softened into a smile, "and if the lifetimes were gentle, successful, the shoes are easy to wear, things go along in this life. But..." Diana's eyebrows grew together, "there have been so many lifetimes, so many, for all of us, that we never know which side, the good or the bad, or even in-between will be the one we land near, when we're born."

"So no one is born alone, dies alone?" Jake's lips turned upward in a slight grin, but his eyes showed Diana how deeply he heard what she was saying.

"Right. We are born into the tracks as it were, of others. Many others." Diana's voice trailed off.

Long moments of shared silence flowed between them, then Diana spoke, "Rinpoche said so many times, you can't do this work, you can't make progress in this lifetime unless you work on behalf of everyone. That means everyone." Diana looked at Jake.

"Living and dead."

She nodded slowly, "When I found out I have a...proclivity towards the dead, towards helping them, I knew it was the path to my freedom also. No separation. Their freedom is mine."

"And have you?"

Diana looked at Jake, "Have I gained in freedom?"

He nodded.

Diana, "After what I told you about the rape, those hours of torture, I shouldn't be here, talking, living normally. I should be in a loony bin someplace, chewing wall paper."

Diana wasn't sure Jake believed her. "A psychiatrist told me, using those very words, 'After what happened, you should be chewing wall paper somewhere.' So I know what Rinpoche said is true: save others, you save yourself. No other way."

Jake looked out at the lake, its blue reflecting the shades in his eyes.

At last he spoke again, "Usually I'm the one who has to let people know, this is not the only lifetime. I'm the one who has to tell people, we're only here, now because we were there, then."

Diana waited.

Jake said, "Diana, are we going to dance this dance again? One more time?

Tahni's Life

1640's

Tonawanda

Having made it back to the village away from Chaytan and his frightening ceremonies, Tahni went immediately to seek counsel with Macawi.

"Did he give you anything to drink?" Macawi's dark, concerned eyes searched Tahni's. The younger woman felt the warmth of those eyes, their fire of love and knowledge as she sat in the warmth of Macawi's medicine hut, relating the incident at the lake, her companion Medicine Man, his strange chants and animal ransoms.

"Did you take anything to drink?" Again Macawi's tone of intense focus.

"At the lake, then again in his wigwam." Tahni watched Macawi's eyes turn slightly hard.

"He gave you," Macawi told her, "medicine. Medicine laced with herbs." Macawi waited for the words to make sense to Tahni.

"I, I..."

"Yes," Macawi said softly.

"I had... I was..." she began again

"Start slowly. Tell me also," Macawi's soft voice conveyed the importance of what she was about to ask, "did he breathe with, did he use his breath with you?"

Tahni remembered sharing the pipe with him. "Yes, once when we smoked together."

Macawi tried to turn her face to keep her sadness away from her young friend, but Tahni's quick eyes caught the look.

"Tell me everything," Macawi encouraged.

"He was there. I was at the lake and he was there. It was so painful." Tears began down Tahni's face. "It was so painful," she whispered the phrase.

"Yes." The older woman's warm brown eyes flashed with concern. She knew some women who lose a baby are in danger of losing their own soul, unless the tears and rage find a way to complete their journey to this surface world. Otherwise, the feelings rotted, deep inside the heart, making both heart and mind of the woman rigid and hard.

As Macawi held Tahni's body, felt the young woman leaning in for strength, Macawi recalled the one woman she had known whose tears and rage had remained inside. The decay of her heart had eventually turned the woman's eyes to rock, her voice to lead, until no life spirit came from her. Macawi vowed she would not let that happen to Tahni.

"I woke at his place and there was a...a...spirit in the corner, a dark, foul smell in the hut and he...Chaytan, he made the spirit leave, then I went outside and he had killed rabbit, raccoon, and beaver. With rabbit he baited Wolf and I watched him take the soul of Wolf then offer it to the...the..." Tahni grew confused. It sounded suddenly much less clear to her. "Then he cured me," she finished, ashamed of her confusion. "He healed me. I am healed," Tahni insisted.

"Physically, you are better." Macawi paused. "But your heart and mind have been given a deeper scarring."

"No, I was scarred before I...when I was in my tent. You left. You weren't there!"

"Your fever had already broken," Macawi's look told her this was true.

"Then why did I, how did I get to the lake?"

"The fever you felt then was not of the body. What was the dream you rose from?"

Tahni recalled, her heart shrinking, the dream she had had of Takoda, of him reaching for another woman, of her own mute voice, unable to call for him. She turned to stare into the fire, unwilling to put words to something so close to her own soul. Finally she told Macawi.

Macawi waited, praying silently for her young friend to soften, but saw Tahni's pride stiffen her back even to the warmth of Macawi's gaze.

"Well, you must come to your own understanding," she said softly. Surprised, Tahni felt herself grow tighter.

"Yes, I must," she said. Her voice sounded in her own ears like small stones falling around Macawi's feet. Macawi sat silent and still as Tahni rose to leave.

"Rest as much as you can," Macawi said sincerely.

Tahni nodded her reply.

Macawi took up her rattle and began to pray.

Outside, Little Bird rushed up to her friend, hugging her, "Tahni. I am so happy you are back."

Tahni thought, "I wasn't gone that long" but the anger in those thoughts made her stop.

"Everyone in the village is so happy you are back," Little Bird whispered as the two young women walked arm in arm toward Tahni's wigwam. There was something different about Little Bird, Tahni could see, but she herself was exhausted, needed to follow Macawi's advice.

Outside of her wigwam Tahni said, "I need to sleep."

"Yes, of course you do," Little Bird murmured, putting her head down demurely.

Alone in her home Tahni's head whirled. Had she been so aroused by Chaytan because of the medicine he gave her?

She built a fire and sat staring, trying to work her way through the inner maze of emotions which threw her thoughts around until one no longer followed another, but each tangled up with the next.

Tahni tried again to think. She recited what she had believed all her life, "Great Spirit loves us all. All the villagers make up a single unit of life, each giving to the other. This connection of one with all means when loss happens, we turn to Great Spirit as our comfort." Try as she might, Tahni felt no comfort from the thought of Great Spirit.

She continued, "The ways of Great Spirit are revealed through the world, the elements, the seasons, and all the animal and fish life, winds and weather patterns, this is how Great Spirit speaks to us," she argued silently.

"And now," Tahni thought grimly, "Great Spirit has brought us the White Man, and sticks of lightning. Great Spirit brought death to my baby and took Takoda to love another. Chaytan is not wrong. Great Spirit saved my life, in the same moment taking away everything that meant living."

Tahni sat before her fire until the sun began to rise. She did not attend the morning prayers with Macawi but listened. The sound of Macawi's voice eased the shredding she felt inside, until she stood up, left her wigwam and picked her way through the crowd of villagers, to Macawi's side. The older woman put out her arm, took Tahni underneath it.

"I am sorry, Macawi. I shouldn't..."

"You have been through so much," Macawi's words brought tears to Tahni's eyes.

"Can we speak some more? I have so much more to sort out..." Tahni asked.

Inside her wigwam Macawi stirred the fire, then whirled around, staring directly into Tahni's eyes, answering the question she saw there.

"It wasn't only water!" Macawi's brown eyes drilled into Tahni's.

"But I, it was wet, I drank..."

"Yes, but it was the most delicious taste you've ever experienced, no?"

Tahni's mind pulled the memory up. "Yes, yes it was as you say, the most...exquisite...I thought that was because of my fever."

"It was water," Macawi's voice softened, her eyes sad. "It was water, but not only water. He uses potions, he creates them..."

Tahni's arm spontaneously reached out for Macawi's. "He had herbs in that water, so the liquid..." Tahni stammered.

"Yes" Macawi said.

"How much of what happened out there in the forest really happened? What part was this world and what part was from...came from..."

"From his magic. That is the question." Macawi regarded her for a long pause. Then she said, "Remember all the details, as many as you can. Then check each one against what you know." Macawi waited to see if the words might enter Tahni, and light up her understanding.

"So...." Tahni replied slowly, "It isn't that one world is right and the other wrong, one real and the other false."

Macawi waited for Tahni to finish her thought.

"Both are valid, but what must happen is separation of the two. Am I right?"

Macawi smiled briefly but soon began to question her young friend again. "Did you notice any warmth toward him, any yearning?"

Tahni held her eyes on the fire and said softly, "Yes."

Macawi withheld a sigh, but Tahni picked up the subtle sign. "Why? I know it was wrong, I know I shouldn't feel this, especially with Takoda..."

"You are not required," Macawi interrupted, her voice soft, "to keep your feelings with Takoda. According to your dream, he has left you, and us." The older woman paused. "No, it's about how the two worlds, the Shaman's world and this one, how they weave. There is one seam, one way in which the two worlds unite and it is said this cannot be broken, not even by death..."

"Sex. But I did not take him inside me." Tahni felt tears beginning behind her eyes. One part of her triumphed, exalted, wanted to run up to his wigwam instantly, fling her arms around him, because he did want her. Another part huddled deep inside, cradling her head, trying to feel her heart, its tender ache for her beloved, Takoda.

"You did not lie with him. But you will." Over Tahni's weak protestations, Macawi said, "That is why he gave you the herbs. So you would feel your life energy and his as one stream. It is most helpful when used to bring another person back from illness. It is only ever used most sparingly, only in the most extreme cases."

"Was I that sick?" The question erupted from Tahni.

"He believed so. Or else..." Macawi waited.

"Or else he used the illness as an excuse to create this, this seam between us, so now I...no, what if I don't want to?" Even to her ears the question sounded petulant, unconvincing.

"You can try," Macawi said softly.

"But why, how does this seam work?"

"When we lie with someone, it is sometimes for the pleasure of the moment." Macawi spoke the known truths of their tribe. "When we lie with someone we love, emotions open up and our soul speaks with our beloved, weaving knowledge of them into our own bodies and souls."

A strong pang thrust through Tahni's body pulling memories of Takoda's love for her, hers for him. She willed herself to stay present.

Then the question erupted from her, "Does...can this seam be created with more than one person?"

"That opening, that speaking of our souls creates a seam between us, so in the afterlife, when we return to the Soul of the village, we still recognize that special person who has shared with us. Now," Macawi's voice grew sad, "When we add those herbs, Chaytan's knowledge of which herbs to use, the seam does not require we lie together. The seam is created because the herbs open our souls to each other without sex. Then our souls call to each other. This goes on after this life, into another and another, forever the souls call to those with whom they share this seam."

Tahni's heart beat fast in the silence that followed, one feeling in her body chasing another, her mind tumbling: she would lie with him, he would be hers, he had wanted to share this seam, or whatever it was, he wanted her, and Takoda and she had shared a seam...

"Tahni," the older woman's voice beckoned. "Do not try so hard to get all the thoughts and feelings figured out at once."

Tahni recognized with a small start that Macawi, like Chaytan, had read her mind and heart.

"Yes," Tahni replied with language, then found herself inside a stream of words Macawi was giving her without sound, about how any who train as a healer often find one or another of these mental abilities opening up. It is a natural side effect of the training in concentration.

"Now," Macawi said with her voice, "We know a few facts. Takoda has gone from us." Macawi said this softly, without flinching. "You are the Chief until another is appointed. Chaytan has, for his own reasons, committed his soul with you, and now your own life course is changed."

"Yes, his reasons. Why? Why Macawi did he do this? I do not feel it is only because I...because he..."

Macawi watched as her young friend stumbled through these thoughts. Then the older woman spoke softly, "You are beautiful child, it is true. That alone is one reason he has created this seam with you. But you sense something more and that is true also. He and Takoda were deep rivals." Macawi waited for Tahni to feel her words.

She did, and her shoulders relaxed even as her face sagged.

Tahni wished desperately at that moment to go back to the safety and inner calm of her previous life, without this turmoil, without Chaytan, only Takoda...her heart sank again and the inner demons of bitter thought scattered through her. "Takoda left you! When will you get it?"

"You cannot go back to what was," Macawi continued. "You are aware now in a different way and that will take some time getting used to. For now, you must rest. Go to your wigwam. Sleep as much as you can." Macawi rose, signaling their time together was over, for now.

At her home Tahni lay down, still unable to fall asleep. It occurred to her she was, as Macawi had said, in Takoda's absence, the Chief of this village. This thought among all the others rose to the surface and she focused on it. She fell asleep, and rose with the early dawn. Purpose giving her strength, she walked outside.

Tahni prepared herself to greet the rest of the villagers. They needed to see her, their Chief, healthy, strong and among them again. So it was for many months.

Spring came, a soggy late event, but finally the sun shone. As the snows began to withdraw, Tahni sent out a search party. Although they were the best warriors, best hunters, still Tahni was not surprised when they returned with no news of Takoda.

Out to collect early spring herbs, Tahni walked into the forest that circled the lake. Her training with Macawi had remained the center of her world since her illness and loss. She had carefully contained thoughts of Chaytan and if sometimes the thoughts roamed beyond their fence, she corralled them back with consistent common sense and will power.

For this morning at least she was deeply engrossed. Moving toward the deeper parts of the forest, she knelt down on her knees, grubbing around in the hard mud wherever her fingers told her. Her fingers expertly, lovingly combed through the forest floor. That dark smell, rich, wet and pungent folded into her nostrils. Her fingers, black with digging, flew in and out of the earth, small animals following their own instincts.

So intent was she, she almost mistook the toe, large and dark, under her fingers. She looked slowly up, fascinated with the muscles of his legs until about a third of the way above his knee she saw the beginning of a large, ugly scar. She flashed to his hawk-like face, his intense eyes.

"You like the sight of a man's war wounds?" His voice mocked. He lifted his leg, the loin cloth fell away and she saw the jagged line of raised white spread just at his groin into a mass of white ridges like tree roots.

"It must have been terrible," she said softly.

"Of course you would think that, with your medicine of chewed skins." The rebuke filled her face with blood.

"Chewed skins," she managed, feeling as though she was running with White man's feet, awkward, slow.

"All soft and giving, all Great Spirit and whimpering," he taunted. "You know so little of pain, understand so poorly what makes us strong. This," he pointed to the white ragged scar, "was the beginning for me. I lost Great Spirit," his voice was a snivel when he mentioned the name, "and found my own strength. My life. My strength. Great Spirit did nothing to help me in those hours of agony. I figured a way out. I did that."

"You must not speak of Great Spirit that way," she warned.

"Why? What has Great Spirit to bring now? More sticks of lightning our people cannot defeat? More diseases from the white man?"

The imperious tone of his words made her feel useless, uninformed, a child.

Still she had to ask, "You have heard of this sickness?"

Dread filled her. If he had heard rumors of the illness scything through tribes, leaving those alive with pocks...her fingers wanted to climb to her own face but she resisted. Tahni felt her chest constrict. She rose dumb before him.

"Of course I have heard. I have seen with my own eyes what happens. But Great Spirit," he sneered, then softened slightly, "has brought you here, to me." His hand was on her breast and in spite of the jumble in her head her blood roared with need.

Thoughts tumbled, demanding her attention but he pulled her body down on top of him. For the first time she was not able to fully connect to the offering of sex. She felt things in her body, but her mind did not flow with them. Sensation rose from her lower body but her mind continued as though those sensations were not, until, in frustration, she threw her legs around him, pushed his penis into her as she lay across his body, felt his hard pubic bone against her bud, his hard root inside her cave, and she rocked with determination, providing focus for her mind, direction for her senses and finally, sweet release.

His arm lay over her, his sweat mingling with hers, as sunlight sifted through the still bare branches. The weight of his arm was comforting. She knew from his breath he had returned from the brief place of rest, the peace which sometimes comes after the storm of sex. He did not move and this surprised her.

"You do not...you speak of Great Spirit..." she began.

"Great Spirit is a name for what we do not understand. If your medicine under Great Spirit was a strong as you believe it to be, why was Macawi not able to heal you?" his voice was strong, but not threatening.

Tahni considered contradicting him. She would tell him, "You are wrong, Macawi did heal me, and you, you..." but she feared the searing retort she believed would follow. Her mouth, following her mind's confusion, lay dumb.

Her faith in Great Spirit battled in her with the reason of his words. Yes, Great Spirit might not have given Macawi the strength to save her. Or was that true? Had she been already physically healed, but fevered from her dream, when Chaytan took her across the lake?

"Your medicine, what you practice without Great Spirit. Will you teach me?" The words, her words, startled her. She felt his smile and knew he had planned this, had figured what he wanted from her and was now getting it. She felt happy but at the same time frustrated, angry. Did he believe she was a child to be toyed with? Still she had pleased him. She could not pretend she was not in turn, pleased.

He held out his hand to her. By the time she was fully up he had slid his hand from hers, slipped back into the forest and disappeared so smoothly she almost believed none of it had happened. Gone. Into the forest and the world only he knew.

Slowly she walked back to the lake's edge, then round the shore. She stood for a long time, trying to calm her heart, but a beast inside her, one with wild wings, raced against her chest. She felt torn but alive again.

In the days that passed, Tahni couldn't tell if her energy rose because of Chaytan and her constant hope of seeing him again, hope that slammed in her heart against the anger she knew because of his taunting about Great Spirit, or whether the spring, and time itself was soothing some of her grief.

Chaytan began to appear whenever she most needed, in the forest, around her wigwam deep at night when the Sun in her mind refused to set. Then he would arrive, and when he left she was whole again. Their sex, not the deep and life changing slowness she had experienced with Takoda, was passionate, intense and left her filled with a wild energy for life. Sometimes she believed she lived for being with him. At times his appearance surprised her, but often her skin rippled and she felt him, knew he was coming for her before he arrived.

When they met in the forest she asked him questions about plants of the forest and field, mushrooms and moss; he taught her about animals and birds, taught her to see with the eyes she had and hear with her ears. He never gave in to ideas about Great Spirit and gradually Tahni stopped talking about it. In her heart she harbored a belief but it was chosen now, something she was aware of as a conscious choice. With consciousness of that choice came doubt.

One night Tahni tried but could not settle. Her body jerked, tossed around until long after dark. She slid out, pretending she needed a walk, telling herself she wanted some air, exercise, but she headed straight to the lake, took a right turn, scrambled over the rocky path to the clearing where his home and the shaman tent stood.

As she reached the clearing she heard voices. Little Bird! Silently Tahni crept closer. Chaytan stood with Little Bird in front of the fire, bantering and playing at grabbing hands. Then she saw Chaytan place something into Little Bird's hands.

Just as he did, the young woman threw her arms around Chaytan's neck. He pulled her to him, his hand commanding Little Bird's bottom snugly into his body. They kissed, hard. Tahni watched, growing aroused. She hated herself for spying, but she was powerless to move. Then jealousy stripped her insides.

Tahni walked slowly back to her wigwam. He had lied. He had lied to her for how long? No, her mind argued against her heart. He had not lied. He simply had not told her the whole truth. She felt dirty. And Little Bird! Had she known about Chaytan and her, about their union? What did Little Bird know?

It was no loss of face for Tahni since her people did not care about who lay with whom. But it was a betrayal of her heart. Had she known he was intimate with Little Bird, or anyone else, she would never have lain with him. So she told herself, the thoughts rising within her as snakes of anger and jealousy that whipped her insides.

Tahni turned to the fire and surprised herself by falling asleep. Next morning she rose to join the others who gathered to greet the day with prayer.

She stood outside, looking around, then saw Little Bird pull the sparkling necklace out, proudly showing others.

"See. I just found it lying on the forest floor."

"Little Bird," one woman said slyly, "only you would find such a fine thing lying around. Who do you think made it?"

Little Bird ignored the implications and continued to display her prize as though she had won it. "White Man made it. He makes many marvelous things." The small group of women fell back then, away from Little Bird, their confusion around this positive mention of the White Man pushing fear.

Tahni, gazed for a moment at the glittering object. "And with the necklace she has Chaytan," Tahni thought. Envy laced her, for a single moment, followed quickly by a quiet calm.

"Look," Little Bird tried to draw Tahni's attention, but Tahni pretended not to hear. She was afraid the slash of bad feelings inside would spill onto Little Bird in front of the others. She was still their Chief. She had to act the part.

As their Chief, she sat in Council. Macawi sat with her and these two women with their ability to listen deeply to others, helped broker peace with the neighboring tribes, a peace that lasted. The peace rose also from the spread of the White man's disease, its sickle having cut through the numbers of other villagers until no tribe could afford war.

In all that time rumors of the White Man's wars and the natives who joined against their brothers flew like flocks of predatory birds. Rumors about the sticks of lightning continued to arrive, but more threatening stories were those of illness wiping out one village after another.

Still, no one pushed her village warriors into battle, neither Whites nor other tribes. She and her people lived without the curse of the white man's diseases, a blessing Macawi insisted was bestowed on them by Great Spirit.

So it was for many years. Tahni's village thrived and in these peaceful times they developed ever more elaborate ceremonies, ever more profound celebrations.

A new Chief had been elected so Tahni, still attractive, but softer in her curves, wider in her hips and with more lines on her face, concentrated her energies on helping the dead and the dying in their transition beyond the Between Worlds. Her work gave her a deep inner sense of being connected, being useful to her people and if she waited some nights for the loneliness of her life to pass like a cloud away from the usual light in her heart, she told no one.

Now it was the time again for the young men to have initiation into manhood. Since this celebration meant their warriors appeared in peaceful costume, unarmed, to welcome their new brothers out of childhood into being warriors, no one knew until a few days before the exact day of the event. This year, the celebration would take place in early autumn.

The ceremony involved boys retreating into a special building, with no outside contact, following the guidance of priests and other warriors. What rituals went on, how the elders prepared the young men by enacting a death to their old life as children tied to women, how they helped birth them into their new existence, as Warriors, no woman knew, not even a Chief, or a Medicine Woman, for so Tahni now was.

"One morning just before the ceremony, Tahni dreamed..." *She stands above the village, her feet planted somewhere on solid ground so it seemed, a sound like thunder rippling the earth, earth shaking from...horses, so many horses, then she watches as a vast flood wipes her village and everyone in it, away*. She woke, sweat on her forehead, under her arms. The dream!

She walked out of her home, putting her moccasins onto the autumn earth, listening deeply to both the outer world and her inner one. She witnessed again that rising darkness just below the surface. She brought her eyes up and saw the usual morning tumble and jump of village life, heard the normal cacophony of voices, two and four legged, as well as the winged life. Nothing unusual, except with her inner vision she could not avoid the underlying darkness, spilling invisibly everywhere beneath her beloved village, her people.

Mary's Life

1883

London, England

She was almost dressed, or undressed, in the French garment when she heard his footsteps outside. Quickly she wet the palms of her hands and rubbed her nipples, until slightly wet and puckered, they rose above the material. Theodore opened the door with a sweep of his hand and saw her standing in the middle of the room.

"Oh, Mary," he groaned, then strode across the room and gathered her in his embrace.

He tore at the laces and stays. In his passion he did not notice how for a moment Mary stood extremely still watching him. She watched him and if he had seen her, he might have noticed a change in her eyes. No longer innocent, her eyes shone with determination, and confidence. She would get him. He would be hers.

Mary, tired but still flushed with the joy of last night's dream, for so her time with Theodore seemed to her, took the broom in hand and began her daily chores in the small dark space she knew as home. Her mother's figure, bent over the needle and tallow, shook with the cough that clung to her now.

"Mother," Mary said softly, "Mother, a doctor?"

"What…for?" her mother's breath came stuffed, short

and labored. "I have herbs…"

"But it's been weeks!"

"Enough! I have work…"

Work! Mary's thoughts took over as she swept. That's what you have all right and that's all you've ever had! Work and more work. What's the point of a life where all of it is work, night and day? Suddenly the words escaped, "Mother, we don't need the money now Theodore is looking after us, you don't have to…"

Beatrice's darkened eyes and ever more stern face, her lips drawn tighter still, turned on Mary. Mary took the dark look as a reprimand and through years of training, backed down, saying, "I'm sorry, I'm sorry mother…"

Beatrice sighed deeply and started coughing again. "Mary," she began, not unkindly, "I have something to show you." She stood up, the cough temporarily quiet, took a few steps and put her hand behind a small piece of window sill. It came away.

"It's something for you…and me, of course" Beatrice said. Mary saw there a pile of coins gleaned from the money Theodore had been paying her mother.

"Mother," Mary knelt down, "You won't need this. Theodore will take care of us, now."

Beatrice's long experience with the world looked back at Mary from the darkness of her eyes. "I hope so," was all she said.

"I know! Why don't we take a bit of this, just a small amount, and…" Mary wanted to give her mother a proper meal, or a bit of wine, not the cheap, vinegary kind Beatrice bought them once yearly, at Christmas, but a small taste of the really exquisite wine Theodore lavished upon her.

"No! No, Mary. You are to have this, in case." Beatrice's look told Mary further discussion was not possible.

Her experiences with the Fieldworths, their mansion, food, clothing, manners and oh, that first night of dancing…Mary's young mind returned easily to recent memories, the triumph of her naïve beliefs in a world made easy by love. For Theodore Fieldworth, son of the richest people she had ever known, loved her.

"Are you," her mother's words broke her thoughts, "going out tonight?"

"Yes," Mary smiled, "as usual."

"Ahh," came the response, with the hacking cough trailing behind.

"Mother, a doctor?" Mary tried again.

"We have no money for a doctor, Mary! I have herbs…" her mother's breath caught in her throat and carried her along its rapids for the next few minutes.

Mary blanched slightly at the sound and sight of her mother, racked with cough, bent over and unable to stop. "Can I…" instinctively Mary's hand reached over to comfort her mother.

"No, don't!" The command, dark and fierce as ever, froze Mary on the spot. She did not know her mother's terror the disease might spread to her daughter.

So it went throughout that day, with the cough as their intermediate space, the place where Mary attempted over and over to connect with her mother and her mother staying firmly, stubbornly in Mary's view, behind the disease, unwilling to reach back.

At 8pm the carriage arrived and Mary, clothed in the latest sumptuous dress, hat and bag Beatrice had created, daintily put her foot up, held the coach man's hand as she slipped into the dark interior with its satin wall coverings, gold curtain tassels, and enjoyed its rocking pace. She let go of any worry or concerns. Her mother would, as ever, be fine. Besides, Mary contemplated, she had offered. Her mother had refused. What more could be done?

This evening the teacher, that short, brown skinned man Mary thought of as a kind father was visiting again. As her coach pulled up to the back door of the garden, Theodore was there, offering his hand and saying, "Hurry, we're going around front."

Mary felt more comfortable than ever walking for a third time up those grand front steps. She found herself thinking, One day I will be mistress of this house.

Everyone seated as before, the small man at the front of the room began to speak. Mary was quickly caught in his words. If her mind did not take in the language or its meaning, her eyes and body took in the intensity and interest of everyone present. She felt a glow around her and a warmth inside she believed was because of Theodore. Although they again sat a few seats apart, she saw his eyes once or twice glancing at her.

She recalled him standing in their cottage, for so she now thought of it, answering her question about why they never went out. He had walked over to her and holding her tightly whispered, "It's because I think of you as a treasure, and I don't want to share you with the world, yet." Her heart had melted as her mind clung to the last word. So she felt secure in their outside arrangement, as she did in their night world inside that tiny garden cottage.

The next minute it seemed she was standing up, applauding, the spell the Teacher had thrown over them all broken. He was a wizard. She saw the effect again on the faces of those around her and marveled a little at how some folks seemed so easily affected.

She took another look around the room. People standing, shaking hands and talking with each other, moving toward the door of the room and there, there was her Theodore…smiling down into the eyes of Brigitte! She could just overhear Theodore talking about their Teacher. Mary's stomach clutched in that almost painful way but she focused on what she was hearing, pushing the bad sensation far away. She overheard everyone exclaiming and trying to express what they had experienced by being in this man's presence.

"You'd think," Mary thought suddenly, "they'd each been given a mountain of money…" Then with a shock that registered through her body, she realized they already had this. The thought grew in clarity until she saw how it was. They lived secure in the knowledge that today and tomorrow and the next day would bring food, good wine, clothes, parties, gatherings, and finally marriage and a family. No question existed about where they might land, no possible threat of being homeless, penniless, without food.

For the first time she knew her life as a valley of uncertainty; she recognized some of her mother's bitterness. She suddenly understood that these people, no better than she was, navigated the world they inhabited by a completely different compass.

A fierce determination rose in her to have what these people had, to live among them and know every day when she woke up that food, clothing, and beauty, for which she thirsted most, were waiting for her.

Out of the corner of her eye she saw Theodore, again with Brigitte on his arm, walking out with the Teacher. She knew he was her key. She moved until she was beside him as he passed through the great hall.

"Theo, I…" she began.

He returned her look with a chill in his eyes she had never seen before. "Not now…" he clipped softly between set teeth. Confused, she stood silently as the others all piled by her, led by Theodore with Brigitte now close to his side.

She walked, head high toward the front of the house. With each step she grew more conscious of a plan. She would win Theodore completely, captivate him and when he was so in love with her he could not refuse, he would marry her. If life had not bestowed on her by birth the same privileges as others, then by God, she'd create it for herself.

Back in their cottage, she had a few minutes to reflect as

Theodore finished his hosting duties. An emotional scene would not help. She needed another way through this night. She planned carefully, and lying on the bed coyly let the cover slip across one bare leg. She was naked.

When Theodore opened the door to their cottage, he barely glanced at her but sat on the couch in front of the fireplace.

"Theo, Theo," Mary's voice was a singsong.

"Ah, come here, my dear." He sounded as though she was an afterthought, but he held out his arm, his eyes still on the fire.

Confused, she pulled the satin robe with its embroidered roses across her body and went to be near him. She needed more than ever before to feel him inside her, to know she had his interest, his attention. She needed to know he loved her.

He gazed into the fire. Finally he said, "There's to be a trip. We are going on a long trip."

"We? Are we going Theodore?" her heart rose in hope.

"Ah, Mary you know that's not possible. I mean, the group of us, those people you saw. The Teacher has arranged for a trip to India. We are going."

As high on hope as she had been a moment before, she now crashed. "Not possible?" Thoughts chased themselves through her mind: not possible because I have no money? I have money! I have the money you paid my mother. Not possible! Again Mary's training, years of biting her tongue, held her in check. What she said was, "When?"

"He wants us to leave immediately. I believe the plan is to leave at the end of this week."

"This week!"

Theo sighed deeply, his hand digging into her shoulder more tightly and turning from the fire to look into her eyes said, "Mary, my love, you must understand. I am doing this to learn, to understand more about life and the things the Teacher talks about. This is an opportunity for us, for you and me.

I'll come back and tell you about all of it. I'll tell you everything." He leaned in and kissed her.

Mary asked meekly "When will you be back?"

"It's to be a long trip." He looked disappointed at this. "I'll miss you, Mary, yes, I will." He kissed her again, then said lightly "And I'll be back, I promise you. I'll come back and we'll be together again."

"How long? How long a trip?"

"Mary," he said in a voice that sounded like her mother's, thin and slightly threatening, "don't let's fight tonight. We haven't much time. Let's make the most of what we have while we can."

That night, although every action was as before, she felt his distance. She told herself this was due to the trip and all the planning he must be about. She told herself he would return. As she told herself she began to believe.

When the grey light of dawn crept toward them across the patterned carpet, she stirred, began to dress. Theodore looked at her as she sat on the side of the bed, reached up, kissed her lightly on the cheek, then turned away, his face to the wall. She heard him snoring before the door closed behind her.

The unusual lights flicking at this time of day through the window of her home might have warned her. Mary got down from the carriage and walked slowly toward the front of the house. The door opened so easily it may have been a second sign, but Mary, her heart full of Theodore's impending absence, did not notice.

What she saw first was the Doctor's white haired frame in the doorway of their bedroom, putting his instruments away. She approached, then stood looking at her mother's lifeless body. Still her mind refused.

"Dr. Fletcher," she demanded at last, "how is my mother?"

"Your mother," the doctor said softly "will suffer no

longer."

Even then it was unthinkable that the woman who had sat as judge and jury on every part of her life, the woman who had once, only once, said she loved her, whose kisses and affection were as rare as a February blossom, could be gone.

Mary choked back her grief in the next question, "How did you know to come?"

"Your neighbor, Mrs. Reid, sent her boy Jack to fetch me."

Just then Mrs. Reid, an ample woman who had lived next to them for many years, came in. Her arms stretched around a basket full of food: cheese, bread, some few cuts of meat, and a bottle of wine.

"Mrs. Reid, come in." Mary stated the unnecessary welcome, for Mrs. Reid was in and laying out the provisions on the sideboard, talking all the while.

Finally Mary interrupted her, "How did you know to send for the Doctor?"

"Well, I was 'round to see Maddie Semple, you know Maddie Semple, the herbalist, nothing meant to your own honourable self, Dr. Fletcher but my littlest one, Bessie, Bessie Junior we call her, although Mr. Reid he calls her Little One, anyway my littlest one Bessie had the croup. Now the rest of my brood never got croup, never got ill hardly at all, that's why of course I had no need of your own kind services, Dr. Fletcher, but here was my Bessie, now as the youngest some say the others just send their ills down the line onto whoever is the youngest and maybe that's why but there she was sick as might be and the sound of that croup so I says to myself, Bessie, take yourself over to Maddie Semple and ask for some herbs to help with the little one's cough." Here Mrs. Reid's eyes looked around the room as though seeing it for the first time. She paused only for a moment before ploughing ahead with her story.

"All day and all night she'd croup and cough and cough

and croup but then, you know, in the middle of the night, " here Bessie Reid stopped for a fraction of a second, then began again in a slightly lowered tone, "because the head of her bed is up right up against the head of the bed of poor, poor Beatrice, and I could hear her, too, night after night, first one, my Bessie, crouping and coughing then poor Beatrice, coughing for all the world like she too had croup only not the same, not as dry but more rumbling, like a rack of thunder…"

Dr Fletcher cleared his throat and looked directly at Mrs. Reid. Mary felt herself begin to fidget, her mind wandering back to Theodore and she too cleared her throat, then glared into Mrs. Reid's eyes hoping to help that women get to the point.

Mrs. Reid continued, "Well, then I went as I said to see Maddie Semple and she said to me, now Bessie, she says, I know you live next door to Beatrice Eagleton and I also know she is a proud, proud woman. But she is very ill, and as strong as my herbs are, sometimes the ways of the world and the illness being what it is, well, I want you to keep out for her. That's how she put it 'keep out for her' not 'keep on the lookout' or anything else."

Mrs. Reid caught the disapproving eye of Dr. Fletcher again and carried herself as quickly across the flooding stream of her mind as she was able, "So I said to myself Bessie she's been as good a neighbor as gets, you know a bit reserved and all, but," Bessie looked over at the graying corpse on the bed and burst into a sudden shower of tears. "She didn't deserve this, she didn't deserve it, she, she, she..." and Mrs. Reid was escorted by Mary to the chair in the living room where that kind neighbor continued to sob.

Seeing Mrs. Reid was completely occupied, Mary walked to the window sill, knocked the bit of wood away and pulled the small tin from its hiding place.

The Doctor took one of the coins she held out for him, then pressed the others back into her hand saying, "You will have more need of this now, than I." His kindness increased her sense of loneliness and Mary felt a thickness in her throat and a large sob in her chest, but she held it all in check.

Mary walked Dr. Fletcher to the door, thanked him and turned back to what had to be done. She put the kettle on for warm water and gathered clean rags to wash her mother's body. She opened the door of the one closet they had shared and saw there all the beautiful gowns her mother had created. She shut down tears as she took the black bombazine dress, her mother's best one, only a little frayed and laid it on a chair.

She had just finished washing the corpse, and laying her mother's dressed body out when Mrs. Sweeney arrived.

"Hello, my dear," that sweet woman put out her arms and embraced Mary, who stood quite still. "I have brought a few things," and she pulled out of a brown paper parcel a few slices of ham and lamb, two jars of preserves, pickles and a loaf of bread.

"That spread will do," thought Mary, "for the small group who will visit. I won't spend more on them. Besides, Mother wanted the money for me."

"Thank you," Mary murmured, hoping she sounded grateful. Her neighbor heard the sadness of grief and the monotones as loss, not lack of enthusiasm.

"Oh you poor dear," the woman cooed, "you'll be right, then. It takes time, seems you'll never get over it. But it comes right again." When this goodhearted woman again put her arm out to pat Mary's, Mary moved beyond reach. She did so with such grace the woman barely noticed. "And Mr. Sweeney sends his sympathies," she said.

"Thank you. You are very kind. Please thank Mr. Sweeney for me." Mrs. Sweeney then went over to Mrs. Reid and with all the pent-up mothering her heart contained, hugged and consoled her.

Mr. Axle arrived next, again with a basket of provisions,

including Mary noted, a better quality wine. He came in the door, looked around, blinked a few times, then stood stock still. Mary motioned him toward the room where the body of his beloved lay. He entered the room and from behind, Mary saw his shoulders shake, although she heard no sound.

He pulled a large handkerchief from his pocket. This was the white hankie Alfred Axle had intended to hand her when he proposed because, in his mind she had accepted and was already crying with joy. Her cold refusal and dry eyed stare had shriveled its usefulness. He had left it in his breast pocket next to his heart then transferred the square to his top drawer where it had stayed ever since. Now it found its way back to the one for whom it had been made.

Mary would later look at the hankie, noting how fine the linen was, and how beautifully stitched the initials, B.E in one corner and A. A. in the other. She would marvel a bit that her stern, disciplined mother had once ignited such passion. For now, she stood by the door, in front of the sideboard as full as it had ever been of food and drink. Mr. Axle bowed to Mary, murmuring his condolences and left.

Mary tried to ignore the growing thorns of resentment. Its presence, biting at her heart with more strength than her sorrow, alarmed her. How long would this take, now, and how long would all this keep her from Theodore? She had only one week before he was gone! It was not fair! She had been awake too long. She longed for solitude and sleep but Mrs. Reid, still crying and wiping her eyes, announced she had to leave. Mary let the last of mourners out and locked the door behind.

She turned and heard the silence. It was not the silence she had known all her life, but a deep, lonely quiet stretching throughout the house. In the fading daylight she sat and let her thoughts wander about. Had anyone asked, had she been trained in thinking ahead toward such things, she might have thought she would grieve, but not unduly. She had been more aware of her mother's insufficiencies, more aware of her as a block against life than as friend or comfort.

It came to Mary as a sudden shock to realize that block had been a stability, had offered a steadiness and support she only now recognized because it was gone. It further surprised her to feel tears welling and spilling onto her cheeks and down along her throat. She sat like this for a long while before her mind turned to Theodore.

When it did, she saw how far apart their worlds really were. She could not send a message to him telling him what had happened. He had no way of knowing, in his warm, bright world, what had gone on in hers. The gap between them increased her sense of being alone and she wept with abandon, until from sheer exhaustion, she fell asleep on the floor.

She woke in the early hours, raised herself up on one elbow and surveyed her world. The small living, kitchen, dining space needed sweeping but the marks and chips on every inch of the walls would never be mended by cleaning. The tiny sideboard was full of food, some of which the mice had begun to peck at overnight. Mary stood then and began the necessary movements toward saving the rest of the food, preparing the room with a sweep and a small fire for the visitors who were sure to arrive. Then she washed herself in their bedroom, her mother's newly dead body just behind her back.

All emotion had been drained from her. She felt a rare tiredness as though she were sixty, not sixteen. Yet she leaned over her mother's body, kissed her once lightly on the cheek.

"Good morning, Mother. I see your cough is much better today." Mary's language rose from a tide of death humour. While she was this close she made sure no odor had started. A glance told her the body wrappings were still in place, nothing swollen or burst.

A few visitors did arrive, most of them people who had

known Beatrice in her youth. They offered their sympathies, stayed long enough to feel their duty discharged, then left, glad to be away from this reminder of their own thoughts about a life of poverty and struggle and its certain end.

This was the last day of viewing. She managed through it, murmuring many "thank yous" and "it is so kind of you" to people she barely knew. As far as she could feel anything, the presence of these people did bring a sense of peace to her. Her mother had been known and would be missed, by more than one person.

On the third day the body had to be transported to the part of the cemetery reserved for the poor. Mary walked along behind the death cart, the wooden wagon onto which had been loaded her mother's simple casket, as was the custom. A few who had known her mother, and a couple of street beggars hoping the sympathy of death might open wallets, joined Mary's march.

The body in the deep hole, a simple wooden marker prepared, the attendants shoveled dirt back into the earth's gap. Mary stood without moving. She had stopped crying, which the rest of the funeral party took as a sign of deep mourning, they agreed to each other as they moved away, back to their lives.

Mary watched until the last shovel full had landed. The attendant, unused to people paying this much attention to his work and moved as much by her beauty as Mary's orphaned status, tried to ease the moment.

"Ye've not so much to grieve…" the man began to lean toward her.

Mary saw the dirt on his body, his face, the broken, blackened teeth, stubbly finger nails rounding on the shovel he held onto.

"He believes he is my equal," she thought with a start. Repulsed, she turned and without a reply walked stiffly away.

"That," the thought rang clearly in her head, "is that."

Diana's Life

2005

Toronto and near Toronto

Diana walked up the two steps set at the corner of the street. A real crossroads, she mused as she pushed the door open and walked to the back of the inner most room, where Debbie, the waitress, stood.

"Hi Debbie."

"Hey, good to see you. It's been a while."

"Probably nearly a decade," Diana laughed, "and nothing much has changed. Does Chuck still work here?"

"Yes," Debbie cried loudly with a half laugh, "he's still here. Still saying the same thing: no place..."

"...else I'd rather be..." Diana chimed in.

"David's playing tonight," Debbie's voice held a question.

"Yeah, I know," Diana withdrew her energy slightly, just enough Debbie would get the boundary.

"What can I get you?"

"Just a beer. You still taking those night classes?"

"Yeah, graduated last month!"

"That's great, Debbie," Diana's warmth was real. "You going to do more?"

"Oh, I'll see. Wait to see how the money goes."

As soon as Diana sat down, her mind flooded with Jake. Jake who called her almost every night. Jake who showed up at the meditations on Sundays, but had told her he was there to see her. Jake who was becoming a fixture in her life, one she felt more and more drawn toward. Jake who would want an answer, soon.

Jake who didn't know she was seeing David.

Again? Diana thought, or always?

On David's fiftieth birthday the previous year she had booked a room in a hotel. Standing in front of the check in desk, women in business suits flooding the large lobby, a female receptionist had taken one look at Diana and flinging her eyes over toward her male counterpart, said "Can you book her in for me please?" It took Diana a second to register. This woman was not busy but was asking this man if the booking was good.

Nervous, Diana had tried to explain, saying, "My friend will be with me but not until much later tonight," as the man's eyes had skimmed her clothes, her slightly nervous face, her obvious inexperience.

"Well, we might have one room."

He was booking them into a small back room, which when she opened the drapes displayed a lovely view of all the buildings in the cement puzzle that Toronto's core had become.

One room left in this huge upscale hotel? Diana reflected. It was like always, as though she and David were on the run. From the Catholic Schoolyard, to his grandmother's basement and now...now he was married and they really were...

"Here you are, honey," Debbie's kindness brought Diana back.

"Thanks. Cheers!" Diana lifted the thin frothy bitterness to her lips.

Why? Diana thought for the millionth time. Why did she

run after David as though her life depended on it? Why wait in the shadows, playing through the night skulking and hiding, when she had worked so hard, been so successful at getting the rest of her life on track?

Diana's thoughts ran around as she peeled the paper label from the narrow bottle, and the audio system played its endless stream of rock and blues and the groups of people, women out with women friends, men with men friends, all looking, searching for the same thing, began to fill the dark room.

All it took was moonlight tilting through my window, moonlight and I'd be down here, entering the past through my present. Or... her musings rambled on… or a certain guitar sound slid into my bones and here I'd be, getting drunk, dancing, running wild. Diana smiled in spite of herself. I grew older but never grew up.

She raised the bottle, its beads of sweat trickling down the sides, and pulled hard on the liquid, starting to feel it warm her belly. And the pull towards him had always... her thoughts streamed now, although I tried through willpower to put it, to put him aside. But he was waiting for me, had not forgotten me... Diana almost saw Winona and herself walking again through those doors, the sighs of his guitar singing through that dim air. She had known he would be here on that first night after India, after living out West, had known it and wanted it.

This place, the galactic watering hole, a dumpy, slightly dirty bar filled with absolutely loyal folks who find at the bottom of their glass a black hole from which they and their sad lives shine with a different, softer light, here where the pain is bearable. It didn't escape Diana she was included in this mess of humanity.

The seduction of dancing, drinking too much and dancing, sweating, heaving my body around, the seduction of being right now, in this moment, no thoughts of the past or the future, a pinpoint of consciousness tiptoeing along in a physical frame that barely registered, not the need for food, or sleep, not the need to breathe deeply, just David. His body. That was my answer, my religion. An hour? A night? What does an addict ask of her drug?

Whatever amount of time the drug promises. Diana smiled and raised the bottle again, recalling that night only last year, when she and David had met, again.

She saw herself again get up to dance with Winona, knowing David was not yet aware she was in the room, she felt him in his mind and body thinking, 'Is that her? Is that her?' as he caught quick sight through the crowded floor, of a tall, thin woman dancing. Then he had turned his back to the audience, but Diana had read his mind.

"When am I going to stop looking? It's not her! When will I learn?"

When he turned back, he saw her and their eyes streamed joy, a white almost solid flash of light only they could see.

"Ready for another already? You in a hurry?" Debbie's cheerful banter shook Diana back to this moment.

"Yeah, Debbie, I have a thirst on me tonight."

"I know what you mean. I'd join you but I'm working..." Debbie laughed as she sauntered away towards the bar.

"You look comfortable."

Diana looked up at the sound of the familiar voice.

"Jake!"

Diana's thoughts slammed to a stop. Jake…what...how did you know where to find me?

Jake's sweet lips turned up slightly, "What makes you think I'm here looking for you?"

Diana gulped and blushed. Of course! She wasn't the only person who frequented this dive and she certainly wasn't the only person Jake may have in mind.

"Okay," she laughed uneasily, "You got me. What

brings you to...this place?"

Jake looked around at the mostly male customers, his eyes flickering as he watched David lumber in with a large speaker.

"One of my favorite places. I used to work across the street."

"Across the..." Diana's world had always focused on this place, this one bar.

"A cop? I told you? 14 Division is just across the street. I spent much time on these streets. My old stomping grounds." Jake was not giving her an inch.

Diana knew she didn't deserve any breaks.

"Jake, I...I needed...I..."

"We're adults, Diana. No explanations due." Jake rose from the chair next to her and Diana noticed his warmth leaving with him. She felt suddenly much colder.

"Jake, don't...I mean..."

Jake looked at her, not unkindly, then ran his finger down the ridge of her nose, cupped her chin in his hand, gently lifting her face and brushed his lips against hers. Then he walked steadily out of the room.

Diana watched him walk away, torn between the desire to run after him and her determined course of action: to drill down into what was happening with David.

"One of your lovers?" David's smirk was ugly.

"Thanks." Diana's response was equally nasty. "Not your business."

"No, I guess not," David said in the voice she knew meant trouble.

So be it, she thought. I can't keep this up. He's married, which is stupid of me to even be involved with him, and he's never here, always on the road, or with... again Diana surprised herself with the thought... or with another girl.

Either way, Diana had set her mind to finding out that night what David intended for their future, if they had a future. She sat down again and waited through the first set.

David introduced the band members, gave each a little extra spotlight time, then announced, "We're taking a short break, ladies and gentlemen, so drink up, enjoy and we'll be back soon."

As the dim lights rose slightly, Diana watched David. He walked through the room, right past her, talking, joking, smiling, shaking hands. Very unlike his usual moody self, Diana thought.

Then he suddenly erupted out of the semi-dark, sort of prancing as he slid by her, saying so only she might hear, "Just a social butterfly tonight."

Diana waited it through as she had so many nights lately. Waited whether she was at home and he was on the road, or waited here for the night to finally end, the slamming glasses on the tables evoking one more song from the band, waited as David shot a final tequila, wound the cords around his arm, walked back and forth to his truck, waited as he hauled the speakers and finally his guitars back there also.

Waited until, sometimes standing outside by his truck, sometimes inside, as he walked by brushing her body with his arm, or saying a few words, enough so no one else might know, enough so she knew he was waiting too.

This night he walked back outside, and didn't return for a long time. She sat as usual, the house lights up displaying a sickly yellow hue on everything, then went to the back door.

Silently opening the door, she looked out. David stood with his arms wrapped around another woman, his face nuzzled in her neck. Diana walked slowly over, quietly, her footsteps carefully muted on the parking lot tarmac.

David's face rose, the face she had loved, had seen in all her daydreams about love, true love, real love, his face, her belief he loved her, really loved her—for how many years? His face rose from the flesh of this short, chubby, big breasted younger woman, whose breath was rising and falling rapidly. She turned toward Diana, "Who are..."

"Stop," David shut her up. "Diana, it's not..."

"Yeah, I know, not what I think...tell you what. You keep believing that..." Diana strode to her car and drove away, tears washing through her eyes all the way up the DVP.

She didn't know what she felt worse about, David's infidelity (and you messed with a married man, you stupid girl, she scolded herself, and one you knew would play around) or that she might have lost Jake, or that love was her worst area in life, or that she should have...

Next morning she deluged him, filled his voice box, his emails with long streams of words. Late in the afternoon he responded, that amounts to immediately for him, Diana thought.

Let's get through this. Either he is the love I've been missing... she gave a rueful laugh, right, when we are finished, I'll be free.

Diana paused. Free. Free of having him somewhere in her heart. Free from the constant sense nothing was over, nothing completed between them. Free from the compulsion that made her believe in him, no matter how many times he broke her heart, played around. Free perhaps to really begin again, this time without him and his guitar at the bottom of every love who tried to live in her heart.

She made herself a cup of coffee and sat on her couch looking over the lake.

She had tried, over the years. She had blocked him out only last year, had decided to just cut off all psychic ties with him, deny him access to her, her energy, her life. She put a wall up, a boundary around herself, a meditation wall and left him outside of it.

Now, she had thought then, I'll be free. She who normally thought of him many times a week, if not a day, had found her mind freed of such inner wrangling.

Then suddenly after three months of this, she received an

email from him, no salutation, no greeting, just, “If I ask, will you let me back in?”

That had been it. She knew her sense of being connected with him was not a fantasy.

“That just makes it worse,” she said out loud to no one.

Later that afternoon she watched as he made his way up her steps, walking slowly, as though carrying a heavy load.

When he came in, she saw black holes in his pupils; she noted the place where his soul had shredded from the choices he’d made in life.

She walked into the kitchen to make tea. He followed her and as she stood before the stove, put his arms out, saying, “Sometimes a good hug is what’s needed to fix things” When he repeated this, she moved a step to be inside his arms but noticed he was not keeping time to her changes. He was unable to connect with her, the flesh woman, standing in front of him. He believed, as all addicts do, his own reality was the only one.

They came back to the living room where he patted the couch next to him. She sat on the opposite side of the room, curling her feet up under her, wrapped in a sweater. She felt like a cat.

“You look like you’ve been under a lot of stress,” she said.

He took the sympathy bait. “Yes.” He flashed his empty eyes at her with a slight smile.

“A wife, a girlfriend, now her… wow, it must feel like stress...”

“Yes, it does...” he leapt for her open heart, certain Diana’s lifelong sympathy for his troubles would lead him to have the upper hand, to be the one in control.

She looked directly into him and said, “Self-created.”

He fell back into himself, the trap all round.

He paused again. “You scared me. That was crazy all those calls, all those emails. It sounded crazy...”

She knew he was attempting to make it her problem. All junkies... she heard herself thinking... do the same thing. It's always someone else's problem.

She said out loud very clearly, softly, "I'm sorry I scared you. I am very intense, just not usually like that..." she paused, waiting for him to confirm this, that she wasn't usually that shatteringly intense.

Instead he said, "I just don't want anyone to get hurt."

"How can you say you don't want anyone to get hurt, when you have a child, a wife, a girlfriend and now someone else?" She kept her voice low, knowing that raised tones would give him an excuse to leave. And she wasn't finished with him, yet.

"I've been thinking about that...I've been thinking about that...It's a complicated situation." He came at her again. "Many people who are strongly intuitive are lacking something..." Their past sat between them, Diana's ragged teen years, hanging on by grasping onto him, making him her safety. Beyond that, his own mother, wallowing away into her own sea of crumbled notes, emptied drawers.

"I'm stable. Remember my life. Think about what I've done, what I've accomplished..." Then she grew impatient with herself for taking his bait, trying to justify herself. "Anyone, any woman would be upset with what you did..."

He said, "Long nails and sharp claws." Then he laughed. He went on, "Sometimes when you're sitting there in the bar, I feel pressure. I talk with you, spend time with you but it's hard in the bar." For a split second Diana believed he was going to suggest they spend more time away from the bar then she heard "...and sometimes I just want to treat it like a job, go in, do my work, and go home...don't want to talk to one more person."

Her training as a therapist kicked in, "I can understand you feeling pressure like that."

He said, "If I won the lottery right now, I'd find a forest

someplace, go and sit there by myself...”

“I have never given you, in these four years, a moment’s pressure about leaving your wife or child, have I?”

“No.”

“I left you last summer.”

“I know you did.”

“I figured it didn’t matter, you just go away and don’t contact me, no email, nothing, so I left you. Then you emailed me. Why do that and then this?”

Into the silence that followed, Diana spoke clearly, “You are a drunk, cross-addicted to marijuana. You are using your precious life energies in the wrong way, for power, and if you continue you will burn out.”

He looked into the space in front of him, his head tilted, those dead eyes penetrating something Diana did not see.

“Funny you should say that. I’ve just been thinking about that. Thank you. You are one of the only people who could say that,” he said.

Diana recognized the buttered ego trap and walked herself around it. So what? That and two dollars gets me a lottery ticket, she thought.

Then he said, “I need some space.”

“What about her?”

“It’s a silly attraction, too much Scotch, too little sleep.”

“You’re not going to see her again?”

“You’re so angry!” He countered, attempting again to make this about something Diana had done or was doing wrong.

“No. Not angry. I’m hurt.” Her emotional pain rose in the air between them, a pillar of red energy, soft, pulsing. She watched his eyes follow it.

“There’s nothing I can do about it now,” he said. “It’s there in the ether between us.”

“You can apologize.”

He paused, the musician, the magician in him waiting for

the right moment then said, "I am sorry I have hurt you so badly."

Silence.

Then the moment came when he presented her with the keys to her freedom.

He said, "I'm not saying yes or no to you, and I'm not saying yes or no to her."

In her head Diana heard her own voice calmly state, Pay attention, Diana, this is important. The moment seared itself across her consciousness.

She gazed at him sitting on her couch and said evenly, softly, "So after everything I have given you, you will take the tiny bit I get in return, and give that away, too?" He nodded his head as though this all made good sense.

Diana felt her mind and heart clear.

He seemed to feel enough had been said. He rose to go and she walked to the door.

"So we can call each other, say next year or so?"

Diana registered the stupidity of his comment, but focused only on getting him out of her home.

"So we'll call each other, right?" His tone of slight desperation when she did not reply reached her ears.

"I won't try to block you out. It will not work anyway," she said.

He laughed, "No, it won't."

Diana realized he still believed he had all the power.

She said neutrally, "You may call me. I might be here. I might be gone like snow on water."

"Well, I may be a tractor on...on ice," he tried to joke through the air, now thick with her stability.

She watched him pick his way carefully on his oxblood colored boots across the porch stairs, his hand carefully on the railing, and she saw something she had never seen before, never thought she would see. His addiction, how his body language, the curling in of his shoulders, a slight tremor of his hand, revealed the fissure, the chasm too great, his mother's insanity waiting for him there, taking him down those hard, concrete steps.

After he left she took a couple of tablets to help her relax. She craved the oblivion of sleep but knew she had to stay close to herself, to comfort herself deeply, since the shift away from him had been so swift, a crater now appeared where he had lived inside of her for so many years. She wrapped up in a housecoat, lay on the bed and waited.

Mary's Life

1883

London, England

Mary stood at the door of her house, looking up the street. She wondered if Theodore would send the carriage for her this night. It was past the time when he would have returned from India. India! Who knew what adventures he had had or what seas he had traveled upon, or even whether...she refused to finish the thought.

She pulled her shawl around her shoulders and with her head high, walked toward town. Her mind was still quiet with grief. She walked one foot in front of the other, steady, aware of the warmth of her hands, one clasping the other in front of her. She saw one or two people she knew, and she nodded toward them. No words were required, as she was in mourning.

She had just arrived at the candle-makers, and was turning to enter the shop when something caught her eye. She turned her head and saw his carriage, heard the horses hooves clapping along. She stood and watched as the coach man drove right past her, his eyes in front as though he did not see her, and she saw a glimpse, just enough, of Theodore! He was back! He was back and Brigitte was there, laughing with him.

Mary's heart thumped so loudly she thought she would disturb the street of busy people coming and going in and out of shops. Everything looked surreal, like a painting she might see in a house like...Theodore? With Brigitte?

She could no longer feel her hands. She leaned against the building and let her breath, which pumped through her harsh and fast, slow to its usual rhythm.

Nonsense, she told herself. So what if he enjoys a short outing with her? Likely he has to get things, purchase some new…he said he'd come back. She thought this as she recalled his face, sad when he had said he would miss her. Of course he had! He had come back and she should be happy he was home, safe! She was acting like, like… Mary did not want to think it, but she felt she was acting like her mother.

She no longer knew when to expect to see Theodore so she spent time learning a new pattern of life. Without her mother who would be up and stoking a fire before her, she had to do this herself. She learned to take on all the chores, instead of half.

As one week left and another began, then another, Mary started to realize how much it took to keep herself warm and fed. Her mother's memory shone in a different light. Mary took to sitting at the window looking out on the street every evening. Way past dark she found herself still there, staring into the inky pools that wavered between candles in the homes of her neighbors.

Mrs. Reid came by once, to be neighborly, and offered whatever use she and her family might be to Mary. The young Miss Eagleton however displayed the same proud face as her mother had and the kindly Mrs. Reid soon left, thinking to herself the apple doesn't fall far from the tree, no indeed it does not, which she stated only three times to Mr. Reid when she regaled him fully with the details of her attempt at being friendly.

Other than Mrs. Reid, Mary was quite alone. So it was one night four and a half weeks from the last time she had seen Theodore, and four weeks since she had put her mother into the ground, she was startled to hear the horses' clopping hooves on the cobblestones, startled to see the carriage stop in front of her house.

Evening had just gone dusk, so Mary reckoned it was slightly past eight. She held open the door, barely daring to breathe in case this vision was a dream. She saw the same silver plate and on it, the embossed creamy paper. Shaking, she took up the paper, opened it and read there the shortest, sweetest words in her life: "I am back. Come to me."

She instructed the coach man to wait, then flew around her house, preparing as best she might for this, the fulfillment of her dreams. He was back and he loved her, he wanted her and she was his!

The coach man let her off as before just outside the side gate to the large garden. She took the same flagstone steps to the door of the cottage. There was the fire in the grate as before and a large basket of food, two plates set on the table, a bottle of wine and on the bed, a length of gorgeous silk material.

Mary crossed the room quickly and felt the green and blue shot silk with the edge of her fingers. It was clearly the highest quality. When she held up the piece, bordered in gold, she noticed the embossing all through the silk itself: flowers and leaves.

Then she saw the booklet sitting next to the luxurious material. She opened it and saw instructions for how to turn the piece of silk into a full dress, called a Sari. Eager for this new game, willing to go to any lengths to please him, she tore off her clothes and began to follow the directions.

Just as she had finished wrapping the piece around her body Theodore arrived.

"Stand there," he whispered. He saw her young, firm breasts swelling beneath the exquisite silk, which fell over her tiny waist and draped sensuously around her hips.

"Mary, Mary, at last..." he said and swept her into his

arms. He ripped the silk she had so carefully put on.

She felt the familiar tingling as he thrust back and forth, eight maybe ten times, then the warm gush of his release shot into her. She felt the weight of his body relax on top of her, her arms clutching his back, his arms, her lips smothering his face with kisses. She stroked his hair and listened as his breath returned, marveling to herself how much she loved him, had missed him, how happy she was to be here with him.

"Theodore," she began.

"Mary, Mary, I am so glad to see you. Do you like the new dress I bought for you? It is special silk. I knew it would look good, but it was even better than I thought…" Theodore's pleasure in his gift was clear. Mary nodded, and tried to hold his head on her breast, but he was up and pulling his pants back on.

"It was an incredible trip. I must tell you all about it. But right now I'm famished." Theodore pulled her up and over to the table of treats, and began without ceremony to feed himself. When she sat opposite him, he began to feed her too.

"Mary," he turned his head from the food in front of him and saw her. She had a small bit of strawberry in the corner of her mouth. He leaned over, saying her name over and over, and with the tip of his tongue flicked the strawberry bit into his own mouth.

Mary held on to him as though he was the only solid ground left in the world. If she was crushed beneath his weight, if she felt uncomfortable, the only words that escaped her mouth were his name. When she felt him relax, then her own eyelids fluttered. Soon he was tired and led them to the bed where they slept the night through.

Their pattern returned quickly. The carriage came by her house. She was ready in a short time. Clothes and sometimes things Theodore called "toys," feathers, scarves, or costumes were laid out in the little cottage. Mary, blissful in her expectations the future would continue into a time when she would be Mrs. Fieldworth, did not press him. She sensed any mention on her part, any request would be greeted as a demand, so she waited, focusing on the happiness she felt each day.

Even when her period lapsed, and her breasts grew sore, when she began to feel nauseous, she believed fully in their future. By the window in her house late at night, Mary fantasized. She saw him opening his arms to her, his eyes shining with pride and love when she told him about their baby. She felt herself embraced by his strong, solid arms, and heard him tell her she was his own and now their baby completed them.

She knew he would move her into the main house, once they were married. She pictured the wedding ceremony in every detail, her dress, her attendants, the groomsmen, and she knew down to the last moment the details of the reception. She wanted Theodore to make a speech, telling everyone about their love, their passion and commitment to each other. She practiced the feeling of having all eyes on her, the most exquisite of brides, as his words made her blush with love and pride. These thoughts warmed her on the nights she was without him.

Now Mary heard the carriage on the cobblestones and said to herself, "This night. I will tell him our secret tonight!" Exhilarated, she gathered the few small things she needed before climbing with a large smile at the coach man, into the luxurious carriage.

As the wheels rattled along the cobblestones, her heart pounding in anticipation, Mary looked out the window upon the world she would soon be leaving. They passed the milliner's shop, the dry goods, the butcher's. A tiny moment of nostalgia tugged at her heart before a burst of joy warmed her with thoughts about her future.

As usual she arrived in time to put on the costume he had left for her, a dancer's outfit. This one had a bustier with just enough stays to push her breasts up, but no material to cover them.

Finally Theodore opened the door. She saw from the bulge in his pants he was ready for her, but she held up her hand. He stopped, a sly smile playing on his mouth, his eyes moist with desire, expecting her to enlarge the scope of their game. He saw her white breasts bobbing slightly, with their full pink nipples and was further aroused. He brushed his palms eagerly against them.

Pain ripped through her, "Owww."

"What? Did I…" suddenly Theodore stopped. He looked. He saw something else, something in her face, a roundness he had not seen before.

"Are you all right?" he asked neutrally, staring at her. Mary felt his gaze as though it dug through her, probing for a truth she did not want.

"Yes, of course, I…" Mary hesitated, "I missed my last… I'm pregnant!" The words burst from her full, happy heart.

Theodore blanched. When he spoke his words fell methodically, slowly and precisely around her. "You missed…?"

Mary felt a tightening in the room, as though the walls had leaned in. She didn't like this place where she felt herself under a weight, as though the air pressed upon her. Her eyes scattered around the room for a way to take them both back, back a few minutes, a few hours, anywhere away from this terrible pressure.

"Well, yes, I am…I mean I missed…I am pregnant." This came out as a whisper.

"And you chose not to tell me until now?" Suddenly, Theodore saw her. He saw beyond her creamy skin and voluptuous shape for the first time. He saw her, the timid, uncertain child whose lack of sophistication threatened to bring his life as it was to an end.

"You knew and you did not tell me until now?" he repeated. A strange power flicked behind his words.

Mary again looked wildly around, searching for a way back to his love. She felt his stare and rays of shame rose in her, colored her face. “Well, I…my mother died, and it’s not unusual...I mean, I… did I do something wrong?” Mary’s heart burst and she began to cry.

“What were you thinking? What did you think was happening here? Did you not use something?” By turning his sense of shame, fear and confusion lose on her, Theodore escaped them. Those hounds picked up the scent across the space between them and ravaged her.

“Stop it! Stop it! Stop that sniveling.” This Theodore, this cruel, mean man was a stranger. She wanted her Theodore back, but he was nowhere near so she came back to the man in front of her. It was Theodore, but what she saw made her stomach lurch and her heart sore.

His lips curled, his teeth bared, he snarled at her, “We have to think. This is a mess and we must find a way out.”

Mary’s heart dropped to stone. Then abruptly she had no feelings, at all. What she wanted was to run away, to find a hole and bury herself inside it, with no future and no past.

“I know someone who has herbs,” she finally said, the dead tone in her voice lost on him.

“You would!” he sneered at her. “That is so out of date! We need a doctor, one who can…”

She had heard about what happened to girls who let doctors take care of them. The instruments were rarely sterilized, the doctors gruff. She had even heard of doctors who administered chloroform to these young desperate girls, then helped themselves to those unconscious bodies before ripping open their wombs. Too many had died. How much of what she had heard was true was not important to her. She would not have a doctor.

“I am not going to…” Mary began but this Theodore was above her, his hard eyes staring down into hers, his finger at her face.

"You are going to do as I say. You are going to do exactly as I tell you. I will find a doctor, we will get rid of it, here in this room. You will say nothing to anyone about this." Theodore turned, walked to the door and looked back once at her, "I expect you back here next week. I'll make all the arrangements for one week from tonight. For now, be gone in ten minutes." Then he left.

Dazed, she pulled her clothes on. In the coach a numbness spread throughout her body until as she opened her front door, lit a candle and sat by the front window, she thought of nothing. She felt nothing.

Finally a single word flitted through her mind. It. Theodore had called their baby "it." Not my baby, son or daughter but "it." Would get rid of, like vermin, like pests. Dusk fell across the cottage floor, then dark. She sat in the darkness, still and quiet for most of the night. This nothing was a strange sense of freedom, a letting go of all the cares of life. She no longer felt any compulsion to participate in what her life had become.

When she came to she had no idea what time of day it was. Or night. It was dark outside. Confused, she went to the bedroom, lay on the bed and fell asleep.

She woke hungry the next morning. She knew the little baby inside her needed to eat. She herself was full of an emptiness that kept the hounds, those thoughts that would hurt her, away.

She went to the cold-storage and saw there was nothing. She had eaten through the stores brought by visitors to her mother's wake, and her last meal had been at Theodore's. Theodore! The name sliced through her body. She convulsed and wept as though a flood gate opened. Gone! She was never to be…she had no…

Then, just as suddenly, she was quiet again, still and unfeeling. "I know," she thought with such clarity it impressed her, "I must feed the baby." Without changing the clothes she had been wearing since yesterday, she threw the old shawl her mother had used, still on the peg by the door, over her shoulders and began to walk through town.

To the next person she met, a soldier from the nearby garrison, she said, "I need something, it's a baby and babies have to eat…"

The man looked at her. He saw an elaborately dressed street walker, one of hundreds who roamed like ghosts, homeless, friendless, good for a quick one in the alley. Her gown was of higher quality than what he usually saw, but her wild eyes gave her away. Although he had used many such unfortunates as his needs dictated, this was on a main street. Someone might see! He shoved her away. "Go back to yer hole," he swore softly at her.

She spoke to no one else until she came to the butcher's shop. She walked in and looked around, staring as though surprised anything this ordinary existed. Frank Hodges saw the woman he had been in love with for as long as he had known her.

"Hello, Miss Eagleton, what can I do for you today?" his large, heavy frame lumbered out from behind the counter. His butcher's apron, full of blood, flashed before Mary's eyes and she gagged.

She managed to choke out to him, "Thank you and I need some bacon and a bite of beef, if you don't mind. If you have any eggs, I'll be grateful…" She put one hand on a post as dizziness swept over her.

The butcher, his huge body moving with grace in the small space, put together the items as Mary named them. He looked at her as she paid at the counter, and noticed her pale, pale skin, an odd emptiness in her eyes. His large heart opened more as he believed her deep grief to be the cause. "I kin drive ye home, Miss Eagleton, sure I kin close the store and drive ye. It's close by and we're not busy."

Mary considered, found herself weaving on her feet, then

said, "Yes."

Frank Hodges took much care getting her into his carriage. He stopped at the green grocer's on the way and bought, from his own funds, tea, greens, porridge, potatoes and such that might keep her fed for a week.

Mary turned to offer him her hand before stepping down. "I am not able to offer you tea at this time." Her voice was quiet, her tone very intent.

"Sure, you go on inside now. I have to get back." His face flushed beet red as he watched her walk in the door. As he slapped the reins, he thought, "She's taken it badly, she has. Well, it's the mother, and that's a hard one," as the horse trotted on.

Mary closed the door behind her. She passed the remainder of the week inside her house, afraid to go out. She sang to her unborn child, told her baby stories, and wept. She imagined the tiny perfect baby born to her and Theodore, the Theodore she loved, not that cruel man who looked like him. She knew that when her Theodore found out, the cruel man would be gone and she and her unborn babe would be safe. She saw their future more clearly than she saw the dirty dishes or bits of food rotting on her counters.

Finally the carriage arrived. The coach man stepped back when he saw her, but Mary did not notice. Imperially she swept by him, looking down her nose as she offered him her hand. He took it gently, helped her inside and turned back to his work.

Inside the cottage, a short, fat man with delicate hands that seemed to slide off his wrists sidled up to her, his shoulders hunched as he began to mewl, "I try to be of assistance, my dear, for girls, eh, ah, women in…in…some difficulty." A long mustache swept across his small mouth as he spoke, accentuating a weak chin.

Mary looked past him, as though at some distant object of great importance.

"I will go through this ritual," she thought, "then my Theodore will be back. He will fix everything." A small warm glow registered far away. She must get to it, hold on until it came closer.

A man who looked like Theodore approached her. She knew it might not be her love, so she was polite, regal, in the way she knew her Theodore appreciated. If it is my Theodore, she thought triumphantly, he'll recognize and take care of me. If it is that other one, then I have my manners, have acted to make my Theodore proud and not given anything away. Secrecy was important now, although she couldn't remember why.

Theodore stared at her. She had not changed her clothes, washed, or combed her hair since the previous week. His insides curled in contempt and disgust. She had bewitched him, tricked and used him. This char girl, this servant had made him think he was attracted to her. He shuddered slightly, then nodded to the doctor who attempted to bring Mary by the elbow to the bed.

She threw off his touch and walked with her head high across the room. She lay down, preparing the pillow as though for a night's sleep. Then the doctor clamped a cloth of chloroform across her face and she was out, drifting, until a searing fire ripped through her mind accompanied by the voice of a woman, screaming with pain.

"That woman better stop screaming," she thought, "Theodore doesn't like his mother being disturbed." Mary couldn't remember if Theodore's mother had died recently or if the bed belonged to the other woman's baby. A series of dark images imploded through her, roses heavy with snakes, fetid water weeds waving into demons and again she heard the screaming, this time followed by deep, heavy sobs.

"That poor, poor girl." Mary thought, "Someone needs to comfort her." Mary now felt quite comfortable. She knew her role was to wait, wait for her Theodore to return. She felt no pain at all until she woke up between sobs, her pillow soaked.

Between her legs a fire raged, slowly burning her flesh. The heat spread up into her chest and face, where sweat dripped down her cheeks. A deep physical agony throbbed beneath that fire. Mary's mind focused for the briefest second, "Oh, here, in the cottage where, with the baby and, and..." before a towering wave of raw emotion, horror and guilt knocked her fragile sense of self. She floated out of range, above and beyond where the wave might touch her.

She lay in the semi-dark, aware of noises and hands frantically stuffing cotton inside her, or trying to but she could feel her blood streaming. She felt thick clots pass between her legs just before she passed out.

Later it was hard to open her eyelids, but she willed them to crack wide enough for the sight of Theodore and a different doctor. Theodore was saying, "Yes, I found her wandering the streets, bleeding and thought I can't let her go on by herself, so I brought her here. You can see she's been treated badly…"

Mary felt this new doctor gently pull her legs aside. He grimaced with the smell and the sight. "Yes. It's a botched job. Some butcher of a doctor…"

A sharp pain now ripped through her belly as he pulled the old cotton stuffing out of her. A small fire again as the needle drew through her flesh, then the gentle hands of this doctor placed more padding inside her.

"She will be barren. Not a bad thing, considering her life."

Mary heard the words spoken about some poor young woman who had been having a bad time.

"The problem now," Dr. Woods was saying to Theodore, "is infection. If she can't hold back the infection, I'm not sure. She looks very thin."

"Well, I suppose she might have had trouble finding

enough to eat on the street."

What was Theodore talking about? She didn't eat on the street. She didn't walk on the streets either. He knew...she passed into a welcome chemical tranquility, brought on by the laudanum Dr. Woods had administered. The pain in her body diminished until she felt good, better than she ever remembered. The constant ache in her center, the loneliness welling from it which had been her companion since childhood, all fell away as she felt herself floating, as though in an endless sea. No thought, no feeling, this nothingness felt good, complete and full compared to the emptiness of the void she had known as her life.

Mary next widened her eyelids enough to catch a vague outline of people in the room. The effort exhausted her. Everything ached, everything including her fingernails and hair. Even when she thought she saw Theodore standing there, next to his mother she was too weak to speak.

"You've been giving her the laudanum?" Dr. Woods deep kind voice radiated toward Mary.

"Yes," Agnes Fieldworth nodded. "She has slept the last three days, since you were here last."

"No food, water?"

"She has taken some water but whether she remembers or not..." Agnes Fieldworth's voice trailed off. "Her eyes are...strange."

The good doctor moved closer to Mary, lifted her wrist and timed her pulse. He checked her forehead, pulled down her bottom eyelid noticing the pale color there, listened to her heart. He pulled up her nightgown to check the cotton padding between her legs. No new blood showed and the smell indicated an improvement.

Then putting his instruments away, he turned to Mrs. Fieldworth, saying, "She is improving, physically. The infection seems to be abating, her bandages continue well. Change them tomorrow. Make sure she starts to eat something, as soon as possible."

He placed his bowler hat on his head and bowing, said, "You are a lady of great heart to take in such a stranger, Mrs. Fieldworth."

Then he placed his hand on Theodore's shoulder. "And you've done good work, here, Master Fieldworth, a brave, Christian act of kindness," before heading out. Mary heard it all through a haze of confusion.

Mrs. Fieldworth turned to Theodore, "A brave, Christian act indeed," she sniveled. "What were you planning? To keep her here without my knowing until she died? How many lies have you told, Theodore? Including the one about going to India…"

"I told you Mother, I was tiring of the girl. I wanted to give it a break, to see what would happen, to see if she would come to her senses. What else could I do?" Theodore's voice was a whine Mary barely recognized. She heard the words but instead of taking them in, she floated above them, far away where there was no pain.

"What did you think would happen? She was never someone you would marry. You knew that at the start."

"I know, I know, but she seemed to know it too, she seemed, it all seemed as though she understood so well…"

"She understood? She understood? You left it all to her? Now she is so sick she may die." Silence. "Well, I blame myself as well," Agnes Fieldworth spoke in a quiet voice now, her anger gone. "I saw what was going on. I didn't speak up sooner."

Mary heard the words. She knew their meaning. He had lied to her, had not gone to India, had never intended to marry her, marry her, marry her. As she floated she saw in front of her a beautiful meadow in late autumn, with tall grass golden from the summer sun. She saw flowers and heard birds, strange lovely birds in the forest beyond the meadow. It was much nicer here. Much nicer. Stay for a while...

Every day thereafter Agnes Fieldworth called upon her mountain of guilt to persuade herself into the small cottage. Servants might talk so she tended to this herself. She brought food and juice for breakfast, trays with soups, cheeses and meats for lunch, special delicacies at dinner. She spoke to Mary, comforted her, washed her body and changed her bloodied cotton padding. As she moved about the room, plumping Mary's pillows, supporting her back with one arm while she spooned in food with the other, Mrs. Agnes Fieldworth thought hard about her son.

He has long been a disappointment. His charming, fickle ways ...but this, this goes beyond all boyhood caprices. My own grandchild...but it never was, couldn't be. Cuts to my soul. He's a man, or supposed to be! Twenty-four years old, soon to be twenty-five and still not taking responsibility…I should have put him in military school. I should have been strong, sent him away to boarding school, someplace he would have learned some discipline, learned how to grow up and be a man. Instead, my loneliness after his father died, my heartbreak, my only child... took him everywhere, took care of him myself, and, and letting him get away with it all but it seemed such childish stuff, what did it matter he lifted a ring from my mother so she said, but I never believed… So Mrs. Fieldworth thought and in thinking believed she was atoning for the very pattern she was in fact repeating.

Mrs. Fieldworth saw Mary begin to sit up, at least when she pushed her up and steadied her with pillows and cushions. She saw Mary open her mouth and take in food, whenever Mrs. Fieldworth helped her jaw move up and down. Then Mary would swallow. Mrs. Fieldworth needed Mary to be mending, and through a lifelong habit of determining the outcome of events according to her own needs, convinced herself it was true. So it came as a shock to her when Dr. Woods visited the following week, walked the few steps to Mary's side, and asked, "How long has she been like this?"

"What do you mean? The infection is better, she is eating…"

"She eats, you mean. She is not feeding herself." His stern

tone set Agnes Fieldworth fluttering around the room.

"Why, no she doesn't exactly, I mean I feed her and she eats, but not by herself, if that's what you mean..."

"What I mean Mrs. Fieldworth," and his voice softened as he remembered what he took to be an immense generosity on the part of Agnes Fieldworth, "what I mean is, she is clearly in dementia."

"Oh, dear, oh, no, how did this...what could I..."

"We don't know anything about what her life has been to this point, but it can't have been easy. She has withdrawn, completely."

"What can we do?"

"We can put her in a home. That's the best we can do. Benham House is as good as any."

"Why, yes, of course. Yes, if you think that's best, Doctor," Mrs. Agnes Fieldworth brightened as this path out of an uncomfortable situation presented itself.

Benham House accepted indigent people who had lost their way in the Christian world. Government subsidies barely covered the wages of a few workers and the building's maintenance. Everything else, food, clothing, personal care for the inmates all depended upon the charity of those whose amassed sins had not, like those of the inmates, emptied their pocketbooks.

So it was that Mary Eagleton came to live at Benham House, an unlicensed house for the impoverished and insane.

Diana's Life

2005

near Toronto

"Diana, so glad you could make it," Wayne greeted her with a peck on each cheek. "We're almost ready to begin."

Diana made her way back to the meditation room. Wayne and Andrea had reconvened the Group in a last ditch attempt to clear whatever was holding the land hostage. Whether that freeing meant they would be able to stay on the land that had been their home for over twenty-five years, or would have to leave was less important than the belief the land needed this now, from them. A return on investment of a kind.

As Diana sat to wait for the others to join her, she looked around the room, noting the shelves holding various Buddhist icons, Buddha rupas they were called, statues of the Buddha in different positions. Her eye caught on a lovely glass vase, used in Buddhist initiation ceremonies to hold blessed water, now reflecting a beam of sunlight splitting into rainbows in the room. She took a few slow, calming breaths and began her meditation with a request for protection.

She had barely completed the prayers when a wall of blood on her inner vision rose, washing towards her.

She opened her eyes. This was going to be a meditation

like no other.

"Hi Diana," Jake's sweet smile was only a little forced, his voice a tiny bit clipped.

"Hi Jake," Diana heard the slight mournfulness in her own tones, felt embarrassment slide across her features. Whether Jake noticed or not, whether he even cared or not she didn't know. She did notice the thought of him not caring sliced through her once, a sad feeling. Then she closed her eyes.

Wayne, Andrea and Hazel filed in and the group took position, holding hands, creating the mind platform in the center and just above their heads.

The meditation had just begun when Diana saw herself walking along a dusty road. An old woman, she felt good in the sunshine, happy to be in this place...again? Was it again? Diana slid herself into the scene completely.

She is approaching a native village. In the village, walking, no, yes being pulled by children, children glad to see her, happily pulling on her hands, saying, "We are so glad to see you again, Grandmother." A few adults, serious, intent, gather around her as she nears the village. Their words mean, 'the need is great, it's serious, heavy, you must come.'

Diana's years of meditation practice take hold and she waits, with a question she feels without language. The strong energy all around vibrates with danger, so her question asks for a sign. Is it safe to continue? A large, dark blue shell appears, a dark blue shell all around her, then from above she sees it below her, sees the large white cross at the apex of the dark blue shell. The sign is positive.

Immediately, she hears wailing, women wailing but her focus goes to the bodies of the young men in front of me, bodies dismembered, blue-grey colored body parts stuffed into mouths or bent in abnormal postures. No odor or sense of flesh, but a dank dampness. Diana knows in a flash these souls, unable to complete their transition to the next life, live out the horror of their dying moments, over and over.

She calls mentally to the imprisoned leader of the boys, "You are dead. You must leave. None of this is happening anymore. It's over." He looks at her with shock, then recognition, turns his head to the East and dissolves, not even dust left behind. The others follow.

The wailing grows louder. Diana focuses on the woman whose voice is strongest. It is the mother of the leader just gone. Diana's mind pushes through veils of grief toward the woman.

"He is gone. He is dead. You are dead, also, you have been dead for a very long time. It is over."

The woman's brown eyes blink once, then her mouth relaxes out of its twisted torment, her body lies directly in front of Diana, laid out as if in a coffin, or as if, Diana thinks, responding to a memory of some death ceremony that must take place, then in less than a second decomposes fully into dust that blows away with no wind.

Then Diana is walking toward an old woman who dances in a patch of sunlight while the cries of her people rise and their blood spills in all directions. This woman dances, one leg up at ninety degrees to the earth, that foot placed softly down, her yellow skirt and beaded top shimmering as she shakes the rattle, an elaborately decorated wooden piece, fiercely shakes the rattle in her hand. She turns her desperate eyes towards Diana, sees her approaching.

Diana knows she is both, that woman and this one. A sudden loud explosion and Diana straddles two times, standing with the dancing Native woman, and sitting in her chair.

Tahni's Life

1660's

Tonawanda

Later Tahni could not recall how the morning went, what she did, with whom she spoke. She would remember only standing opposite the new Chief, watching his fine head turned to see the beautiful strong bodies of all the young people, men and women, dressed in their best ceremonial tunics, beads shining against their dark, healthy skin, who walked regally in procession then stood in line waiting for the warriors to emerge. Sunlight splayed through brightly colored leaves in the still, beautiful morning.

For a brief second she felt the world slow down, time move thickly, felt in her belly that horrifying tingle. Then sound, a rumbling, like in her dream, her forehead already wet with sweat and the ground shaking slightly beneath her feet.

Tahni's eyes looked up, took in a vision, dressed in strange men's pants, a blouse and shawl Tahni did not recognize, a white skinned ghostly woman moving toward her. This white was surrounded by souls, who pulled at her ghostly hands, calling "Help, help us, you must help."

As the woman drew closer Tahni felt familiarity, saw a thin white line of energy running from her own native body to the heart of this other. The white woman moved fearlessly and whether she felt the ground shake beneath her Tahni could not tell. Just as Tahni put up her palm to signal friend, the woman, along with the souls accompanying her, vanished.

The strange apparition of the woman vanished. Tahni turned her attention to the screams around her. Now her eyes took in the impossible...horses, many... the Chief lifted his head toward her, his eyes questioning her as the first note of war cries, first bite of powder, hit those beautiful bodies. Her people toppled, sticks in a child's game.

It took so little time, a knife cutting air, allowing demons entry, white and red-skinned demons flaying her defenseless tribe.

After the first wave of shock she took in the impossible scene. A person on each side of her on the ground, crumpled, twisted. The Chief still looked at her, stunned, then turned his head down the long line of bodies, beautiful red-skinned, muscular bodies of their people, lying now in red mud.

Some ran for horses, but the lightning sticks stripped them of life before they had gone two steps. So many! A vast army that crawled everywhere leaving dead every one of her people.

At least the new warriors would be safe! They might emerge and help. Where were they? Rattle in hand, her consciousness paralyzed by the terror and screams rising around her, her feet began to move to help the souls now emptied of bodies. So many wounded and dying and still the powder stung her nose, bit her eyes. She threw one leg up in square above the earth, then put her foot down. As she turned with the dance, she saw Macawi try to lift a child into her arms, only to fall, blood spurting from them both as the lightning stick bit into her.

Tahni danced and sang, shaking her rattle, trying to keep the soul of her village whole, pleading with Great Spirit to help her honest people to the next life. She threw her other leg up in a square over the breast of Mother Earth, her instincts and training joined in this one purpose: to help the souls of her Village cross fully.

She was aware of the long house where the young men had been in their initiation, entirely without protection, entirely vulnerable, no weapons, no warriors near them. Tahni turned her body to look across the village toward the long house.

Tahni's ears filled again with the moans and cries of those dying in the massacre around her. Her legs moved, her rattle shook, her mouth uttered sounds and she focused on the dying all around her.

A red skinned man pulled his tomahawk out of someone's body, held it up, turned his face to her. She saw the blood madness in him and kept dancing staring directly back into him. He saw no fear in her eyes, just the Medicine Woman of the village doing her work. He lowered his tomahawk, whirled around, took aim and tossed the sharp blade into the back of a child who screamed once, then fell face first into the bloody mud.

Tahni kept moving through the nightmare. A small part of her near the back of her head felt certain she would wake, find herself in her home, this a terrible dream. She searched the carnage for their Chief, hoping to connect with him, see him leading.

Her eyes found him, she saw with relief he was still standing. He looked toward her his palms open, mouth distorted. She noticed blood staining his ceremonial tunic.

"I'll have to clean that," Tahni thought. Then the Chief, standing among bodies that lay like broken dolls, one around the other, at odd angles, bumped forward as though someone had slapped him hard from behind, his eyes locked above her head as his body fell, blood fountaining from the tomahawk in his back.

She tried to move toward him but her legs would only dance. Nothing else. Into her body she retreated, dancing, calling to any of the Village Soul who might hear her, reminding them of the path to Great Spirit, to the world beyond sorrow, where they would meet again, reunite and be one.

So it was the soldiers' saw her, putting first one knee up, standing on one leg, shaking her rattle, turning in an exact half-circle before placing that foot down, carefully not on any of the bloody flesh lying everywhere, taking the next foot up in a ninety degree angle to the earth, singing, moaning the death journey songs.

"What's this?" one White man jeered to his companion.

"An old woman, probably mad. Half are, you know."

The first raised his rifle, set his sights, but his friend's hand appeared on the barrel.

"She's harmless, let her be. Mad old woman. Kind of funny, too. Hey, watch," he poked his friend in the ribs, "Want a partner for your dance?" he called to her.

He slid off his horse, held out his arms as his legs bent in a waltz, the tune humming in his head.

Tahni stared at his arms, held her body in position and waited.

"Bitch," he swore softly, undid his breeches with one hand, grabbed hold of her with his other. His grip on her arm hurt but she did not fight back. From a distance her soul, clinging to one of the trees she had always loved, watched this take place. He slammed her to the ground, forced her legs apart, and tried to thrust his penis into her.

His limp penis fell sideways.

Smelling the rank scent of fear, lust and blood madness on his body, she tried to close her nostrils. He slapped her cheek so hard she passed out. She came to, his stinking breath close to her face.

Then he found it. Fear. Her body emitted a scent he unconsciously chased; her fear meant he had power. He was powerful! His limp penis filled for a brief minute, long enough for him to stash it inside her dry vagina and push himself back and forth, back and forth ripping through her.

She lay perfectly still, waiting for this to be over, her distant soul knowing she was all right, she was fine, it was all right...

His face flushed, he grunted. “What you get for not dancing when a White man asks you.” He slammed the butt end of his rifle once lightly across her face, hitting the bone around her eye. A flash of white light, searing pain and through the blood dripping from her eye, she saw the white man’s sneer, watched as he remounted his horse, rode away.

Confusion crossed her mind, and the word “Why?” Then hate, dark, throbbing and terrible filled her inner world. She was pulled back to this world by the blood falling down along her face, smelling, she noticed, “different from my moon blood.”

She waited on the ground until the last moans had stopped. A vast stillness hung across the space that had been her village, her life. It was late morning.

She stood slowly, looked down at the blood soaked tunic, her celebration tunic with so many beads. “Beautiful,” she murmured to herself. “Beautiful.”

Chaytan saw her, mumbling a little, standing openly among the bodies. He had skirted the massacre, staying within the protective trees, had watched as the soldier raped her, thrust his rifle butt across her face. Now he ran across the open, bloody field, looked into her eyes, saw the emptiness, and half carried, half pushed her toward the cover of forest.

Chaytan stood her up, slapped her once, shook her by the shoulders. The pain on her bruised and battered cheek woke her.

“You must move,” he commanded, “or the soldiers will come back and do to you what they did to the others.”

Bending over, Tahni vomited violently onto the ground.

He put his arm around her waist, urging her forward before she was fully erect.

At his wigwam they sat silently, without a fire.

"So sudden," Tahni said with a shudder. "Why did you not come out to help us?" Tahni didn't know what she was hoping for, but she needed to talk about what had happened.

"'"What could I have done?'" his voice was nearly a whine. She heard his cowardice, the self-absorption behind his words. Nothing about this matters, now, she thought.

As if it was of little importance, she continued "And Little Bird? She is the only one of the villagers, the only one who I did not see. Is she..."

"Alive," he said with words. Then she heard his thoughts. How he had been lovers with Little Bird; she saw him again giving Little Bird the necklace. She heard, too, what she did not want to know: Little Bird had revealed the date of their ceremony, had told their enemies when they would be defenseless.

"No Great Spirit," she said into the dusk, as though this made sense of Little Bird's betrayal. It was as much to herself as to Chaytan, who leaned his body away from her.

"If that is possible," Tahni thought bitterly. Soon she asked into the deepening gloom, "Why?"

"They promised her," Chaytan looked at Tahni with guilt, "us, they wanted trade. Only trade." His voice fell on the last word, his eyes like trapped birds flew first to one side then another, no safe place to land. He saw the look in her eyes, beyond horror, a kind of softness with no end, as though some inner barrier that had kept her in this world had let down completely.

"They told us no war. They only wanted trade," he repeated.

"You knew. You both knew," she said softly. As the words slid off her lips, her heart shattered. The Whites, with their lies, had made this happen. But her lover, and Little Bird, her friend, had set them all up. She recalled the eyes of the man who had raped her, his hatred. Then her mind went grey, as though smoke covered everything, infiltrated everywhere, her memory, her reason. It felt soft and comforting.

Chaytan soon began to speak again. "We must leave. Many of our people are going north, far north, to regroup away from the White man."

Tahni shot him a look.

"And other tribes," he said.

Tahni's mind returned briefly to the present and she felt the pull in her chest. Her purpose, the only one left, was to dance...what? The whole village? Without the bodies in front of her how would she call to the souls? If she tried to dance with the bodies in front of her, the White Man might return, kill her or worse. Now the bodies were there, still lying where they had been shot, or hatcheted, or arrowed, already corrupting, decaying with no dance or sound of rattle, no voice to coax the soul toward Great Spirit, to return to the home all had come from. She turned her head slowly from side to side, as though looking for something.

Chaytan waited.

"I do not know what I am to do," she said sadly, tears forming, one sliding down her bruised cheek. "I am the voice of the dead and dying, I give them direction, my rattle and song show them the way across. But the whole village? At once? Without the bodies! I cannot, we cannot go back there even for this..." confusion took over and she fell silent.

A few minutes later she said, "No. I will not go north. I have to find the souls, the ones from the village who remain yet in the Between Worlds. I am the only one left who can help them cross so the Soul of the Village can be whole."

Tahni found herself praying silently, spontaneously, "Great Spirit help me!" The prayer surprised her because it was genuine. She felt it push against the part of her that wanted to give up, lie down right here, stay, build a warming fire, let the soldiers come.

"No." Tahni said again. Her chest felt stronger, more

certain as the word arrived to her lips. She knew the real enemy: despair, depression. She tucked the immensity of her grief inside, for a time when she might be able to heal it properly. For now, she must deal with the horror, its memory coursing through her blood still, ramping her mind to strange paths, peculiar sensations of not really being here, at all. Those sensations of numbness crept up within her, took her. She fought to stay present.

She heard his words, “It is not safe here now. We stay one night, then we must leave. They are everywhere.” Chaytan looked into Tahni’s eyes and saw desolation.

The autumn dawn crept with chilly certainty across her face. She felt with her fingers cautiously along the line of bruise on her cheek, then slipped out of the skins. He was already up.

“They have not been too close,” he said.

They dressed in some of his skins, for protection from the cold which with certainty would stretch across their world soon, taking all warmth and food with it. They knew the winter would be harsh, but Tahni began that day with a strength summoned from Chaytan’s home, the last connection with their past.

She found a berry bush. They gorged, hunger overcoming them. Then they carefully selected paths that were not as worn, rare paths through the woods and out toward the plains beyond what had been their village.

The second morning, they emerged from the forest and crept out towards the plain, staying next to the forest but not quite in it, keeping their eyes and ears open for any signs of soldiers, other tribe members.

“No one,” Tahni suddenly thought, “no one can be trusted.” Sadness rose in her, a sadness she carried but soon noticed she had forgotten why. Then grey confusion rose, like fog, smothering her focus. The fog was comforting, calming. She wanted to give in to it, lie in it, let it take her. The reason she had to shut something out eclipsed from her. What was it, she thought furiously, frantically, what was it? She knew not to let Chaytan know any of this. She knew he too, for some reason she again could not remember, posed a threat.

She saw the back of his body now, creeping in front of her, holding his ear to the earth, his eyes scanning in a circle. The sight of him reminded her, soldiers, natives, they had to be careful, so careful.

As she put her eyes and mind on the plains, her focus returned. She remembered riding here with Takoda in what seemed now like another lifetime. The memory, flushing up from within, provided warmth and energy to her badly depleted system. Upon its heels came another: the meadow where she and Takoda had joined as husband and wife. She turned that memory jewel over and over, keeping her eyes and ears sharp to the movements of the plain and the forest in this moment, and darting back inside herself to the regenerating sensation of that other time, when happiness was natural.

Later that day as they skirted the plain they found at their feet a small circle where the plains grass had been crushed, probably by deer, the night before.

Chaytan lay down in the gentle autumn sunshine. She lay down beside him, spontaneously putting her hand on his chest. The warmth of his body through her hand felt reassuring and she let go into the physicality of her lover's presence. She felt his heart beating quickly and saw the bulge in his crotch. He lay beneath her, holding his hand on her back. It meant stay still, don't move.

Their ears then were free to listen. He knew this union was for healing her, not for him. They stay still, him locked inside her secret walls, his strength for life, his life force itself straining to leave his body and join hers but held in check.

She did not move, not even to clamp her muscles around the warm length of him that filled her. So they lay for an hour or more as trees shuddered slightly in the breeze, the earth moved, as planets crept along their ritual orbit, they stayed completely still, breathing together.

She felt the roar rising from within, a distance at first then closer and closer, a tide of energy she met with tender resilience. By not flinching, not moving she met the column of vital fire that now spread through her, racking her body in rhythmic spasms of bliss over and over. The column completed its rise up to her neck, face and head spending itself completely.

He gasped, letting go, the warmth of his juice spilling inside her. Panting, her tears on his shoulder fell down his chest. He kept his hand on the small of her back. She felt clarity return. If she did not want to be alive, at least she knew she was.

Diana's Life

2005

near Toronto

A sudden crashing noise, a sound like a bullet cracked through the room. They opened their eyes, looking at each other, still holding hands.

Diana looked at the shelf, to the place where the vase had reflected rainbows not a half hour before, its pieces scattered on the floor, on the carpet.

She scanned the faces, heard Wayne say, "Take a moment and breathe in deeply. We'll go one by one around the room to give our reports since as it seems...we have been ended." Some chuckled at his weak joke.

"Wayne, do you and Andrea have any alcohol around? We could all use a sip of something," Jake asked.

Wayne came back with a bottle of Port in his hand and five small glasses on a tray he passed around.

"What happened, Andrea?" he began.

"I didn't see much, but was aware of a group of people, native types, in funny dress, nothing I recognized. I just knew they were Natives. They seemed glad," she paused, "...really glad we were, we are here. They seemed, they needed something... I never learned what it was exactly, but it seemed to me they felt sure we would give it to them. Next thing I knew I heard the crash of the glass," Andrea's pale face looked from person to person. "That was about all."

Wayne nodded toward Hazel, "I too felt a group but it seemed like I knew them. I was in terrible fear and when the crash happened..." Hazel's tears rolled down her cheeks, "I thought it was gun fire and for some reason that felt more horrible than anything. Gun fire. I'm so glad to know it's only glass..." she shuddered.

"It was a very short meditation, of course..." Wayne's voice calmed them all, as he continued taking inventory of what happened. "We arrived, sat, and went in, as usual. Everything around us is as it was except the shattered glass."

"That's what you call it," Jake offered, "I call it the place where times meet. I felt someone, saw someone hurl an object toward a line, the line was both in that world and this one..."

Hazel broke in, "Yes, yes I sensed that too...now that you say so, I remember a split second after I recognized it was not gunfire I remember a sensation of being both with those others and here, in this room." She looked around. "That world...someone wanted us to end, it was the end, we...completed what we came to do."

"I didn't see anyone hurl anything, I didn't...I wasn't in both places at once, but I do remember being somewhere with a tribe, or group, or gathering of some sort. Many people," Wayne continued, "many people and shouting, some sense of calamity but it seemed at the same time, far away, distant, as though I sensed it through cotton batting."

Everyone turned to her now. Diana began, "As soon as we began I was on a dusty road, walking, only I was an old woman, well, older than I am now, even..." A weak joke, but one they all needed, "...older and then children, calling me, pulling me by my hands," her arms reached up as though being pulled, "and then a group of adults, telling me how important it was and that it was very...serious, or heavy or something like that." Diana closed her eyes a moment to try to recall exactly what happened next.

"Then a body of a young man, several young man but one, the leader, in front of me..." she relayed the experience of his body releasing, then of the body of his mother releasing. "Then the woman, the old woman dancing in a yellow skirt, one leg positioned at about a 45 degree angle above the earth, her eyes, totally uncomprehending, really I've never seen anything..." Diana stopped, a sob erupting from her chest.

"Take a sip of Port, Diana, it'll help," Andrea was at her side, her arm around Diana's shoulders. "You've been struck by something in the middle of what the rest of us just got as edges."

They carried on talking for another hour, determining in the end to keep in contact that weekend.

Then Wayne nodded, folded his hands at his heart in prayer posture signaling the chants that ended each meditation session. Everyone was still quiet as Diana stood. As she walked down the hall she was so absorbed in trying to just stay present, to keep centered, she didn't hear Jake, right behind her, until she had the door handle under her fingers.

"Diana?"

She turned, smiling weakly.

"Diana, I'd like to come by again, right now, if that's okay with you?"

"I'm all right, Jake, really..."

"I know you're all right, Diana. But you have been through something here, and I want to just sit with you. On your dock? If that's okay with you?"

Diana felt anger stiffen her back. She didn't want Jake to know her so well. Another man she can put her dreams and hopes on who'll disappoint her in the end? Better let him know that sooner than later.

Mary's Life

1883

London, England

Mary saw the meadow, as usual just beyond reach. But this time as she watched, its softness flooded her, its warmth began to poke a hole in her mind that descended into her body. The meadow itself began to fade as she felt a tear slide down her face.

She looked around, even as the secret internal shroud continued to cocoon her senses. Her mind did focus, at last. She looked down. Dirty, bare feet emerged from straw that should, she noticed vaguely, have been thrown out long ago. A dingy tunic she didn't recognize covered her body. She dropped her arms from carrying the ghost infant and cramps shot from her biceps to shoulders before she shut that down.

She looked dumbly around. About twenty people, if they still might be called that, held to the walls, moaned softly or scuffled aimlessly back and forth across the floor. Rusty brown blood caked on the back of one woman's grey tunic. The woman seemed oblivious. Nausea shot through Mary's body at the sight and she shook with a moment of revulsion.

Then she saw the small, brown skinned man, the teacher from Fieldworth Manor, standing in front of her. He held out his hand to her. Reflexively, Mary grabbed her thin grey tunic with one hand, tried to hide herself with the other. The hand remained. She looked at his eyes. Warm, deep brown eyes, his mouth smiling as his lilting voice said, "I am glad to see you are back, Mary. Now," he grabbed her hand, "let's get out of here."

He seemed to glide them both out of the darkness of that hell, effortlessly toward a waiting carriage where a servant held out his hand to help her up.

The memory of so many other moments, being helped into a carriage, flashed through her mind with a slash of pain that stripped across her insides. Theo! Mary stared coldly at the door man, grabbed the door handle and yanked herself up. She crouched inside the small well-appointed space, where Mipham handed her a cloak. It was of very good material, trimmed in fur and Mary liked the softness of it. She threw it over her body against the cold, but did not put it on.

"Do you not like the cloak?" Mipham asked softly.

She looked at him briefly, then out the window. Through the rise and fall of the cloak he registered Mary's breath was in the top of her lungs. Slowly and evenly, without drawing her attention away from the window he began to breathe deeply down into the bottom of his lungs. Soon he heard her sigh deeply.

The carriage stopped outside a modest, impeccably kept three story brownstone. It was on the edge of the fashionable district in town, although whether Mary noticed this Mipham could not tell. She leaned toward the door, then hesitated.

"It's all right. Go on," he said,

She held her hand out to the servant, who might have been assisting royalty. More moments, memories of stepping down, her hand in a white glove, perfume, music from a large building...with a start Mary suddenly realized she must look to this servant like those filthy, hollowed out creatures in the asylum had looked to her. Again she yanked her hand away and glared at him, before scuttling, her shoulders hunched, up the pathway to the door.

It was open. Mipham was right behind her, prompting. "Go in." She noticed he was smiling. He was always smiling. Mary felt her own face rigid and frozen, followed by a wave of some emotion she did not at first recognize. Bitterness sliced through her.

She walked in and stood gazing at the simple carved wooden hall piece, with its polished mirror and large hooks for cloaks. Comfortable, warm cloaks, people wearing them as if everything was fine, good in the world, she thought. Her heart writhed in a flash of pain before her mind shut down.

"Come in, come in," her host insisted. She hesitated then stepped in front of the mirror struggling to avoid its judgmental eye. In spite of herself she glanced and was transfixed.

Her hair lay plastered across her head, dirty strings hanging down to her shoulders. Bone edged up near the surface of her skinny pale cheeks. Her thin skin bore scars of self-mutilation, most noticeably three deep lines carved down her right cheek as well as many discolored pits, signs of long standing infection. Sunken empty eyes, scrawny lips drawn tight as though refusing. A thought straggled across her mind, no one will ever want to kiss me again. Again that powerful feeling, bitterness, sliced through her consciously and she knew self-hatred for the first time.

"That hatred will do you no good, Mary," Mipham said softly.

With a slight start she realized he could read her. So be it.

"What do you know of hatred?" she spat at him.

"So your tongue returns on waves of venom," his words slid across a sudden sheet of ice so palpable she stepped back.

Then he turned, as cheerful and kind as before, and walked down the hall, calling over his shoulder in his usual sweet tones "Come in." It occurred to her she did not know him. No matter. Nothing mattered. Whatever happened to her now did not matter.

In the kitchen, he pointed toward a door on the back wall that led to the scullery. "You will find a tub in there. Soap, towels, everything. Wash," he commanded then closed the door to the rest of the house behind him.

Mary looked slowly around the room. Light fell from a window to her right. She registered that light meant sunshine but as she stood in the beam of light, she felt nothing. Sunshine felt good. This was a memory, without sensation or emotion. Beneath the window a table large enough for four people. Between the table and the door he had pointed to, a sink, with taps for running water.

On her left a grange, an old but reliable stove with pots on top. She registered heat coming from the stove and instinctively reached out her hands. They were chapped, chilled and sore.

She held them over the stove top then moved languidly toward the sink. Oh, yes, a pot. Back to the stove, then to the sink for water. She filled a succession of pots with water, noticing as she walked each one to the stove how her muscles strained.

After the pots were full and on the stove she opened the scullery door.

The back door of the house was on her right, the usual stores held in a scullery, including the tub to her left. She lingered over a few jars, touching their glass with her fingers. She felt no hunger, only a dull curiosity. She saw soap, took a bar, put a few towels across her arm and returned to the warmth of the kitchen.

The first pot to heat she lugged to the sink. There she carefully washed her hair, over and over until all the grease came away in the basin. She piled her hair up fastening it with a comb she had found in that back store room.

Now the tub. Warming enough water for this took more time. She knelt and idly ran her fingers along its rim. Where had she done this before? A body, somebody, washing, she was washing somebody...doesn't matter, she told herself, nothing matters. "Get washed he said to do that I will do that," she thought in a peculiar sing-song way.

She saw the pots beginning to boil. Carefully she poured hot water into the tub adding some cold from the kitchen tap. As she slid into the warm wet a short sigh escaped her. She scratched idly at the lice in her pubic hair, made active by the water and soap she began to apply.

She held up a palm full of soap and watched a couple of bubbles and their rainbows. Good quality soap or there would be no rainbows. Good quality people also get rainbows.

"Not like me," the thought bolted through, taking her breath. She focussed and continued to slowly wash her body, noticing the ravages.

Lice had left their calling cards, small round red spots. She knew these would heal. Her bones stuck out at all angles. She supposed she would gain weight again. Her feet, erupting with infections from being bare and in contact with human waste would respond. Nothing indicated she would die soon, and for this she felt disappointment.

She toweled off, brushing her skin vigorously. Layers peeled off, dry light flakes of what used to belong to her. "Like my life, my old life," and pain shot through her heart leaving her bent double. "Theo, Theo," she intoned softly.

Just then a knock at the door and his insistent voice "You are ready to come out now."

"Noooo," she wailed, giving in to the claw in her gut. What is the point, without him? What is the use with no love, no prospects? She sat in the cooling water, sobbing. Theo gone! Betrayed me, did not love me and my baby, little baby no more...

"Open up, quickly," his voice cut through to her but the pain continued on a flood of memories. Theo in their cottage, their love, the ball gowns she had worn, his hand on hers guiding her to the dance floor, his mother saying he had not gone to India...she wailed, a wild animal sound.

She heard a key turn in the lock. She felt his compact arms pull her to her feet.

“Yes, yes,” he said, “this must happen.” He pulled the towels tight across her body, gently pulled her from the tub, and held her, rocking back and forth until the sobs slowed then stopped.

Mary stood as he instructed and slowly put her hands out for the bundle of cloth he gave.

“Now dress yourself,” he said in his lilting voice.

She held the material in her hands for a few minutes after he left, noticing its quality, much better than what she had been wearing, but not nearly ...Mary’s mind again flooded with memories of her mother kneeling and pinning, sewing and fussing over the glorious gowns she had created for her. All the other fabulous gowns worn by all the fashionable young ladies paraded before her, memories chained together rippling one after the other as if they held hands. She was back at the ball she had so eagerly awaited and attended, paralyzed to the present.

Finally another knock at the door. “Mary, Mary you must open up.”

Why? She did not think the words, still the question was clear to her. So she remained standing silently in the middle of the room, the clothing bundle in her hands.

“Mary, open up and let me in.”

Mary stared down at the pile in her hands.

“I will. I am all right. ” All right, never again, never again all right, all right was then. This is now, not all right, not all right, not ever again.

Slowly she pulled the clothes on. Each movement required enormous effort against the weight of her limbs but at last the task was over.

She opened the kitchen door onto the dark hallway. On her left, another door was open. Candlelight fell softly across the carpet at her feet. She looked into the dining room where silverware and lovely plates sparkled.

"Come in, come in please." He rose as she entered. Small was the word she heard in her head in response to the space of this room, but how she knew this or by what standard she could not say. Small but well-furnished with many pieces of china, vases and other decorations lining the walls, her awareness continued.

The table was set simply and beautifully with polished silverware, patterned plates, gleaming glasses. A peculiar feeling, warm and comforting began to well within her but she set her chin against the rising warmth and it vanished.

"Slowly you will learn to allow trust. Then you will encourage that positive glow to rise." He had read her again.

She looked straight ahead, ignoring him.

"We eat modestly, but with relish," he said as though answering a question while plating meats, turnips, carrots and potatoes in front of her. The smell wafted up. She resisted an urge to lean over, breathe deeply the delicately spiced affair. She waited while he bowed his head, put his palms together and spoke for a few minutes in the rhythmic language she guessed was his native tongue. Then without looking at her again Mipham, her host and captor, cut into and ate, as he had predicted, with relish.

The food found its way to her mouth. She chewed slowly. She knew flavors existed, spices and delicate textures but they seemed just beyond a barrier she could not penetrate. Still she dutifully continued to eat, watching every now and again as her host gave himself over generously to his experience.

She ate sparingly, the richness unfamiliar after a diet of gruel, porridge and more gruel for....how many days? How long had she been in that place?

She waited until he had completed his meal and was sitting back, looking at her. Through the gaslight she saw again those warm, humour-filled, brown eyes.

"Yes?" The word fell lightly from him.

"I..uhm...that is...what day is it?"

"You have been in that place for two years. It is now 1883, Thursday the third of March."

Mary gasped. Her eyes darted from one side of the room to the other, prisoned birds looking for escape. Her hands wrung the napkin over and over. "But I..."

"Do not think about it." His soft voice was a command. She felt an instant of relief.

Yes, she thought slowly, better not to think. She passed out. She woke several moments later, still at the table.

"I knew a woman," he continued as though there had been no lapse, "who passed out, right there in front of you. She just fainted right away, without moving."

Mary listened, his voice beckoning her back toward a world she did not want, a world without Theo. Theo! With the name anguish rose in her belly, consuming her chest until she could not breathe. Mipham felt the constriction, released his own breath with a deep, purposeful inhale and spoke.

"Mary, you will learn to hold your mind where you want it to be, not trapped in the past, or yearning for the future. You are here, that is all. HERE." His raised voice scattered the demons inside her and she felt present, if only for a second.

She took a glass of water, raised it to her lips, drank and felt the cool liquid slide down her throat.

"Good. Excellent!" his soft voice had returned.

Mary accepted his ability to follow her mind, to be inside her head. She accepted this without question, because question took energy. She had none to spare.

"You are a prisoner," he continued, "of the mind. That is the most difficult prison of all. You are free of Benham House, no longer a prisoner there, but you still exist inside your own mind and emotions as a prisoner. The past will continually rise with its hooks. Hate and anger poison the moment you are in now, only you do not see that it is the poison of your own mind."

Tahni's Life

1660s

Tonawanda

Now they kept their minds on the next meal, both scavenging roots, berries and the occasional kill. They moved at night, attempting to keep both cold and the White man away. Sometimes while the soil was not yet frozen over, they dug pits to sleep in during the day, covering themselves with branches and what remained of summer's leaves.

As they walked one night, she started to hum, not loudly, but enough he had to touch her shoulder, turn her around, had to put his finger on her lips. When he did, she looked at him, startled, then suddenly recognized where they were, how it was for them now. He saw her startled look, but took it to be a momentary lapse, even an indication her sadness and despair were lifting. It did not cross his mind she was not right. To him she was still Tahni, a full medicine woman.

She kept from him her inner confusion, how quickly she noticed herself shifting out of the world around them, her mind huddling toward some soothing grey nothingness she yet recognized as an enemy.

For the first couple of months as they wandered Tahni found herself drawn to return closer and closer to the earth of her village, to the place where the corpses, having been piled near the perimeter of their village, and covered with dirt, were rotting.

She stood within the forest, as close to the village as Chaytan permitted, and danced, her rattle held in his hand to prevent sound. She danced and imagined one or another, sometimes a group of her former village family, waiting for her, hovering in the Between World, damp, grey, cold, calling for her and her dancing, a sight which warmed and encouraged them. Once a crow flew left to right exactly overhead as she finished her dance. She believed it was a sign that one, maybe more, of the souls had made it across.

As the months dragged through winter's darkness, they huddled more against the cold, their primary enemy. Dancing at the edge of the forest, even for the souls of the dead, was for later, when warmth and hopefully food would return.

Her tunic had shed all of its beautiful beads, falling like tears following the massacre. The beads had continued to drop as they ran into the forest, waited for dark before washing in the lake, learned to shy away from full moon light. What had been their constant friends, sun and moon, stars and seasons now had to be reconfigured against the potential that air would split open, spitting deadly fire from lightning sticks at them.

One morning she woke to Chaytan's moans. He had been extremely tired for several days, and the nausea which accompanied their diet as a matter of course had kept him from eating even the small bits she could provide. He lay next to her, the heat drained from him.

"I am in pain. Everywhere," he stated. Tahni looked at him, felt along his arms and legs, then moved quickly through the forest. When she found the right tree, an evergreen, she stopped, prayed. It seemed to her the tree's vital energy thrust forward a little, as though giving permission, so she carefully removed some of its foliage.

She returned with the medicine. "Chew these for the rest of today, as we walk." She helped him to his feet, and held his arm to keep him steady as they again began their daily routine of walking, walking, moving.

Over the next few days Tahni continued to administer the foliage of the Northern White Cedar. Its green virtues wiped out the scurvy which had threatened Chaytan.

He said to her softly that night, "You could have left me to die. That illness would have taken me, as I am, we are..." he did not finish. They both knew that after months of walking, of winter's ravages and hunger's constant presence, they were dangerously weak.

"Yes," Tahni replied. She returned to the silence which had become habitual for them, as much from the need to conserve energy as from having nothing to say.

In early spring, when the ground was barely released from ice, they returned to what had been their village, again at Tahni's insistence. This time they saw the White man's building, insides of trees standing up naked in a square, like the bones of an animal, like, thought Tahni, the way they left our people to rot to bone, then dust. This thought had no energy behind it. So little food for so long had stripped them of the luxury of emotion.

They stood looking at the sight that sealed their past to a deep grave, their future to an unknown, for several minutes. Then Chaytan said softly, "We can go upriver."

For the first time Tahni agreed.

As the sun began to warm their world, they moved farther from what had been their home. With the sun's continued warmth, animals began to dig their way out of hibernation, plants to poke through the soil and Tahni and Chaytan had more to eat.

Peering from the veils of the forest that lined the Tonawanda River's edge, they came across a hut, a derelict one, grey with weather. They waited a full day watching for any one, soldiers in red or blue, both uniforms of the hated English, or Natives from other tribes.

Then they walked carefully, silently toward it. Off to the side of her vision Tahni saw beautiful early wild roses, her favorite. She moved toward them. Chaytan grabbed her hand, shook his head and pushed her toward the door. She was disappointed. Didn't he want her to have the roses? Didn't he love her?

Inside dust motes floated in streams of sun coming through the walls. On the square floor in the back corner lay a pile of things she didn't recognize. He pulled a soldier's coat from that pile, tossed it aside. She saw it with her eyes, but her mind went blank. He pulled out a dark brown bottle, checked it. It was nearly full. Carefully he laid it beside the soldier's coat. He turned, said he was going to hunt. She watched him walk outside, into the autumn woods. Whenever he left, she expected it to be for the last time.

Tahni had discovered a place inside herself. She went there whenever he was gone. It was silent, neither dark nor light, with no sensation. She sat for hours in her place, until he opened the door again, tossed four small dead rabbits softly on the floor. She saw him lean over, move the door silently with his foot, enter with ferns piled up in his arms. As she looked up at him, he registered her eyes held nothing.

The soldier's coat lay where he'd left it but someone had ransacked the pile; the peculiar white woman's skirt now lay under Tahni. Chaytan lay the rabbits at her feet. She stirred, began to move, walked outside carefully straining toward distance, any shadow or muted sound. Nothing. She put her head down examining each small stone, found what she wanted, walked silently inside.

She slid the skin off each rabbit with the sharp side of the stone. He had made a very small fire.

They roasted the rabbits layer by layer, letting the fire grow large enough to heat and cook the outer layer, stripping this off and hungrily devouring the delicious meat while letting the fire grow small again as the smoke cleared through large cracks in the walls.

Greasy fingers, greedy mouths, the loudest of hunger's wail finally silenced, they lay back, listening intently. Their ears grew around them, taking in their world. No sound, no hooves, no voices, nothing. Sound was their enemy, their oppressor. Silence meant freedom.

He lay back on the bed of ferns, licking the last of the grease off his fingers.

"Here." He tipped liquid from the brown bottle onto her mouth. "Take some."

The liquid flowed to her belly, spreading warmth inside. Ah, she saw, the White man has put sun in this container. Liquid sun. He took the bottle, upended it. They looked at each other, then passed the bottle back and forth, back and forth gorging themselves.

He held his hand up, signaling her to watch him. Tahni watched him walk out the door, then return a few moments later, his hands full of rose petals. Cradling his full palms above her head he showered the pink pieces all down upon her. Liquid sunshine shifted the room, the world, turning it over on itself.

"Ish wall shtraigh?" her tongue skidded around her mouth. Then laughter, erupting through the inner sun, laughter cleared a path to this moment.

"One good thin' White maaan..." he announced tipping across the floor at the end of the tunnel Tahni saw through the empty bottle, waving good bye. Blackness.

Tahni woke with small pebbles in her mouth, rasping down the sand in her throat. She stumbled up, disturbing his snores so he too woke. She grabbed the water skin, drank half of it before gesturing to him. Up. He drank the rest. Move.

All paths used to lead to more forest, to lakes and valleys, to the great forever. Now every trail, every road or course took them to soldiers. So many soldiers. With the soldiers came other White people, men whose loin cloths grew around their legs, women in skirts that puffed out even when they were splattered with mud. These people had things in their hands. They bashed those things around and soon trees became thin pieces, then those thin pieces which would have fed a fire, became an enclosure, what kept the natural world out.

They watched from the forest as one small building after another, then two and three stood on the ground that had been their home. For the most part their own people, the other tribes, had fled. Up north was the last rumor they heard, but they knew everyone else from their village besides Little Bird and the two of them, had died.

Something else they watched: the men took bottles, passed them around. Bottles might have the liquid sun in them. And where the White people were, there was a sure supply of food. So Tahni and Chaytan watched, waited. When the invaders left for the night because a building wasn't finished, they raided, taking bits of leftover food, keeping their eyes out for those dark brown bottles.

They wore the clothes from the shed, Tahni now in a White woman's dirty blouse and dark brown skirt, no underwear, he in a pair of soldier's pants and the soldier's coat. He hunted and killed, but the dangers of fire meant raw meat. And sparse. It had been the harshest winter they could remember and the animals had scattered farther and farther away from the White man's infiltration.

They continued upriver until one day Chaytan took a special interest in watching one building. Tahni followed his gaze. She saw Natives mingling with Whites around the building. It was the first time she had seen this. The sight somehow increased the constant sense of emptiness inside her.

She turned back to where she rested against a boulder, keeping her mind carefully trained on what was before her. Trees lined the large river's bank. Trees she knew the names of but right now could not recall. Green carpet of forest stretched out beyond the fringe of those trees, boulders creeping out from under that green carpet. Focusing on the moment was the only sanctuary she had from the inner beating of thoughts, or worse, from that grey fog that threatened to overturn her entirely.

Tahni sat upon the new spring grass, regarding the river below, and the buildings being erected on the far side. She attended to this moment with great care, since the fog inside her was so close.

"You have been watching." Tahni turned at the voice. She recognized it, but her mind refused to put a face to the sound. She looked up and there was Little Bird, smiling. Tahni noticed the flesh on Little Bird's body, her strong energy, health. Little Bird's eyes shone with vitality and her freshly brushed hair gleamed. In an instant of comparison Tahni knew she herself was worn beyond skin and bone.

"Yes," Chaytan replied. Tahni now looked at Chaytan. She saw the light in his eyes, the gleam of desire, need, whether for Little Bird or the food and shelter she represented Tahni did not know.

Little Bird sat herself down, patting the log for Chaytan to sit beside her. Tahni watched with no reaction as Chaytan meekly obeyed, his knee conveniently close enough that Little Bird's hand found a home there.

"You can come, you know," Little Bird looked at Tahni now, extending the invitation as though it was to Little Bird's own wigwam.

"You can come and stay with us. We have food, and drink, and...and..." Little Bird's eyes slowly drew for Tahni the picture of what she must look like, withered, wrinkled, ravaged and dirty. With a small start Tahni saw Chaytan's filth, the dirt of his nails, greasy hair hanging around his face. Shame filled her.

"...and a bath," Little Bird concluded.

"I, uhm... no," Chaytan replied uncertainly. Tahni turned away. She tried to focus her mind on what her eyes saw before her, but her focus dragged itself along the path of Little Bird's words. She didn't remember why, but she knew not to trust Little Bird.

"It's all right," Little Bird's voice went on behind Tahni's back, "they are all right with you, now."

That word, the last one, the word "now" shuddered through Tahni's body. It meant Chaytan had not been allowed to go with Little Bird before, it meant he had remained with her, Tahni, only out of desperation, out of having nowhere else, no one else to stay with. Tahni felt no strong emotion, just clarity.

Then revulsion spilled through Tahni. They, the White men who had massacred their innocent village, were all right now? Fury hurricaned the words she needed back onto her tongue.

"You mean, the people who wiped out everyone you loved, or said you loved, everyone you knew, they now say it's all right, so it's all right?" Tahni's thin body shook.

Little Bird tossed her head, imperiously, as Tahni had seen so often in the past.

"Where have you been?" Little Bird demanded. "Have you been all the way up river, like I have? Have you seen the numbers of Whites, greater than all the leaves that fall in autumn, all up and down the river? Have you seen the buildings they have made, everywhere? Do you think," she drew her lips back into a thin grimace, "they are going to go away? Besides," Little Bird's face showed power, a sense of control Tahni recognized, "the White Man is going to give us our own land! They have said all they want is for us all to be together, they will gather us all and once we have gathered, they will give us a large stretch of land where they will leave us alone. So you can stay here and scramble like animals, until the Whites take everything from you or you starve to death in filth. Or you can come with me."

She looked triumphantly at them, as though she had settled something.

Chaytan listened, his head to one side.

Tahni took in the vision Little Bird painted of the many Whites crawling through her beloved lands, forests, rivers and plains, stripping the trees, turning them inside out, crushing the meadows under their bleak buildings. The last tiny rag of hope in her heart dissolved. She returned to silence and trying to focus.

"If not now, then think about it. If you want to, you can come and find me. There's food." She threw this word at them both, a weapon. "Food and clean clothes." With a withering glance up and down at Chaytan, she disappeared again.

Under the beautiful spring stars that night they lay together, Chaytan and Tahni, in the silence which had cloaked them together for so many months, their bodies comforted by each other's presence. At last Tahni fell off to a fitful sleep.

She woke to a different silence. The sound of Chaytan's breath was gone, his body no longer as close as her arm.

She wandered then. She could not bring herself to take up Little Bird's offer, even though she knew there was nowhere to go. She wandered, eating sometimes, but often forgetting to eat. Sleeping sometimes, but often forgetting to recognize whether it was night or day. She wanted to see Macawi. Why didn't Macawi come out? Tahni sensed she ought not push that question because it lay somewhere close to a nightmare she skirted by.

She scavenged enough through summer to keep herself alive but when the cool of autumn began again to settle on the world, her health and energy depleted, she walked past the upright logs of the barricade, into the small town still being built directly over what had been her village. Her wanderings had returned her to the place which had been her home.

Tahni recognized the smell of freshly cut trees. "Everywhere, the White man brings death," she thought.

Standing in the middle of the town built upon her former home, Tahni began with a chant, a death chant. She wanted to contact the souls of her people. Rattle in one hand, she intoned, sang and danced a few steps.

A couple of White people doing town business, coming out of stores, stopped and stared. Soon a crowd ringed her. Oblivious, Tahni kept moving and throating the deep sounds of her people's songs.

"Yeah, keep going Injun," the jeers and taunts flowed. Dazed with hunger, uncertain what these white ghosts said, she danced, asking Great Spirit to guide, protect her.

A soldier came out of one of the buildings. He raised his rifle to his eye and the crowd thinned. Then the sight of this woman, emaciated, withered, cut through to one part of him.

"Ah, now, stop that," he said, his hand waving in the air. Tahni knew from the way he held his hand he wanted her to stop. He looked around at the crowd, seemed to decide something, then motioned for her to follow him.

Tahni shivered on the dirt floor, the bars in front of her, a thin grey wool blanket wrapped around her. She stared between the bars of her cell, looking for ways to communicate with these half mad people who had chained her up like a mouth foaming dog.

Two young men in uniforms pointed to the structure to her left, a bed of sorts. No soft skins, but a dead tree, its insides laid out side by side. A bed of death. She ignored them, kept to the floor.

They fed her slops from a bucket, tried to get her to dance for them in exchange for food. They mimicked her, parodied her movements in the street.

"Come on, now, you kin do it," one of them said. He was so young. She saw he was not much older than the warriors who were to come out sometime, would come out from their initiation, and when they did, he would be dead of their tomahawks, she thought. Her brave warriors...her mind traveled to places she could recognize, refused to come back.

Without the forest, without the earth, sun and stars, her heart stopped sending fresh signals to her mind. Instead her heart stayed behind in the world she knew. Her mind followed.

"Here you go, a little piece of meat." He wagged the scentless beef in front of the bars. Hunger drooled on her lips. She came forward to take it and he snatched it away.

"O lookie, Jebediah, she's right gone."

Their language, their sneers, meant nothing, but the food did. She stood at the back of the cell, coy, smiling at him. If she was nice, if she might convince him he could have her...and she was willing. The meat was life.

"Ahh, Injun bitch," he suddenly snarled, Jeb jabbing him in the ribs.

"She wants you, Daniel, look the Injun broad wants you."

Later when Jeb left, Daniel took the key, unlocked the cell and raped her. She waited far away in the forest, for her warriors to emerge from their initiation.

"They will get you," she whispered. He thought it was a love sound. He finished, threw a piece of meat in at her, sneered, jabbered in their ugly language and left. She ate the meat. It was cold, but had been cooked.

Her guards' games grew more complicated and soon involved the liquid sun. They offered the bottle to her through the bars, and she whimpered, danced a little, begged. They held the bottle back, fed her some scraps which she devoured, then gave her just enough of the booze to soothe her torn soul. She loved that first sweet trickle running down her throat, loved the way the pain would soon ease.

They raped her, sometimes taking turns.

Then another soldier, in a different uniform, came, opened the cell and led her out. He took her arm and helped her into the street, steered her towards one of the buildings where food smells came from. He sat her in a chair, the other men gaping, and got her a meal. She ate with her hands, stared at him.

He threw some coins on the bar. Then he threw one shiny coin down, and the man behind the bar poured liquid sunshine into a small clear cup. Her guard threw his head back, drank the potion. Inwardly Tahni drooled.

This man said some words to her, took her upstairs and showed her a tub of water. He left. She bathed, slowly, and put on the skirt and blouse laid out for her. She did not do up the buttons. If she offered herself to him, he might give her some of the liquid sun she craved.

She came out of the room with her breasts, flaps of wrinkled skin, uncovered. He saw the dugs, saw the look in her eyes, murmured Christ to himself softly and pulled her blouse together. He took her downstairs and escorted her outside. "Go now, get away from here," he said pointing.

She thought he meant dance, so she started to dance, all the time imagining the liquid relief pouring through her.

"Crazy, they are all fucking crazy," he muttered to himself, went back inside.

Soon someone did come by, take her round back. He gave her no shiny coin. She learned quickly after that. She stood outside the bar, leaned against the wall and waited. Another White man came by, looked at her and she knew what to send through her eyes.

But first, she motioned with a finger on her palm. This one took her inside, made her sit by herself while he and his friends laughed in her direction, but he bought her one of the small cups of liquid sunshine.

Now it was simple. That was what she lived for.

One night in summer the rain pouring down on her, she staggered around the street, a full bottle in her hand. She mumbled incoherently, hatred rising in her for these fake humans, these evil spirits in white flesh.

Two soldiers, familiar enough with the sight of her but recently warned by their captain to clean up this town, took the bottle, smacked her for trying to get it back. One raised his rifle, rammed the butt end into her chest as she lay in the mud.

The soldiers left. Tahni sighed, a bubble of blood rose from her mouth. Hatred smeared through her vision, a dark spectre. As her breath slowed, the anger and hatred passed. She was standing among large rocks, warm sun shining on her back. The rocks formed a small half circle around a bit of land where shrubs and trees grew. She did not know this land yet it seemed familiar. She turned to her right.

"Takoda!" Her heart leapt. Her trembling hand reached for him and he held his out for her. He had been waiting for her! His eyes, his arms around her, Tahni passed from this life.

Mary's Life

1884

London, England

Mipham continued, "This moment is the only way out of the prison of your mind, the chains of your emotions. First learn to be present. That means with all the pain. You will cry and feel desolation. As the process works, you will feel worse than you ever have. That is the price of coming back."

Mary blanched inwardly. She did not want to come back. She did not want to feel. Where she was, in a state of suspended emotions, feelings left unfelt, was all she desired.

"You will change your mind. You will want to be here, again. Not in the same way, but you will accept life again. For now, you need suitable activities, activities that will train you to be here in a stronger, clearer manner. You will begin to learn how, this very morning."

Mary was in the front room of the house, a room with high windows and little by way of furniture.

Mipham intoned, "Palms clasped above your head, keep your chin a little tucked in like I showed you, Mary." Mipham's sing-song voice made her sigh. She pulled her arms straighter, felt her chin tuck in slightly. Slowly she brought her palms down to the middle of her chest, a place Mipham referred to as the heart center.

"Good. " He giggled at her from his place at the front of the room, where he sat on a dias covered in plush carpet and soft cushions. He smiled at her and as always that warmed her. As he smiled at her, she heard his next instruction, "Put your left foot against your right thigh."

She tried and toppled, grimaced at him, stood up, positioned her palms and tried again.

"Yes, yes, very good." He toned this in his singsong way, as Mary felt herself sway, tilt and then buckle again onto the floor.

"Why is this important, anyway?"

"Ah, Mary, the discipline of the body is much easier, no matter how hard it seems, than the discipline of the mind. With the body you have something physical to grasp."

He said this as she again toppled.

"Why can't I do this simple thing?" she wailed, tears splashing down. "It's not difficult, why can't I do it?"

"You have never asked yourself to be balanced before."

His unending patience slammed like a rock against which her inner turmoil raged, "That's fine for you to say. You've never had to... had to..." and she cried.

"Yes," he was patting her back, "yes, it's true. You have it most difficult. Having to live here, in this house and with me." He sighed so deeply and looked with such mock sympathy at her that she started in spite of herself to smile.

"Good. Let's try again," he said.

So it went. He let her fall, time after time. She counted internally, two-seconds, three...oops and over she went.

After about half an hour of this, Mipham looked at her innocently and said, "You may put your right foot on your calf, as an alternative posture."

"What? Why didn't you..."

He huddled into himself as though her words lashed him physically.

"Stop it!" Mary yelled, "Stop acting like I'm hurting you..."

"But, Mary, you are." He gazed at her sadly, his large brown eyes full of pain.

"It's only language...it's not like I'm hitting you," she almost sneered.

"Are you sure?" he dropped his eyes from her and whispered this so she had to lean forward to hear. "Now, Mary, try again. Maybe you would like to try with your right foot against your calf instead of your thigh?"

Mary stood, sucked in some air, focused away from her emotions and into her raised palms. She let go of her breath and put her right foot snugly on her left calf. Her arms flailed out as she found balance, then slowly, she brought them back to her heart center where she held the posture for what felt like a long time.

"Good. Over thirty-seconds. That's enough for today."

"No!" Mary's emotions drove her. "No. You made me fall and fall, over and over again all the while you knew this other posture would work. Why do you want me to look like a fool? Why do you torture me like this?" Her voice grew louder and louder as Mipham sat watching.

"On the floor. " His voice issued this order.

"No! No I won't keep doing what you say. You say things but how do I know you aren't just doing the same thing you just did? Setting me up for something difficult I mean. How do I know this isn't another set up?"

"All right, "Mipham got up quickly and slipped out of the room as though nothing left behind were disturbed.

Mary's thoughts tumbled as she paced the room. Her breath raced and her jaw clenched, she thought, "I'm leaving. Had enough of this. This is too much. I have to go." Where? She knew there was no place she would find the safety she had with Mipham. A single, uneducated woman, she felt her facial scars gingerly with a finger, now without prospects the only path she might take outside his front door led to a brothel, or the street.

He walked back in again as though expected. "Mary, try this. Lie on the floor on your stomach."

Since there was no place she could go, and he was the only person left in the world who knew her, she obliged.

"Now, pull yourself up so your bottom is the highest part of your body. Yes, that's it, bend in the middle so you are an upside down V shape, with your bottom up."

Mary felt the blood enter her face and head. She felt her arms strain and begin to shake.

"Now," Mipham continued, "bend down so your body is parallel with the floor, raised by your arms."

Mary tried, her arms collapsed and as her chest hit ground a large wail sounded out of her. What is the point she thought. It's not Mipham's fault, it's mine. I'm the useless one, no good for anything...

"Now, Mary, now, put your bottom back up!" he commanded.

Mary struggled up again into the inverted posture, her chest heaving with sobs. Then she threw herself onto the floor, her arms flailing as she tried to regain her focus on her body. The dark enemies of emotion driven thought hovered along her body, ready to enter and slice her in two, ready to send her back to that place…

Her mind gone again, she lay folded in a fetal posture, wailing and sobbing in front of the platform where he sat.

Mipham picked her up and helped her walk around the room. The large windows picked up bright winter sunshine, spreading a coat of extra warmth that helped the fire in the grate. Mipham walked with Mary, then stood beside her, breathing.

Very soon she returned to him, her hand grasping his arm.

"It's all right," she said, tonelessly.

"Yes, it is," he smiled gently.

So Mary began the active meditation of yoga.

In part she continued out of respect for Mipham, but mostly she performed the postures, bringing her body to the floor, stretching out with her arms above her head, pulling herself rigorously through the routine again, and again, because the teeth of her thoughts ripped at her if she did not.

They waited until she lost focus. Then they descended, "stupid girl, what made you believe he could love you? Anyone could love you? What made you think you were special enough, important enough? Of course he doesn't love you, who would...and now, no one will. No one will ever..." The words rode waves of self-loathing, filling her body with dark weight until she was paralyzed.

Yoga kept the thoughts at bay. She still heard them, but from a bit of distance, just enough distance she was able to keep breathing.

"Mary, thought is energy. Energy is ...you might say alive in some way. So the thoughts create the action, the actions do nothing to release the thoughts. The patterns get bigger, more easily performed. For example, when you first came here, you struggled to wash the dishes, yes? Now, it is easy and other things are difficult.

"How did this happen? It happened because you had to use specific actions, actions that did not come from your thoughts but from consciously applied direction. What would you have done, left to your own decision?"

"Tried to see Theo." Mary said these words slowly. She could say his name and feel less about it. He was becoming a memory, one she chose not to hold on to. With his fading went some of the sorrow about her lost baby, her rage and sense of shame over his betrayal. Only a little less, but enough to give her reason to continue.

"Right. You were controlled by the thoughts and the emotions they rode on. But they, the thoughts, are only thoughts. Little energy packets. When we learn to focus our attention elsewhere, those energy packets get smaller and smaller, and other ones get larger and larger. Learning to focus on what is wholesome allows us to bring increasingly good thoughts to mind. Good thoughts in our mind mean our actions will be more wholesome. Actions being more wholesome means we feel good and so on it continues. A pattern, yes but a good one."

Several weeks went by and Mary learned to accomplish a few things every day. She made beds, dusted, cleared up after meals and started to learn how to cook. She continued under Mipham's insistence to practice yoga and slowly began to see her mind clear, her focus grow stronger, her emotions stay more even.

"Mary, tonight we go out." Mipham announced this in his usual abrupt way one night."To Fieldworth Manor."

Mary's heart constricted, her breath refused to move through her body, as though her blood were suddenly solid in her veins. Return to Fieldworth Manor? Now? Tonight? She tried to focus but emotion shoved her will out of the way. "How could you mean...I am not...why there?"

"Because they have asked me to come and speak to them. Your task tonight is to watch." Mipham pushed his dishes away slightly, a sign she was to clear the table.

With a deep, purposeful intake of breath, Mary rose, her mouth set as grimly as her mother's ever had been. She removed dishes, washed and wiped them dry with an attention to detail fired by anger. He had a talk and therefore she had to go and listen! She was to watch him, as though she didn't spend every minute of every waking day watching him, listening to him. He was beyond self-absorbed!

Then Mary began to think, to consider how she might react, what might happen when Theo....Theo! He would see her! Some part of her sang with certainty. He still loved her!

He must, after all they had had together. He would look into her eyes, remember their love and like a bad dream everything else would disappear. These thoughts faded in the cynical self-loathing that followed, "Yes, treat you like he did before and with about as much respect." Hope shoved against reason and in the tension of this conflict she could not get her mind clear.

"Now, Mary." This order issued softly, unarguably, from Mipham as he entered the kitchen just as she finished the last dish.

"But I want to change, to...to..." she protested.

"No. You are fine." He swept his eyes up and down her once, turned and she followed him down the hall.

"Like," the carping voice insisted inside of her, "a dog."

"Breathe." Mipham commanded her as the carriage pulled away from the safety of their home.

Mary surprised herself by thinking of it as their home. She had up to that moment defined her life with him as his. His house, his food, his teaching. Suddenly she found herself feeling the tall, brownstone three-story was her home, too.

"When threat rises from the outside, we naturally define ourselves within whatever safety we know." He had of course read her mind.

"Thank you." Her sarcasm fell off of him like rain on the outside of a window pane.

As the horse hooves clattered over the cobblestones, and the streets with their ordered houses melted past Mary mused. Smiling faces... She had always seen houses with their window eyes and door mouths as smiling faces, full of a kind of warmth and certainty she desperately wanted for herself.

She tried unsuccessfully to settle her mind. In breath...Theo! And Brigitte. The two of them in their house, their home, everyone aware they are the married couple, the ones in charge of their lives while she had been left, to hang...or to die. Brigitte snug and happy, contented, with everything in the world at her feet, wealth, her husband, possibly children.

A ghost of sadness rose through the trunk of her body,

up to her eyes and dissolved there as a single tear. She herself would never have children.

Then her mind offered a picture of the room inside the grand house, with everyone snickering behind their hands, whispering, oh she's the one...Mary felt the tear slide down her cheek trailing her shame.

"That's how little I meant to him." Mary tried to convince herself away from any thoughts, either warm or cold, of Theo and Brigitte. She tried to breathe in and out, to focus. She tried and failed.

In agony, Mary felt the carriage wheels stop. She glanced out. It was the same house, but looked a little smaller, a little less grand than before. She stepped lightly down, her hand on the coach man's hand, then looked up to him with genuine gratitude.

"Thank you," she said humbly.

"Come, Mary." Mipham's imperious tone made her furious. She was suddenly very present. Why care about any of these people, or what they thought, at all? Who were they to her or she to them?

She walked behind Mipham, watching as the crowd on the steps parted, as though he was someone more important than they were, to let him go through. No one noticed her, of that she was certain.

Inside the large doors, through the elegant and beautiful lobby, into the room on the left of the great hall, Mary moved quietly, watching. She noticed the beauty of this building, but noticed also the beauty did not as in the past sweep her away. It was just pleasant.

Mary streamed in behind Mipham and watched. She watched with chagrin as Mipham walked up to their hosts, Theo standing with Brigitte by his side. A large wave of deep emotion, fear mixed with envy, stirred with hatred and a shame that nearly knocked all the other emotions out, rose in her.

She breathed deeply, with purpose, fighting to stay present.

"You remember," Mipham was murmuring to Theo, stepping aside so Theo had to see Mary, "Miss Eagleton?"

"Miss Eagleton," Mary watched as Theo moved forward, looked at her as though with trained interest, took as little of her hand as possible in his and waved his fingers up and down in the air. Mary watched and saw he looked surprised, as though he had not calculated on her being there, with Mipham. Or even, Mary thought suddenly with surprise, that I am still alive.

Theo's surprise offered Mary an advantage.

"Mr. Fieldworth." Mary heard her own voice, calm and even. The slight jarring inside his eyes, as though she had fired a volley that had hit its target gave her added strength. She turned toward Brigitte. "Mrs. Fieldworth." Mary held out her hand.

Brigitte's eyes widened in shock, as Mary took in the changes. Brigitte had put on weight, her hair, dull and frizzy, stuck out of the curls at odd angles, her eyes lay inside the folds of new wrinkles. Mary also saw what was worse, more unexpected. Brigitte's eyes revealed some deep inner loss, some unfathomable sadness.

Startled by what she saw, Mary let go of Brigitte's hand and followed Mipham toward the front of the room.

She watched Mipham's spine, his characteristic walk at once even, unhurried and yet belying a deep purpose. She saw him flick the fingers of his left hand toward the back of the room and she knew, although she could not say how, that was where he wanted her. Mary took a seat as far to the back as possible and waited.

With her back to the wall she felt protected from the eyes of others. She found herself able to gain a focussed calm. Her breath loosened, her palms dried, her heart beat in a more regular fashion. She looked around.

Theo had taken his seat beside his wife in the front center row, but was standing now against the far wall, leaning toward a young woman, who gazed up at him, almost in a trance. Mary's breath caught as she saw directly and instantly the same pose Theo had taken with her, the same flashing eyes, the same smile now shining on this young woman. Mary could almost see the young thing tremble.

It took but an instant. Theo moved back to his seat. Brigitte had her head down as though the shame were hers. As though the shame were hers for his selfish ways. The thought was new to Mary. She considered it, let it go and felt a surge of relaxation fill her body.

At the evening's end Mary climbed into the carriage, pulled herself away from the small window and watched through the curtain as the throng gathered to touch Mipham's hand, to have his eyes fall on them, to speak a few last words to them. She still found this response from others amazing, but then, she reasoned, I live with him. For some reason, this made her want to giggle. What she allowed herself was a small smile.

He sat back. She was struck by a desire to tell him what she had experienced, but he looked at her fiercely and said, "Not now."

Inside their house that night he said to her, "Tomorrow. You will tell me everything tomorrow." He left her at the front hallway.

In the morning she could hardly wait to see him, tell him how Theo had stood and looked at the other girl and how Brigitte had seemed so sad and most of all, how she herself now didn't feel the same. At all. Words tumbled across her mind, and she smiled widely as he entered the kitchen where she had started to prepare their breakfast.

"You must go and get sausages. NOW!" he commanded.

His voice nearly made her jump. Again anger slashed across her insides. How dare he! Even as her insides poured with outrage at him, she was hurrying to the front hallway, taking her shawl off the peg, throwing it across her shoulders, taking the coins from his palm and finally, out on the street, rushing toward the butcher's.

She knew where it was. Mipham had driven with her through the city, pointing out landmarks, emphasizing the turns and names of the streets, in a way she had taken for granted at the time. Now she knew where to turn, which street to take. To the right of their house, down two blocks, to the left for three, then turn onto the main street where a sight brought her to a complete stop.

On the opposite corner several red-skinned men, wearing feathers in a band around their heads, leather pants, with little if anything on their upper bodies despite the chill rain, stood waiting outside the Cathedral. Clearly they were waiting for someone to guide them in.

Mary stood suddenly breathless. One of them turned as if her eyes had called to him; he brought his body fully around and looked at her. Mary's body reached toward him, her cells beckoning with a rush of joy, a new light clarity in her heart and head. He continued to look at her and slowly, slowly, the corners of his beautifully shaped mouth moved upward in the beginning of a smile.

Mary's skin shivered with a slight clammy sweat. Her feet fastened themselves to the road. Otherwise, she thought, I'd surely fly.

Light, energy, a bouncing sense of the wonder of life filled her darkened heart and in those instants she felt alive for the first time. A large spontaneous breath filled her lungs.

Just then the minister issued forth from the dark insides of the Cathedral, his black robe swirling and the group of men moved inside. Her champion continued to lock eyes with her, until he too finally left off, turned and faded into the dark entrance.

She turned to wood. Foolish woman, she thought. When will you learn to stop with these notions, these stupid fantasies? Your life is here. You know what it is. That is all. Accept it! Mary did not know these thoughts were the same ones her mother had practiced, over and over, until they became the dull platform upon which Beatrice had endured her life.

She turned to her left, walked a few steps, then checked over her shoulder. The door of the Cathedral stood as it always did. She pulled on the heavy wooden door of the butcher's and entered the pungent smelling, small room where Frank Hodges sold his fresh flesh products, continued to be polite and kind and continued to love, in his large heart, one much rumored about Mary Eagleton.

His face opened with a deep smile. He moved instinctively from behind the counter, wiping his large meaty hands on the front of his damp, bloodied apron, before splaying them across the back of his trousers then finally offering one, still red, to Mary.

Mary's eyes fixed on the bloodied apron. She gasped, felt her head grow light, felt the room shift and then nothing.

When she came to, Frank Hodges was leaning over her, calling her name over and over. Sweat pocked his forehead, his armpits offered evidence of his hard working character, and his warm breath, so close to her face, made Mary gag. She choked and coughed, turned her head to the side and struggled to sit up.

"Mary, Mary Eagleton," he kept saying as though her name was to her the same charm it was to him.

Where had she heard that before, someone calling her name twice? Mary sat up.

"Ahhh, you're coming to, now, there then, tha's better." The butcher felt better for seeing her move. "Wha' happened to ye?"

"Oh, Mr. Hodges, thank you," Mary felt genuinely grateful for his concern. "I don't really know, I just came in and..." she caught sight again of the blood soaked apron and felt her stomach retch. She leaned herself toward the floor and made an ungraceful but successful attempt at standing.

"There, now, tha's better. Can I get ye some water?" Frank Hodges carried a small pot of water to Mary's hand, where he placed it as carefully as an altar boy places the incense holder.

"That is better," Mary said. "I'm so sorry to be so much trouble, Mr. Hodges."

"Please, call me Frank. Those wha' know me calls me tha'."

"Thank you Frank, thank you. I just came in for some sausage, and then the room...'"

"Now, now think no more on it. I'll get the sausage, wrap up and have you back home in no time."

"No, I believe I am all right, now thank you Mr...Frank."

"Now, I'll nay hear of it, ye fell in my shop and I'll take ye home safe. It won't take no time at all."

Mary realized pressing her case would gain nothing. She submitted to the overly solicitous Frank's generosity although she wanted more than anything to walk out the front door of the butcher's and stand in front of the Cathedral for as long as her legs would allow. She wanted, she had to see him again. She needed to feel that strange sensation of true peace and happiness.

Frank Hodges took her arm, guided her through the back door of the shop, and up onto his cart, pulled by his steady mare, who he then encouraged through back streets thereby avoiding all Mary desired. He delivered her, as he had promised, safely home.

"There now, Mary, can ye manage from here?" he asked as his still reddened hand directed her from the cart to the ground outside the small brownstone.

"Yes. Thank you so much. You really have gone beyond

what was necessary." Mary tried to keep her voice warm and steady.

"Not at all. Not at all." Frank Hodges as pleased with himself as a man might be, climbed up on the cart, and turned back to his shop.

She were always delicate as a flower, that one, Frank thought to himself as he clucked his horse back toward his shop.

Inside, Mary held onto the walls as she made her way slowly to the dining room where Mipham had prepared breakfast for them.

"I went for sausages, you made me go for sausages, and you have breakfast ready without them?" Mary stood at the door, her hand on the jamb.

"Oh, yes." Mipham dismissed the words with a wave of his hand. "Now Mary tell me everything. Leave nothing out." As he spoke, he rubbed his hands lightly together, like a child having a good joke on the adults. "But before you do..." he continued looking at her mischievously, "look!" He waved two tickets, in the air, back and forth.

Mary took the tickets in her hand. They announced the Buffalo Bill Wild West Show! She turned pale.

"What?" Mary was speechless. "How did you...did you set this...how could you have..." She alternately stared at him, at the wide grin on his face, and at the pieces of cardboard in her hands.

"Oh, I see. You don't want them. Oh, well, I'll just have to find someone who does want to go see Buffalo Bill and his Wild West Show." Mipham feigned sadness, rolling his eyes as he pulled the tickets away.

"No, no! I want to see... I want to go!" Mary shouted with more passion than she had shown since before her stay in Benham House.

"Ok. Here they are." Mipham giggled and pushed the tickets across the table towards her.

"How do you do that?" Mary suddenly incredulous, asked.

"Well, I just put some pressure on my fingers, and lean into it a..."

Mary cast him a look. "Not that. I mean, how do you always seem to be one step, at least, ahead of where anyone else is? Did you know just this morning I saw these men, these Indians from America and, and..."

"Oh. You're asking me about time, how time works..."

"If that's what it is." Mary paused. "I believe you are a magician." She concluded, a look of satisfaction on her face.

"All right. Then that's that. And now we go to the Wild West Show!" Into the silence that followed his announcement, he asked, suddenly an adult again, "Is there anything else you want to talk about?" Mipham seemed to have forgotten his request she tell him everything.

"Yes. I mean no. This, this Wild West Show. I had...I experienced..." and she told him what had happened on the way to the butcher, concluding with "What was that?"

Mipham began calmly. "Sometimes the veils of time grow very thin and we are given a taste of something from another lifetime." He paused.

"You believe I had another lifetime, in another place, maybe with..." Mary stumbled.

"Almost certainly with...Theo, Brigitte, and now this curious turn of mind around the Wild West. Have you ever felt anything close to what you felt when you saw this man, these people, or when you think of the Wild West Show? Think. Try to remember."

Suddenly she saw clearly the meadow with its spring flowers, and the lovely feeling she had had before, when she was in... darkness descended on her inner world as she recalled the loss of her baby, and Theo's cruelty. She looked at Mipham with sad eyes and said softly, "The meadow."

Mipham reached his hand out and touched her arm. He

said, "I'm so sorry, Mary."

His tenderness made her flinch and tears started behind her eyes. She wept now at their dining room table, simple, uncontrollable tears, as she felt again the void inside, the place where her baby's life, her baby's childhood, then teen years, then adulthood would never take place. Empty now.

Mipham sat with his hand touching her arm until the last tear fell. She did not know it was the last tear she would ever cry for her child. Her eyes glanced at the tickets, still lying in front of her.

"How do these things happen?" she looked at him with such wonder Mipham couldn't help but smile.

"We reincarnate toward what we love. We also reincarnate toward what we hate." Mipham stopped.

Mary's fingers sat interlaced on the dining room table. Her gaze fell upon the tea pot and stayed there for several minutes.

"So," she said at last, "I may have been born here because of some hatred from another time? I may for instance have been born..."

"Anywhere" he concluded for her.

"That meadow, the Wild West, some place in America..."

"Anywhere," he repeated.

"It is our emotions, then, that direct our incarnations?"

"It is our emotions, and our habitual mind states that direct where we will be born again. You, or who you believe yourself to be, may have been involved in a lifetime in the West, in the Colonies, yes. Then possibly under some circumstance or other, you died with some strong emotion for those from this part of the world."

Mary was not satisfied. "That's why you always talk about patterns and habits, why you taught me yoga, and, and...What about fainting? I fainted when I saw Frank Hodge's bloody apron. What does that mean?"

"Maybe you hadn't eaten breakfast." Mipham smiled and rose to leave.

The warm smell of fresh horse filled Mary's nostrils. Unconsciously she opened her lungs, gasping for more of that scent. It created in her a feeling of anticipation of something good, fulfilling.

She and Mipham filed with thousands of Londoners and English from all parts of the country as well as several hundred foreigners through the doors to see the legendary Wild Bill Hickok's Wild West Show.

Ponies, buffalo, elk and deer stood in cages awaiting their turn on stage. On stage! It was an elaborately constructed miniature Rocky Mountain range, composed of seventeen thousand train car loads of rocks and dirt, complete with shrubs, pine trees, and a meandering stream trickling through its vast grounds.

Mary spotted the village and leaned heavily on Mipham's arm.

"Look," she whispered. Her trembling fingers rose across the paths they walked amid the resurrected wilderness, toward the accurately reconstructed complete tepee village. "Look," she whispered again. She stood stalk still.

Mipham waited patiently, before gently waving her arm. "Shall we go closer?" he suggested.

Mary found tears tracing down her cheeks. She could not move. The crowd milled around these two standing still, the only still point in the dance of these thousands of feet.

Finally Mipham suggested, "Let's find our seats." Mary agreed and stumbled toward the direction he took. Drums began tolling rhythmically just as they sat and there, below them and in the center of the tepee village began the Ghost Dance. Mary's tears flowed without stop. Never had she seen anything so beautiful!

Mipham swayed happily to the music, enjoying every moment, glancing now and then toward his companion, taking in her tears without comment. When the last throb of drum had faded in the air, Mary looked at the brochure in her hand.

"The Ghost Dance is what we just saw. It tells of an after place, where the Native world is restored, all their families come together again and it says here, 'no more sorrow, but laughter, rejoicing and peace encompasses everyone.'

"How?" Mary's face turned to Mipham, almost accusatory, "How can they stand it? They are being wiped out by us as we claim their land, their buffalo and yet..."

"Hard to imagine, isn't it?" Mipham returned her gaze steadily.

There didn't seem to be anything else to say. These people who had suffered so much still had the heart to send out hope to each other through their dance and their belief in an afterlife.

The show continued all afternoon. Proper Native warriors dressed in long braids of brilliant feathers, their naked torsos slick with sweat in the hot lights, rode ponies across the plains in a miniature Battle of the Little Big Horn, or of General Custer's heroic victory at the Last Stand. The red skinned warriors bleated, whooped and yipped as they brandished fake tomahawks at the known winners, White men in their leather fringed jackets, who squatted, shooting counterfeit bullets in an imaginary re-enactment that always and forever ended in the White man's supremacy.

Mary sagged into her seat after the show's finale.

"Well, that was wonderful!" Mipham chirped toward her.

"I'm done, spent, nothing left..." she managed.

"Oh," he looked at her with slightly exaggerated disappointment, "then you won't want to stand in line to get an autograph?" and his arm swept out to his side, pointing down to where some of the Native actors stood, scribbling on the proffered brochures of the happy Londoners.

"What?" Mary leaned forward for a better look. There he was, the man she had seen outside the Cathedral. "Come on," she said rising straight and edging her way toward the aisles.

Mipham followed as she navigated her way down to the main space, and into the proper line up. Mary's heart thumped loudly as the line grew shorter and shorter. Two more people then he saw her! His eyes touched hers and stayed with her, although he managed to be polite to the others.

She looked up at him, his even smile opened as he placed his warm fingers under hers beneath the brochure she offered. Flooded with a feeling of security and ease, Mary ushered one long easy breath and stood staring.

They gazed together for a long time, too brief to record, then he said softly, "Wait for me. I must finish this, then..."

At that moment the lightning which had threatened all day erupted with a loud crash. The lights in the building throbbed wildly off and on and the ponies, rustled, whinnied and broke free of their ties. Voices called to him, he moved gracefully to help, turned back to look at her once, then disappeared into the thrash of ponies, men and blinking lights behind him.

Her feet remained on the spot, as if she had nothing else and nowhere ever to go. But the crowd thronged through the building, a voice over the intercom encouraged everyone to leave calmly or risk further exciting the animals.

Eager to get home out of the fierce rain and now howling wind buffeting around outside, the throng of people pushed against her shoving her, forcing her like a tiny stick in a swollen spring river. As Mary struggled against being shuttled toward the door, she screamed "No, no, no!" but her voice pulsed among the decibels of lightning, ponies screaming, men yelling, crowds shouting to each other. Finally she was outside where the shoulders that had padded against her own let go and she stood on her feet again.

Rain poured, wind howled and crowds still spilled onto the sidewalk, leaving her no path by which to return inside. Mary tried to push against those closest to her, but the sheer numbers of people determined in the opposite direction sent her reeling along with them. After two blocks, the crowd thinned out enough she was able to begin the walk back, but the last of the audience had left and the building was shut tight for the night.

Mary pounded on the door, pounded and shouted but whether anyone heard she never learned. Finally she hailed a cab and sat, watching the dreary streets unfold, grey wrinkles on a worn out piece of cloth, she thought, her customary mind set of disappointment and despair returning more heavily after her brief dance with hope.

Mipham ushered her in, walking in silence toward the kitchen. She followed him mechanically, until he turned at the kitchen door and said softly, "They leave tomorrow for America from Brighton. If you catch this evening's train, there is a chance you may make it in time. I have packed a small case, and some food for you."

Mary's heart staggered, then flew upwards, a winging bird, again. "Thank you," she managed, as she scooped up the small valise, and put the package of food into another case, placed her purse securely inside, shut it firmly and walked back out of the brownstone building she had come to know as home.

Mary stood on the dock in the drizzling grey dawn, watching the ship already in full sail empty itself and with it her heart and hope, from the harbor out onto the sea. She remained for several hours in the freezing spring drizzle, without moving, as though by willpower she might find time reversing.

Soaked, she took the overnight train back to Camden Town. She hired a carriage to take her back, through the growing light, a dull grey misty English spring morning, watching without thought or emotion people leaving their houses, ready for their day.

Mipham opened the door, silently took off her wet shawl, and led the way to the back of the house where he had prepared a bath for her.

Mindlessly she removed her clothes, one by one undoing the buttons, wrapping the cloth of her blouse and skirt up in each other before placing them on the stool. She slipped into the hot tub, noticing her skin turn pink. She knew the water was hot, but she could not release herself from the chill which had entered her bones, a chill that even now sent her shivering and shaking.

When Mary finished drying her skin she put on the dry clothes he had laid out for her. She opened the door and found Mipham waiting with some tea in his hand.

"Mary," he looked at her feverish eyes, glazed, and at her flushed skin, "drink this. Are you warm enough?"

Mary took the hot tea in her hand, which shook, looked at her dear friend with recognition. "You are my dearest friend, Mipham," she said softly. "You are my only friend in the world."

"Mary, Mary, come now." He led her upstairs where she lay on the bed as he instructed, got under the covers as he instructed, tried to get warm as he instructed.

When in the middle of the night he checked in on her and found her delirious, moaning softly about the meadow, her eyes open and more glazed than before, her head and body covered in sweat, he called for the doctor. Mary saw again her beloved meadow. This time she reached its welcoming grass, the soft breezes and warming sun.

"Such a shame, so young," the doctor said, "Is she a relative of yours?"

"No," Mipham responded softly, "she was like a daughter...like a dear friend to me." His eyes filled.

"So young. But as you say," the doctor shook his head, "she had already been through so much, no reserves left to fight the pneumonia."

At her graveside stood one Frank Hodges, his shoulders shaking with the grief of his large heart. Mipham also stood, chanting mantras and prayers to entice Mary to move on to a better place, not cling to this one but to go toward that warmer, sweeter world waiting.

Diana's Life

2005

near Toronto

Diana shivered, the effects of the meditation starting to show in the goose flesh on her arms, in the paleness of her face, her sense that her facial muscles were sagging.

Jake noticed the gooseflesh as they sat on Diana's dock, the water lapping below them, the sun shining warmly through the late autumn afternoon.

After a long silence, he asked gently, "Diana, what...how are you?"

"I'm good..." Diana heard the clipped tone in her voice, "I mean, thank you Jake for asking. I'm feeling what I often feel after...when I..."

"When you return to the grave and back?" the banter in his voice did something to lighten her heart a little.

"Yes. You could say that." She smiled ruefully.

"What about you? What about what's good for you?"

"You were in that room, Jake, you experienced pretty closely what we all...what we all experienced."

Jake was quiet for several minutes, then said softly, "You took the lion's share of it, Diana."

"My job, sir, just my job while I'm here..."

"Oh, sort of 'your mission should you accept it'?" The humour didn't really play.

Diana shrugged, "Jake, really what did you experience?"

"You heard. I 'saw' I guess with what you might call that inner vision, I saw someone hurl an object..."

"Before that."

Jake paused. "I wasn't there, as a...person, I was behind the scene of the massacre, as though I...as though..."

"...as though you were already dead." Diana finished for him.

Diana's shivers hadn't stopped so Jake insisted they go inside her home.

"Would you...there's wood outside, would you build us a fire, please?" Usually Diana hated asking, being vulnerable, but she was beyond that.

With the warmth from the fire spreading quickly through her living room and with the blanket Jake had retrieved from the other chair she began to feel more solid.

He didn't ask questions, as she expected, but sat looking into the fire, his fine profile, and that emblem of the Chicago Black Hawks, clearly visible to her. She studied his face, then said quietly, "I want to tell you about David."

Jake kept his face to the fire but slowly said, "Diana, you owe me no explanations."

"I know, Jake but I want, this is...I have to tell you it's over with us."

"You and me?"

"No, David and I."

"Oh."

Diana hadn't realized she'd been expecting a stronger response. She breathed in slowly and began to speak, but he cut her off.

"Let's stay present focused for a bit. Let's talk about what happened this morning."

"We can, if that's what you want. But Jake, what happened with David and me is part of what took place this morning. I know the two belong together in some way."

Jake sighed lightly, then looked at her, waiting.

"I found David with another woman, that night I saw you downtown. I had felt like he was cheating, but this was in my face. I was seeing him, yes, and I thought, no I did love him, have loved him since we were in high school but it was different this time.

"I was going back to him to see, to push the boundaries and see if he was able to have a loving relationship...I know, thin ground to walk on, when he was already married. If he was capable of being true, surely he wouldn't have been with me.

"But as dumb as it sounds, I needed more proof. That was it, last week. He came here, and what he said disgusted me, revealed who he really is, how selfish and... and I have to be careful because I too have been selfish in response to him, not considering his wife or his child."

"Jake said nothing.

"So when he left, he left believing I'm open to seeing him again, next year after he dallies with this other...the other woman, he really believes..." Diana shook her head.

"Anyway, after he left I took a couple of tablets to help me relax. I craved the oblivion of sleep but knew I had to stay close to myself, to comfort myself deeply, since the shift away from him had been so swift. Thirty five years of him at the bottom of my heart, of me believing he was the one person who really loved me, really understood me..." Diana's tears fell silently. "I wrapped myself up in my housecoat, lay on the bed and waited.

"In a little while, I saw a creature at the bottom of the bed. I mean, when I say I saw a creature, it wasn't with these daylight eyes, it was with the inner vision, the same vision as when I see the Angels.

"The creature was female, human, covered with lice and dirt. Her matted, stringy hair lay in braids but filthy. Pustules, pimples covered her face from lack of nutrition and hygiene. Her brown dress, a kind of tunic affair, hung in filthy tatters to her emaciated body. What remained of her teeth were broken, brown and her breath stank.

"My babies and they raped me...took my babies...you know," her arm reached for me, her dazed eyes roved around.

"My babies," she cried, "They took my babies. Raped me over and over, they took my babies, from my womb, from my breasts, they beat and starved me, they..." I took her in my arms. "...all my babies, they took them...soldiers and those men..." she spat the last word.

"I knew she had lived on the street, no, she was the Street Woman, the Raped Woman, the one beaten and raped by father, husband, brothers, the woman whose babies had been scrapped from her womb, ripped from her arms, she was all that.

"I smoothed her hair back, leaned over her lice covered head, kissed her forehead. She melted. She just melted away."

"Did Diana see a slight upturn at the corners of Jake's mouth? She couldn't be sure.

"I called Rinpoche. I needed his help. I've never phoned him before but he answered my call, or rather first his assistant dialed my number, then Rinpoche came on. He asked me many questions, then said, 'this is happening because of a deep connection through many lifetimes.' That was it. Confirmation.

She was the one who had bound me to him, through how many lifetimes? It was her insanity, my insanity that tied me to David, her craziness that compelled me to make excuses for him, cover his selfishness with my love."

"And she was the one you met this morning, in the meditation?"

Diana nodded then asked, "What do you think Wayne and Andrea will do about the land?"

"There isn't much they can do. They'll be evicted. But at least as of this morning, the massacre is cleared from the land."

"The land is free, I am free...Jake," Diana reached out her hand, "Dance with me."

Epilogue

If you walk along this lane in late summer, you might see two old people sitting side by side holding hands on their dock. If your ears grow large, you might overhear them.

"You remember how this happened?"

"Yes, I remember."

"Tell me again. I found you..."

"You found me, and we lay here on the dock on our bellies, looking at the water. It was spring. That's important..."

"Why?"

"Just because...let me tell the story! It was spring and we were lying here and I read you the riot act. "

"What did I do?"

"You did me the honour of not laughing, not smiling. You rolled over on your stomach, looked at the water and said, "Looks clear from here."

"Yes, that's it. And then?"

"And then you asked me if we were going to dance this dance again. I remember you saying you had to teach everyone about how we've been here before in other lives, and how we go through the same things over and over. And I told you I already knew that, and yes, yes, I would dance this dance."

"You said that later, not at first."

"You are such a sweet child, I love you so much. You love to hear this part over and over. You were the leader of the Bluff Boys. You lived twenty minutes by car from where I grew up and we never..." the woman turns to look into the eyes of her partner, "we never ran into each other. I am so sorry for the time we missed."

"We have now. We have had already more than many will ever know."

Then the two stand and putting their arms around each other, they sway to a sound only they can hear. She looks into his eyes. He looks into hers.

Their intimacy embarrasses us, because it is true. We turn away.

Acknowledgements

Although my heart and hands typed the text, credit for the birth of this book goes to the generosity, kindness and talent of many people.

For ideas and support I owe huge thanks to Kate Gilderdale, Chad Donella, Marianna Balboa, Ronalda Jones, Bruce Allen, Joe Bertin, Brendan Gal, Catherine Sword and Linda Stitt.

For making the cover and layout consistent and beautiful, my gratitude to Sue Reynolds and James Dewar of Stone's Throw Publications knows no bounds.

Many thanks to Rich Helms for a fabulous course in Book Trailers and to Amber Robinson for help with the trailer.

A special debt of gratitude to my partner Harold Musetescu whose distance about the book provided me with space and whose closeness to our personal space created a loving retreat while I was writing.

To my extraordinary and glorious family especially my grandchildren, your being inspires me daily with a desire to be better, do better, write better. You are the reason.